MOVING TARGET

A Novel

by Nik Edge

Prologue

Late September 1974 at 11:23pm on a Friday night in South Central Los Angeles:

He was a few inches under six feet tall with a face almost coal black in complexion; broad in the shoulders, wearing a red bandanna tight over his lower brow, his shaded eyes were darkened by sunglasses. There was a slight hitch in his step that could be seen as basic swagger, or the residue of an old injury. In his right pocket was a small cylinder, casually concealed by an olive green Army jacket that was virtually brand new, but which had been softened and faded purposely through excessive washing cycles.   So it looked weather beaten. As he approached a small Korean corner market he glanced around quickly, only seeing one lone female figure about a block away down Century Blvd, lighting a cigarette and teasing her hair.

He pulled the cylinder out of his pocket.

Across the street, on the second level of a concrete like box of a building built with WPA WWII funds, an old Hispanic man was sitting by his window. He watched the hunched man below pull something out of his coat pocket, then touch the end of a lighter to it. The eyewitness was half raised from his haunches when the glowing object disappeared into the front of the grocery.   The bomber sprinted around the corner, and as the dull explosion echoed down the street, the man in the window had few visual details to later retrieve from memory. Beyond retaining the picture of the short, husky form and the nondescript clothes he would have been hard pressed to describe more.

Acrid and noxious black smoke began to billow out of the grocery and three customers emerged, one teenager briefly hesitating at the door with shoulders hunched, and arms crossed across his face, as if expecting another explosive round, before taking the same quick route as the bomber (later the Hispanic man thought it a bit curious that he was also wearing a red bandanna, like the bomber).

The Korean owner was able to emerge without sustaining burns or much smoke inhalation. He had seen the bomber's arm in motion. Coughing in short fits he stubbornly fought the beginning of the blaze, filling a water bucket from a rusting utility sink in the back of the store, and putting a wet towel over his mouth and nose. At one point he rushed out with a gun in hand, and looked in both directions quickly before ducking back in and returning to throwing the full buckets of water onto the fire. But he had to quickly bow to the inevitable when the flames reached a pile of old newspapers in the corner near the restroom. The blaze became a swirling inferno at that juncture. When he finally came out for the duration of the conflagration the Hispanic man across the street heard his foreign curses, from the depths of his chest, bemoaning his fate. The store owner ran to the nearest pay phone to call in the emergency, but his building was isolated, over twenty yards from the nearest one, thus not endangering any other businesses, so he did not expect a quick fire and police response. It was surrounded by a large parking lot, one which he had long envisioned would allow for a major expansion of his store's footprint.

"Now I will simply have to build again," he glumly noted, even though his insurance could conceivably cover most of the reconstruction cost, or at least grant him a measure of solace with enough funds to purchase another property requiring renovation.

Indeed, as the middle-aged man from the outskirts of Seoul feared, there was virtually no response. A police chopper hovered over for a few minutes when the inferno was at its peak of destructive fury, and a loudspeaker voice commanded onlookers to keep away: "Do not approach the fire. Repeat, do not approach the fire. Remain at a safe distance." He wondered "And what, exactly, is the so-called 'safe distance'?" But after the helicopter buzzed off there were not any more signals of official concern, just the typical gawkers on both sides of the street, and the token thrill seeker ignoring the warnings of other motorists to not proceed. So there were occasional cars, often gang driven, roaring past the fire, some firing a few shots toward the flaming structure as they sped past.

The owner ran to the back and was able to start his car, and pull away with the furious hiss and crackle of the fire as a kind of destructive background percussion. Later he realized how lucky he had been that his car had not exploded, because his gas cap had recently been stolen and he had been resorting to using a small towel as a plug. Such a makeshift cap could have easily led to the machine being ignited, with flames quickly licking up the gas soggy cloth.

Long after the sound of the sirens receded the blaze continued, until only smoke and embers remained. The Korean owner vowed some form of revenge, but the particulars remained hazy long afterward.

One

Cole pulled up, driving the gleaming Pontiac GTO that many admired, and some outright coveted. It was bright baby blue with thick white walled tires, and boasted red pin striping on the doors in a pattern of dueling dragons with a gleaming scimitar between them. Their sharp wings unfolded back toward the dual gleaming silver tail pipes. In fact, one might swear that on that particular morning one of the street's onlookers held up a hand to shield an eye from the piercing light one exhaust pipe created. He grimaced, then returned to regarding his torn up motorcycle, a smear of grease on his yellow-and-blue LA Rams shirt.

Cole revved the engine one last time, and gave the victory sign before shutting it down. His tall and gangly form loped over toward Gordy, his unruly mop of brown hair bouncing slightly with his jaunty step.

"Let's go," Gordy said, hunching up his thick shoulders. He was the same height as Cole, but much wider and bulkier through the chest, and had a complexion similar to the bomber's.

Cole admired a large palm frond swaying in a tree directly over his car. "Hey, hold your horses. I just got here."

Gordy replied "Nah. Today's the day gangbangers are out in force. It's the weekend, you know. You seem to forget what I tell you about the unique danger on these sorts of days. We should move on quickly, not waste any time." He gestured toward the crew across the street.

Cole shrugged. "All right, I might be white and unpopular on your block, but I'm hungry. So before we head to the beach we're stopping for a burger and coke."

Gordy ignored the intent looks of the small throng across the street and pulled open the passenger door. Habitually he commented, "Put some more grease on this door hinge, why don't you?" even though it did not squeak. He did not return the stares of the onlookers across the street, figuring they would be easily provoked, and lash out at him and his "honky" friend.

"Yeah, right. Listen, Gordy. "I've got an idea for a screenplay." Cole turned left on Century Blvd., just ahead of a wino waving furiously at a seemingly innocent bus bench. In the rearview mirror his form became extremely tall and thin, like a slowly decomposing vampire wavering in the early Fall LA heat.

Gordy was a bit distracted. "Yeah? Well, I've got an idea for a poem," he replied. It's called 'Let's motherfuckin' get out of here.'"

Cole downshifted into the yellow light. "We're on the same page, brother. We need a smart project to get us moving forward. We've been too bored. Chasing chicks is fun, but without a dime it's hard to make it go anywhere."

Gordy looked pointedly around the plush leather interior. "You need to spend less time inside this machine. Granted, it's surely a bad motha', but it attracts too much attention."

Cole responded, "I know. We need to be noticed by the big shots in Brentwood, Bel Air, and the hills. Let's bounce some ideas off each other...."

Gordy kept himself from warning Cole about heading into a possible speed trap in the last stretch of road before the highway. "Okay, so let's just say that we do complete the so-called 'project.' Then where and how do we get it to a movie producer's desk?" Gordy started to motion toward someone inching off the curb on the right, but Cole was already filling the lane gap on the left, the engine of the car roaring.

"I have contacts," he began.

"Right," Gordy riposted. "You've got it so figured out you just make a quick authoritative statement, and then expect me to automatically agree."

Cole's tanned face crinkled up slightly. "Hey, Gordy, I know a few people in the industry who know producers themselves. That's the truth. This plan will definitely have some traction. You can trust me on that." He slowed, but did not stop at the Bob's Big Boy they often frequented.

"I guess we're headed to Denny's," Gordy remarked flatly. (which meant continuing to the Marina Del Ray highway without pause).

Cole said "Yes, we are. But back to the screenplay. You can write your poems till the end of time, but keep them to the side for the time being. Anyway, let's do a little brainstorming while we cruise today." He turned on the radio, and dialed to classic rock, which blared all the way to Denny's. It was a bit past nine a.m., and the coastal marine layer of fog still prevailed. Cole rolled down the window and allowed the ocean breeze to soothe his over caffeinated head, the result of an overnight writing session. One impulse told him to defend the sanctity of his struggling writing process to Gordy, another recommended pulling the talk in the direction of sports, an always agreeable common denominator for them.

Lincoln Blvd. went through the Venice-Santa Monica corridor. They passed a record store, people milling around the front, some would say loitering with sandaled feet and cut off Levi shorts and tank tops, passing smokes, marijuana likely one key component of the mix. One guy had on a purple pillbox hat. "Some of these Venice dudes are clearly weird," Gordy commented under his breath. Cole was no longer accelerating, as if the aggression he had displayed on the streets of Watts had already exhausted his determination to exhibit the raw machine power of his vehicle. "Well," Gordy inwardly shrugged, "he is what some of the brothers call a 'hard-headed honky.'"

"So we've got a deal, right?" Cole said, forking up a piece of sausage link, while admiring the Hispanic waitress leaning over across the way.

"Sure. But what's your idea exactly?"

Cole paused, eating a large piece of French toast, even pouring some extra sugar on top as insurance against failing energy. "It will be about LA gangs and Black Power influencing City Hall."

Gordy shrugged. "Hmm. Sounds a bit farfetched. But I know some cats in my neighborhood who might have connects with a few Black Panthers. Could be a source for research material, at the very least."

Cole pondered for a moment. "We could talk to cops, gangbangers, and make a story about the struggle for power. Then give it to, hey, wait, what about a documentary...no, you're right. That might be a bit dangerous."

Gordy made a stew of his steak fries and scrambled eggs, and smothered them with ketchup. "I have an idea. We write out tentative scenes, then go out for research, and push the story forward."

Cole leaned forward. "Yes, we can do this. You don't want a real job, and I've only been getting off and on construction and painting gigs lately. Luckily, I've still got a bit of a small trust fund left."

Gordy laughed. "Hey, don't give up on your little bungalow apartment just yet, not on my account."

Cole slapped some money down on the table. "Let's talk it over more down on the boardwalk. And, by the way, it's called a studio, not a bungalow."

It was 1974, but the hippies were still percolating through the Venice vices of incense, tanning oil, and tie died shirts. There were hardly any overt gangbangers around, here and there a young bandanna clad Hispanic or black with a more casual walk than he could safely deploy in his own neighborhood. A couple of black "brothers" nodded half-heartedly toward Gordy, but he was engrossed in talking to Cole, whose eyes were darting around more than usual.

Gordy slowed his walk briefly, next to a skateboard stand selling RAM trucks. "Hey man, you sure you're not living some kind of suspense movie right now?"

Cole had momentarily hopped out of the way of a skateboarder. "No. Just have this feeling things are about to get started. I've been tired of the usual mess, all the boring routines. Don't care much for house painting. Drywall work, on the other hand, completely sucks." He rolled his shoulders back, grinning a little. "Boss tells me the next project is starting up next week, so I want to get a good start."

Gordy turned his head away. "Look over there at that old man feeding pigeons, cooing at them like he is grandpop bird. I could definitely get some good poems out of that image, that's for sure."

Cole kicked a pebble out of his path. "Yeah, probably. But why don't we get started in earnest on this project? "

Gordy patted him on the shoulder. "Let me get started in my neck of the woods, as they like to say. I'll make a move toward the Black Panthers myself."

Gordy wore thick bifocals, and kept a small notepad in his pocket at all times, in an anticipation of an idea that could be developed into a lengthy story. As he walked down Century Blvd. he passed his Korean grocery, the one where he was known on a first name basis. There was yellow crime scene police tape stapled to plywood crudely emplaced where the blown out façade had been. Because lately he had been resorting to using earplugs to ensure he slept uninterrupted through the late nights he had not heard the uproar. He thought it odd that it had been sealed up so quickly. "How could a full crime investigation be done already?" he thought. He pulled out his notebook and wrote "9-17-74. Kim's place destroyed. Sealed up. Police not treating case as priority?" He walked a few more blocks, to a medium-sized chain store-Sam's- and went directly to the front counter. The Watts Eagle paper had a photo, a bit grainy but still solid, of the destruction on its front page. The LA Times had no such mention, however, in its local section. Gordy rolled up the thin Eagle, and deposited his change on the counter.

"Hey, brother, have a nice day," the young clerk with jerry curls said, already ringing up the next purchase.

Gordy replied, "Oh yeah. Sorry man. I'm a bit preoccupied. Ah, the Korean grocery down the street..." He felt his words trail off.

A block further down he ducked into Pop's Cuts, a font of local information. Along the mirrored wall facing the two patrons having their afros worked over were various oil pomades to slick the hair into better packages of their natural selves. Gordy liked to joke with Enis aka Pop (the owner himself) that he wanted the usual "oil and vinegar dressing." Enis was fussing and clucking with concentration, holding a small pair of shears poised over a young man, who was holding forth, "Dumb frigging niggas. They should ball some like me, get a scholarship or something."

Enis replied, "Yeah, like you? To Long Beach State? You're going to have to be careful down there too, son. No breaks in the game." Enis' clucking had temporarily halted, and he nodded toward Gordy, who took a waiting seat near the corner that had an Ali poster looming overhead magisterially, his massive form preparing to uncoil a jab toward a foe.

Gordy called out, "Just chilling over here for a bit, Pops. Don't mind me none."

Enis chuckled, said, "I wasn't," and went back to his work.

Gordy resumed, "I don't know about that bombing last night, but it's like, kind of, too jarring."

The young athlete turned his head around to regard Gordy with some suspicion. "What you trying to say?"

Enis broke in, "Okay settle down now. You're in good hands. What happened last night doesn't have the markings of the typical gang banging young knucklehead type. Robbery? Sure. Assault? Check. But bombing a place? That's extreme shit. Right, Gordy?"

"Yeah, Enis. And nothing in the Times about it, either."

The young man surged up briefly in the barber's chair. "Yeah, only dead niggers need apply for notoriety. I think Malcolm X said something like that once."

Enis and Gordy paused, struck by the creative wordplay. Gordy had to admit to some envy, because he was the self-professed writer who was committed to dredging up the best expressions and here a local athlete was competing with him in wordplay. "Isn't this something?" he thought.

Enis flourished the clippers quickly, almost angrily, and continued, "Not enough self-righteous brothers left. These rag wearing cats don't know what they're doing. Copying the East LA cholos if you ask me." He applied the shaving cream with one straight razor, and worked with one blade in his partially free hand. "And I even remember the zoot suit riots. Yeah. Those military punks feuding with the military."

Gordy considered bringing up the Black Panthers as possible scapegoats in the group attacks, then rid himself of the thought through the study of his own face in the huge mirror. He was in his early thirties, but the gristle covering his thick jaw was almost entirely gray. His eyes darted in quick response to those of the patron in the barber's chair, who became mute as Enis finished his barber's flourish with styling gels and hair dryers.

Gordy felt the opportune moment, a pause, and stood abruptly, "Sorry to just drop in and out, Pops, but I've got places to go."

"Yeah, yeah," Enis chimed in, "and people to see. All right. Get your ass out of here, and do something constructive."

Gordy smiled as he continued down Century Blvd. past the donut establishment with its giant, cinnamon colored representative above the hangar like roof slowly shedding its pink paint in small, random sprinklings on the parking lot asphalt. He ignored his slightly grumbling stomach and the rich scent coming from the interior, and struggled past the Der Wienerschnitzel, its current specials bannered in mustardy yellows.

Night Shift was a soul food restaurant by day and early evening, night club during the late night. It had an old neon sign salvaged from a demolished Vegas casino during 1969, when the owner, a front man for a consortium of south central business interests, everything from a women's boutique owner to a recreational park purveyor, decided against graduate school studying sociology at Morehouse College in Georgia. His name was Greg Stiles. But at such an early hour Gordy did not expect to see him. They were on more of a casual acquaintance than friendship level, although Stiles called him the Big Don, owing to some of Gordy's popular published pieces in the Sentinel, which were mostly short poems.

Gordy shielded his eyes from the glint off the front picture window, at the same time with one glance satisfied that it was another busy lunch time. The chalk board in front of the register listed one of his favorite specials-chicken fried steak. He poured off a glass of water at the self service station and sat down at one of the two small tables in the corner. Actually, he preferred to sit back and eavesdrop on any talks pertaining to the grocery attack. He thought, "I could always ask a waitress for news."

Along the wall to his left were photos of former LA sports stars such as Jackie Robinson, Frank Gifford, and Anthony Davis, some authentically autographed, others glorified news clippings and magazine covers. Some frames were clearly structurally compromised, held together by wire, toothpicks, and Elmer's glue. A bit off center was a strange, dark ceramic chandelier, hanging from the ceiling with stars, arrows, and moons painted on its sides. Sometimes New Year's revelers boogied beneath it, to the primal thump of Jungle Love.

He lingered over the menu, hoping for some insight from listening to the surrounding patrons, but was stymied by a gentle but persuasive roar surging through the tables piled high with predominantly southern dishes. Finally, when the young waitress, wearing tight purple pants and hoop earrings with a large Afro arrived, he relented. "Hey, sister, before I order, I've got a quick question: "You heard anything yet about who is responsible for that bombing last night?"

She replied, "Don't know, but word around here is that somehow the Black Panthers were involved in it one way or another. Hey, that's just what I heard, all right? I don't want to be adding to the rumors."

Gordy wondered, "Did my jaw drop or something?" He saw impatience, concern, and a touch of fear in the purple shaded brown eyes. "Uhm, thanks for the tidbit. I'll have the chicken fried steak as usual, with a large Coke."

"Coming up within ten." She cocked one hip to the side.

"That quick?"

"The special is always the priority of the kitchen," she replied with vigor, and turned.

Gordy appreciated her sass, but especially her swaying walk. He thought, "Damn. What happened to my nerve? Do I actually need some tips from Cole in the ladies' department?" But once the food arrived he settled in, pondering the possibility of the Black Panthers involvement. Recently, word on the street was that, sobered by "ass whippings administered by cops," militants had adopted a more secretive and less publicity seeking entity as a foundation to work from. As Gordy speared a gravy slavered piece of steak, he looked over the room full of diners and wondered who might have more than simply a passing interest in the Panthers. "There is a palpable nervousness here," he thought. He left the cash on the table, and took advantage of an extra breath mint on the way out.

Cole picked up the phone receiver after rushing in from the kitchen, where he had a beef patty with melted cheese crackling on the small stove. He looked out over the North Hollywood complex swimming pool, where a topless girl, indifferent to management's non-nudity lease provision, did her early evening laps.

"Gordy?" he said, maneuvering a chair so he could keep his eyes fastened to the girl.

"Sure enough." Gordy was in the habit of using a different response every time he picked up the phone.

Cole smiled behind his phone receiver. "What's on your plate? I just got back from another day of painting. Now I'm treating myself to my famous pounder burger."

Gordy replied, "Not bad, man, all things considered. But I had the chicken fried steak down at my local eatery. You can't beat that. A scrumptious sister served me, too."

On his end, Cole thought the bathing girl was looking directly at him as she slowly, even tantalizingly, climbed out of the pool. "All right. You get anything?"

Gordy said "No, not yet. But quiet rumors point to the Panthers. Hey, truth is stranger than fiction, as they say." Gordy clicked his television remote until the Rams football game came on his black-and-white television.

Cole returned, "No kidding. Someone had to see what happened. Well, maybe not. The bombing took place around midnight by my calculations. But isn't that a busy street?"

Gordy responded, "Are you kidding me? Remember the night we were almost jacked up by those gangbangers in the lot behind the grocery? They were all lined up against the wall, staring at us with clear menace."

Cole chuckled to himself, because he was still staring at the bare and partially tanned breasts in his pool area.

Gordy watched the Rams quarterback being mercilessly pounded to the turf. He was laid out flat on his back, unresponsive. Even the Rams cheerleaders stopped their sideline routines. "Man, the Rams quarterback looks dead on the ground. I partly blame the coach for switching off from one to the other too often. They need to keep our brother Harris in all the time, as far as I am concerned, or he'll never get comfortable."

"Really?" Cole stood and walked to another seat, resting precariously on the edge of the bar ledge, with its cheap, peeling laminated edges.

"Oh, man, his arm just twitched, the trainer just gave the thumbs up sign...no, he's not dead." Gordy turned the volume down on the set. "All right. Now I'm finally focused."

"This is it," Cole almost gasped in excitement. "We document the case on the side, then shill it to the studios. But, hey, we can still make some shit up along the way. And you were the one who already mentioned it, how the cops might not care enough about this case to pursue it, or there's already some kind of political cover up going down."

Gordy paused. "Okay, now I know you've done some suspense stories. But you sure this screenplay business is almost the same? Different format, you know? We're both writers, and we both know how difficult large projects can become. Things can get messy very quickly."

Cole winced as the girl below noticed him ogling her and gave him the middle finger. "What ever happened to the summer of love?" he thought with some despair. "You're right, Gordy. This is our first collaboration, and there will probably be nothing easy about it. But look at it this way. When the facts elude us our fiction will come in, and vice versa."

Gordy replied, "Man, we could be in for a bunch of lawsuits if we go ahead with this, if it goes too far, if you catch my drift?" Despite his doubt, however, he was quickly being taken in by Cole's initiative, which although sometimes tending toward recklessness, was a solid and persuasive character trait in most instances.

Cole laughed. "Well, if that happens, if someone 'sues our pants off' they will be left staring at my dirty third eye, if you know what I mean."

Gordy replied, "I get your point. But, hey, I've started doing my part, getting some intelligence on the bombing. It's time for you to get rolling on your motion picture contacts."

Cole thought, "Damn. He can really be impatient." He reached into his refrigerator for a Tab soda, and popped it open with his right index finger after setting it atop the counter. "Man, you're all revved up. But that's good, for both of us. I know a girl from LACC, met her in a writing class. Her Dad's a producer at Orion pictures. But I don't have her number anymore, so I'll have to do a little sleuthing. Anyway, along the way I might find even better contacts."

Gordy replied "All right. I'm signing off. Got to get going on this new long poem I've been planning. Then tomorrow I'm going to snoop around the grocery again, see what I can find out. Maybe a way to start sifting through the rubble."

Cole replaced the receiver with his left hand and poured the remainder of the Tab into his glass with his right. A part of him was surprised, and invigorated by the pace of the developing plan. Another questioned the wisdom of involving himself in potential danger. He returned his attention to the Rams game on his small bar top screen. He noticed the formerly unconscious quarterback sitting on the sideline bench, hair a bit askew, his face muffled by the trainer's towel most likely laced with some sort of alcohol and/or smelling salts to help revive him. He thought "Gordy, our game is just starting."

Two

Gordy lived in a converted garage behind his grandmother's house. It was equipped with a hot plate, a small refrigerator and, most importantly, enough wall space to hold many book cases for his ever expanding library. Even before the Rams converted a field goal to clinch the game, his eyes were wandering beyond his television set to select a future reading item. He thought Dostoyevsky's *Notes from Underground* might be a good catalyst for his poetry, even though he had yet to read it. "But best title ever," he thought. He briefly considered *Anna Karenina*, but one college professor, in a particularly unguarded moment, had assigned sections of the writing to a certain category of "filler." "Listen, Gordy," he had said. "You're sharp enough to know instinctively that even the classics have their own so-called "'surpassing mediocrities' interspersed with their more spotty, brilliant passages."

Gordy felt a small, ironic smile crease the corners of his mouth as he approached the book case, which he had inherited from his grandfather, who had been one of the first black reporters at the LA Herald. His grandmother was still living in the small house in front, regaling her walls with framed cutouts of her husband's proudest moments, such as his prize winning journalistic depiction of the 1965 Watts riots. Gordy tried to help her with errands and house duties, but she only, and begrudgingly at that, allowed him to keep up with the yard work. But he had never shied away from physical labor. Once a week she rewarded him with his favorite dish-beef stroganoff-and let herself into his space when he was not in, depositing the food platter on the old but sturdy coffee table.

He was almost permanently unemployed, but he was able to suffer only minor qualms about it, since he had created a reading and writing schedule for himself that equated to at least a part time job. And he was proud of the evidence: Next to his typewriter was a stack of poems, which he tended to sift through periodically, pulling out a handful to rewrite. He called them his "verbal critters."

A slight breeze wafted through the window above his kitchenette, urging the aroma of a thick slice of banana bread his grandmother made the previous night. His parents had dropped him off with her when he was five, promised to return, but never did. Their bodies were eventually found in a culvert on the outskirts of a small northern California town. They were believed to have been the victims of random violence, possibly the detritus of a drug deal gone bad. Gordy felt a rogue biker gang had to be involved at some stage of the murderous plot, and Cole had given his theory some support. Over the years, his hatred of his parents had morphed into a cold indifference. He wondered if their violent end had eased his anger into a more mature acceptance of their faults. "Well, at least Pops got me into music, and Mom herself was a poet," he thought. "And I'd like to think they'd support this project Cole and I are planning."

Cole had a painting job to complete, so he dumped his stepladder, paint, and tools in the trunk of old pickup, and tore out of the complex lot with a lusty Santa Anna wind brushing the thin palm trees arranged around the teardrop shaped pool, their shadows chasing away a family of lizards living out of the corner lot, in a patch of pampas grass. He swerved around the pothole that the manager kept promising to have filled/repaired, and dialed his car radio to classic rock. His destination was a quaint cottage in Studio City, in a quiet cul-de-sac off Reseda Blvd. He was encouraged and a bit surprised by Gordy's initiative in getting their project started. "Was he just waiting for the right spark?" he thought. "But did I detonate a larger grenade than I expected?" He rolled down his window as he passed a gas truck readying to turn right onto the 101 freeway, because a slow trickle of a gas leak was spitting off a back wheel, fouling the air. He thought "Must have overtopped when it was filled."

The side door was unlocked. The young couple Jen and Wally did not believe in protecting possessions, because they did not completely believe in the notion of ownership of anything. Consequently, most of their belongings were hand-me-downs. An orange alley cat that they fed leftovers to, even artichokes bathed in olive oil, hissed at Cole as he entered. He left the door slightly ajar to allow for escaping paint fumes, and shoved aside an empty Coors beer can lolling on the white linoleum kitchen floor, a pattern of spill in the shape of a snaking blood trail, making for a sticky patch.

Cole recalled that an old Hollywood acquaintance, one he had known since they were both five, tended to patronize a popular Hollywood bar called Rattlesnake. He thought he would stop by later that day while he scraped around the edge of the opened paint can. Then he burst out the side door, but by the time he made it to the street proper, the offending beer can was rolling away from his car. "What a scurvy town this can be," he muttered, and flicked a dried piece of paint off his thumb pad on the way back in, toward a stand of ice plants. "Yahoos throwing cans off the sides of neighborhood cars," he thought.

After an hour of rolling paint onto the living room walls, he sat on the floor and opened a can of Dr. Pepper his temporary bosses left him before beginning their hallucinogenic laced spiritual journey to Yosemite. Jen had walked nonchalantly past him bare-breasted, watering a potted flower in the kitchen sink. "Geez, don't be so nervous," she had said. "If you get a hard on it's no big deal, no pun intended." Wally had flitted by with the comment, "She's a little whacked right now. On something, uh, I'm not really sure what actually." Presently, Cole's gaze fixed on a tracery of spider web in the far right corner of the living room ceiling. "Didn't I get rid of that already?" he said, standing up for a final rolling session.

Cole's mother was a schizophrenic housed in the Camarillo Mental Hospital. Before her forced move, Cole periodically assisted her on small weekend projects, building up his young, mediocre strength by toting the gallons of paint from truck bed to living room, trunk bed to kitchen. One day when he was ten she reported a voice telling her warningly "You're cutting into corners." She started taking more cigarette breaks and neighborhood walks over the course of working days to calm herself, but over the course of five years her work production waned steadily, until she was constantly being threatened with termination, or being laid off permanently. Later, when Cole visited her in the huge cafeteria-like lobby of the hospital, she said, "Well, I guess I did, indeed 'cut corners' work wise. So they had no choice but to fire me." He recalled the walls of the institution being a light lavender color, but wondered if his young, fearful mind had distorted the picture, because the lack of wall color was supposed to be more soothing for mental patients.

She had started calling him Colby, which he later found out was the name of her high school sweetheart. He brought her a Celine book she had requested and a chocolate bar she insisted she would save until the first day of the new month, what she termed her "emotional purging day." He had not visited her for almost a year, and felt uneasy about it on certain days, especially on the ones where his own struggles with house painting chores attacked his spirit/ego and sense of belonging. At times he drank to excess, yet despite some aggressive behavior, he never went to the extreme of physical assault. On one occasion, before entering a restroom after more than a couple of tequila shots and beer chasers he calmly told himself that he would trash the inside of the bathroom once inside, but not touch even one hair on one person afterward, and he proceeded to do exactly that. In fact, he simply tore a small mirror off the wall and broke in in the sink. Music was thumping heavily in the small club, so that as he exited, no one could be certain when the damage had been done. That incident led to his first novel, about a former boxer who repeatedly broke his hands during the process of punching brick walls in frustration about not being able to make money any longer from doing what came naturally to him. Cole realized he always had a certain level of self-control that protected him from the most vicious acts borne out of disenchantment with life. To Cole, just as there were comforting associations with the repetitive motions of painting, his first book gave proof that order could indeed be wrested from madness, and that he could create something enduring. He thought, "Gordy is the purveyor of verse; I'm the purveyor of prose." If he had been more contemplative, he would have admitted to himself that his idea for a screenplay was a way for them to push each other to the outer limits of their shared dedication to craft.

He waited until most of the paint fumes had dissipated, then closed the windows until about only one tenth of an inch remained between window ledge and window frame. Because he had brought an extra white shirt along, he simply washed off above the waist, and pulled a can of Miller out of the refrigerator to smooth his ride over to the Rattlesnake bar. He revved the engine before tearing out of the driveway, causing some leaves to tremble and slide off the wide hood. Momentarily his mind fixated on the young blonde he had espied cavorting around the pool area. "So she gave me the finger? Just forget about it. Perhaps there will be others even more violently dismissive."

"I must be on my third beer already," Cole thought as he glanced around, within the walls of a barroom created to resemble on older version of itself, with framed lariats, horseshoes, and spurs alongside photos of barely clothed females. One had a special plaque proclaiming the "Texas Rose," her bare shoulders turned toward the camera so that the nipples of her otherwise bare breasts did not show. Cole had studied the ten or so faces that had entered over the previous two hours, as he sat behind one of the three round tables near the restrooms. One girl gave him a quite savage look as she sauntered by, a black widow tattoo behind her neck. She was also wearing spiked heels that Cole thought must actually be as sharp and as pointy as knives at their extreme ends. He thought, "Is it because I am sitting alone, and too near the restrooms, that some consider me a perverted threat of some sort?" There was a token hippy type, waving his hands with supplication toward a biker who was having trouble keeping a smile off his broad, scarred face. As Cole admired the long, tanned legs of a couple of girls in short shorts and long, striped socks, he thought "Beach bunny paradise." One guy who looked part Hispanic leaned back against the far wall and moaned loudly to himself from time to time, his voice deeper when a new song came on the jukebox. Once or twice he roared, "Goddamn it play fucking Santana!" but otherwise he was largely ignored. Only the previous week he had tried to convince one of the grizzled bartenders that he should be provided with ample free beer in exchange for ensuring the smooth running operation of the jukebox, and had almost earned permanent ejection for his nerve.

At that time of day, the overall vibe was of such a bleak character that Cole finally despaired of engaging anyone in conversation. He finally took a bar stool and leaned in a bit toward the bartender, who had his elbows up to soap suds floating on top of the wash sink. He gave Cole a cautious glance in the mirror before turning, and slapping a coaster down. "What's your poison, friend?" he asked. Cole's attention briefly fixed on the bartender's lazy left eye.

"Uh, I guess just a beer. Uh, actually let's make it easy. A Bud draft."

"Tall glass I presume."

Cole noted a slight hint of an English accent. "Why not? I'm in no hurry. I'm hoping to run into an old buddy or two of mine." He did not receive an immediate response, so he returned to the study of his surroundings. In the slightly smoky reflection of the mirror he saw the Hispanic guy point his index finger toward the back of his (Cole's) head.

"So you're looking for someone? Well, that's what bars are for." The barkeep shrugged his wide shoulders and paused momentarily, grinning wolfishly. "All right, we'll cut to the chase. We'll talk, and if I think you're okay I will answer some of your questions. This is the first time I've seen you, so I might even choose to put you off at first. No offense. I like to be as direct as possible with patrons at the outset. It seems to keep things from getting confused down the road. It's my standard speech to newcomers. Can you bear with me?"

Cole thought the line of questioning a bit odd, but overcame his reservations quickly. "I understand. You run a tight shop. If it's any consolation, I'm looking for a girl, and I'm not a pervert of any stripe."

The barkeep simply glared for a moment, and briefly returned to his sink. Still with his head over the soap suds, he said, "I'll be the one to judge, partner." He wiped his hands and forearms with a towel, and Cole noticed a rose tattoo on the underside of the left forearm. "You are blunt, which I like, but also a bit pretentious, which I don't."

Cole glanced back for a moment, then relaxed. "Okay. I guess you've got a point. I guess trying to impress sometimes gets the better of me, makes me sound off. Ah, man, it's just I want to cut to the chase."

The bartender smiled a bit unkindly. "You've got a way with words, but your body language is off. I was an MP years ago, and I still have the knack of sniffing out stuff. You're working some sort of angle, that I know for sure. So you've got to understand that I need to see you interacting here a bit before you get a so-called 'hearing.'"

Cole slid his beer mug ahead a space. "Okay. That's fair, I mean, I'll be around.   Actually, I'm kind of doing research."   It felt unconvincing even as he said it. "Alright, I'll spit it out, as they say. Me and my buddy are doing research for a screenplay."

"Research for a screenplay, you say? Hey, how much does it take to write a Hollywood trash fest?" The barkeep laughed openly. "Just kidding. Really. Good luck.   You look old enough and intelligent enough to know what a snake pit the picture business is.   The Rattlesnake will provide you with plenty of material over time. I'm sure of that."

Cole nodded his head. "That's what I like about this area of the city. Things are really humming. My buddy crows about places in his Watts 'hood, but I don't go for shootings and fire bombings. Bar tussles and sports and arguments over music are more my style."

"Well, regardless of your style, it looks like you're really starting to nurse that beer. Looks like you won't be around tonight."

"Nah. I'm going to do a bit of research, maybe a bit of writing." Cole dispatched the rest of the beer in one gulp. "I'll be back within the week."

"Okay. Be good, hombre." The barkeep moved to the far end of the bar, where a patron had dropped his head over a spilled shot of whiskey. He tapped the old man's head, whose long hair had contacted the spilled liquor. Cole heard the responding yawn as he exited. He put on his large, dark oval shades, because the sun had taken on its fierce late afternoon trappings. Cole thought, "I feel like an ancient Aztec exiting a blood-smeared temple." He chuckled to himself when he saw the edge of a ketchup packet smeared on the edge of the curb. He wetted a finger and wiped a small tear of the red condiment that had spotted the rim of his rear wheel. The ketchup splatter radius had been very large, indeed. "Another random attack?" he thought. "First a beer can bounced off my ride and now this?"

When he arrived back at his apartment complex, the pool area was thrumming with a large radio and loud voices and massive amounts of beer. One guy was bragging how he could float his Coors can in the water without spilling a drop of its beer, which prompted his girlfriend to punch his flabby stomach. Once inside, Cole pulled the curtains close, and turned on a large floor fan, one he compared to the design of a hockey goalie mask. Then he pulled out his small writing pad and sat on his couch, struggling to pen words in the deepening dusk.

Three

He had tea in the morning, with milk and sugar, English style, alongside a few leftover links of sausage, which he dipped in French mustard. Gordy walked briskly down Century Blvd., noticing the police scene crime tape still bracketing the front of the bombed out Korean grocery. On a hunch, he walked around to the back of the building, into a small alleyway with its predictable doses of broken glass, crushed cigarette butts, and cans in various states of decomposition. Momentarily he was self-conscious, looking across the street toward a few decrepit Ford sedans to confirm that he was not being watched. A wandering dog paused briefly, sniffing at something in the yard of a property across the way, then continued on its way. It appeared briefly as a greyhound, but only because it was malnourished, its ribs jutting out, the parched tongue hanging out at a cockeyed angle. Gordy turned back to the alley and imagined the Korean grocer barely escaping the blast radius of the bomb a split second after realizing that the projectile tossed into his store was not a mere bottle of beer or liquor. There was an acrid and sweet smell still emanating from the destroyed structure. In a momentary, obsessive mode he tried to separate the smell of candy bars from beer. His eyes fastened onto a large crack in the exterior plaster, where a smudge of shadow evidenced a clear opening, if narrow. He noticed a wheeled dumpster, one corner edging out from the touch of a still intact storage shed. "Hey," he thought, "I could roll that over underneath the hole and work on widening the opening so I can shove my bulk through."

The thought captivated and scared him at the same time, because it was patently illegal, a scheme to pull evidence from a crime scene.

Yet the LA Times had still not covered the story. What if he was officially deputized as a private investigator in some manner in order to legally investigate it? Could he and Cole make a screenplay actually based in fact? Could some details and people be skewed to some degree in order to still create essentially a work of fiction? It would be a magnification of their original plan, which was seeming more and more to be taking on a life of its own. He thought "How about a show called 'Cole and Gordy PIs'?"

Gordy's foot pawed at a smudge of trash and mud near the dumpster while his eyes scanned for onlookers. "Should I tell Cole about it?" he thought, moving around the shed so that he could not be seen from the frontage street. "Will he try to dissuade me from breaking into this joint if I choose to do so?" He was feeling a bit reckless. "Hell, I don't have to tell him either. We're working together on a project. That's the agreement. No more. No less." It was partly a conniving part of himself that was urging this tack, as he was well aware at that moment, while his eyes fixed on a shallow scratch on the ribbed exterior paneling of the storage shed.

He continued to ponder as he neared the donut shop that locals called simply The Big D. It never ceased to amaze him that, despite an increasing number of shootings in its parking lot, it still had a huge and proud sloping pane of glass fronting the sidewalk and street. The three patrons seated at the counter all had varying doses of stress hunched up in their shoulders. One was a true "soul brother," with a huge afro peeking out of a flowing purple cape that was rakishly draped over one shoulder. A larger man with a shaved head faced the street, stirring gobs of sugar around a cup of coffee. He studied Gordy closely for a moment as he took a stool halfway between the two. He sensed they would have preferred he sit with his arms resting on the counter closer to an old bespectacled man in a suit devotedly reading his morning paper. He cleared his throat loudly, which clearly annoyed the big man on the other side, who was spooning whipped cream into his still drink neglected brew, though only a few crumbs remained of his chocolate glazed donuts. The old man folded his paper loudly, pulling at the edges to make a tight snap, and the big man grunted and spurted, "Old fool," which drew a slight smile from the young Hispanic waitress in her cloud blue smock, tapping at her order pad with a dull pencil. She placed a coffee cup in front of Gordy, and widened her eyes in questioning. "I'll have a large coffee roll," he said, and watched her head flinch a bit to the left, as the sun splintered, hitting the edge of the roof, and planted itself on the back wall of the kitchen. Of course, her unfortunate head was blocking some of the bright rays. "Give it up, girl," the old newspaper reader said. "Get this guy his roll, and I'll let you know if you're needed."

The cape-wearing guy in the middle said "Speak for yourself, Riggs. I might be here a while still. Just keep acting like you're going to find a job."

"Yeah, creasing that paper ain't doing shit," the big man in the corner said. "And clearing your throat ain't getting rid of the taste of vomit in your mouth."

Gordy tensed up as the old man responded, without seeming rancor, "I love you, too, brothers. Honestly, some days I look for jobs, some days I don't. And I only drink when someone else does," he chuckled. His left hand swept over the corner of his mouth, but almost delicately, while the waitress covered the laughter gurgling inside her throat.

"Right, right, old man Redbone," the big guy continued. "Act above it all while our markets get firebombed."

"I heard it was Korean," the waitress said, arms folded over each other. "I mean, not black owned."

The big guy stood, knocking over the last gulp of his syrupy coffee. "Don't get confused. My cousins got along with Mr. Kim alright. He is either dead or disappeared. No one can account for his whereabouts. Maybe he has gone into vigilante mode."

"All right, all right," Gordy intervened. "She's probably not from around here, brother. But I'm down with what you said. Heard Kim was a decent cat. I stopped going there a while back, because some young Crips have a beef with me, and I didn't want anyone else to get hurt by the conflict."

The caped one to his immediate left adjusted himself briefly on his stool. "Word's that some guy across the street saw the heinous act go down. No idea how old he is, but supposed to be some hermit type. When anyone asks him his name, he says his first name is simply The and-"

"What the?" the muscled one almost stood up to his full height.

"Hold it there, man. His last name is Statement. So his full name is The Statement. He refuses to answer direct questions, so word on the street goes-"

The older, suited one said "Great. Another drugged up wacko. My guess is he is lying, just trying to draw attention to his sorry ass. Lots of people around here will say or do just about anything to stay on the government dole."

The big guy responded, "No offense, but it's not just the brothers and cholos." Gordy sensed that, appearances aside, that the big guy was the velveted one's bodyguard.

The old guy crisped the edges of his papers with sugary fingertips. "No one cares about Watts, that's all. Only when there is something major, major indeed, like back in '65. News helicopters need footage of not just one joint like that Korean grocery, but the entire neighborhood in flames. Anything less makes the news hounds yawn. Now the Vietnam War, napalm bombing, rioting in the streets, all that made the news wires light up."

"Listen to the old man," the big guy said, looking pointedly at Gordy. "Getting philosophical on us. Next minute he'll start saying his name used to be Shabbaz X and shit. Comes in here, sits down and thinks he's some Zulu chief or something."

His boss chuckled. "Yeah, wouldn't surprise me, either. But Driggs here is alright. It's these so-called gangbangers that are the problem. Probably one of them that bombed out those Koreans. Potheaded punks who don't understand business. Koreans, like other immigrants, take care of their own."

The big guy countered, "Yeah, well, some brothers think those Koreans are a bit too aggressive in how they treat their black customers. Always paranoid about things being stolen from them.

36

Will even follow kids all the way around the store and stuff. It can get disrespectful very quickly."

The waitress recovered her position behind the counter. "You guys arguing again?" She raised a slightly teasing finger. "People really stressing out about that bombing? And I've got a long ride up Olympic every day. Guys on that bus make you guys look like gentlemen."

"Imagine that," the old man added.

The waitress and Gordy both laughed while the other two cringed out two guarded smiles. Among the five, Gordy left the largest tip.

Cole had his writing implements out, but he kept hesitating, wondering how fact-based the proposed screenplay should properly be. He had some library books opened, some sociology texts, others collections of LA Times articles, but all equally devoted to describing the decay of inner cities. He was especially drawn to a book chronicling the infamous Detroit riot of '67, where raw National Guards troops had such a tight grip on their weapons that many black juveniles were killed unnecessarily, a few actually shot in the back as they fled to safety. "Why am I drawn to this shit?" he said aloud, closing his blinds for a deeper shade of security. "Should I spice things up just a bit, for a better, cinematic public performance?" He realized that a concept, fully formed in his head, would be more difficult to translate into a screenplay, even though he had managed to create a couple of manuscripts in his spare time. "Who has ever done what Gordy and I are going to do?" He stood and walked to his bedroom, spare except for the books bulging inside and outside two old, rickety bookshelves. He turned to the left, and placed his hand into a small black case, thinking, "Hope I don't need you." Inside was an unloaded .44 Magnum, which he had never used. "I'd better take some target practice soon if I think I might actually be using it in the near future."

His grandmother's lawn was a bit overgrown, so Gordy filled up a 7-11 plastic cup with ice and soda and perched it on the bottom of the back steps, where he could conveniently access it while cutting the back grass. But first he had to scalp the front, an area of pride for his grandmother, who still weeded around her plants and shrubs, especially attentive to the bright green shoots of her aloe vera patch. A half hour later he was walking down Century Blvd., quickly approaching the series of government subsidized apartments that fronted the destroyed Korean grocery building. The concrete block structure had originally been built for returning WWII veterans, but eventually fell into disrepair and was ceded to the city, which converted the battleship gray exterior into a less drab and comfortable cream color, but otherwise did only minor renovations to the vast interior. Gordy had never set foot inside, and was unsure if he could simply walk onto the community grounds, a predictable rectangle in the center of the property with a half-hearted playground built a few years prior, and a roving security guard in a golf cart. Presently, he was in the far corner of the complex and, as the gated entry door was unlocked, and he did not see a NO TRESPASSING sign, he entered smoothly, without incident. He took note that the buildings facing

Century Blvd. and the grocery were marked A and B, and had numbers ranging from 100-290. He briefly considered jotting it down, before entrusting it to his short term memory bank, which rarely failed him. Gordy was thinking "How do I ask about someone named The Statement without appearing a complete fool?"

There was a figure sitting on the steps of the olive building D, hunched over in camouflage pants and a still crisp Army jacket. He did not notice Gordy until he was halfway across the grounds, in part because of the interposition of a glinting ray of midday sun. His nervous hands described somersaults in his lap, and he sometimes used his left arm for better balance atop a small pile of newspapers that he also used as a doorstop to let friends in at night. It was rounded at the edges, and accumulated dirt and dust had been worked into it with moisture. His head jerked from side to side, until he visually fixed on Gordy's approach. Then he started thumbing his improvised arm rest with a heavy hand. Gordy thought the beat approximated that of a recent popular funk song.

"You don't live here, do you?" The guy was in his early forties, with a thin physique and a sloped posture. His skin was a light cocoa color.

"No, can't say I do. Live around the corner. I didn't see any warning signs and..." Gordy began as the man stood.

"Alright, man. No sweat." He took one more step toward Gordy, then relaxed. "You seem alright to me. The management here at the property refuses to pay for security, and too much shit has been going down lately around here."

Gordy responded, "Yeah? I'm thinking the same thing. I'm looking for someone who word on the street says saw something or someone the night the Korean grocery-"

"Was torched? I wasn't in the 'hood when it happened." The slight tension in his shoulders loosened again.

"Not torched actually," returned Gordy. "Bombed. Not something gangbangers are known for." He tried to sound casual, but he sensed that he had failed in the mission.

"Man, you're sounding a bit like a cop now. It was just a grocery store anyway. And your interest in it?"

Gordy replied, "Yeah, I'm familiar with the owner." He allowed a blatant lie in the guise of an innocuous generalization. "Cops seem to be dragging their heels..."

"I see." His pause was prolonged, while he looked with wonder into the blue sky, a nervous tic in the corner of his right eye. "But who is the cat you heard probably knows something?"

Gordy chose his words carefully. "Know it sounds crazy, but I heard the guy's name is The Statement. Yeah, I know, strange. First name simply The. And last name Statement."

Sputtered laughter rippled inside his cheeks, and his hands once again did somersaults in the air. "Man! That is one strange dude. Claims he is black, but white as the driven snow. Must have taken too much dope when he was in 'nam, or The Shit, as he calls it. Now he says he's a Rastafarian Revolutionary. Wears weird outfits. One is called The Court Jester, with all sorts of frills, lace and crap. Never aggressive toward me or any of the brothers and sisters here, but people give him his space all the same. Used to live in Topanga Canyon, starting acting too weird even for the hippies up there. So the government got him on meds and moved him here. If you're looking to write an article or story about someone colorful, he's the guy for you."

Gordy brushed away a fly that was obsessed with his nostrils. "Sounds like what I heard about him. Hard to talk to him, well, that is only based on the fact that he only makes, uh 'statements.'"

The reply was quick. "You've got it, brother. So you'll have to be patient if you want to get any info out of him. He won't answer direct questions. He's a pretty smart cat, too, so if you try to suggest a subject, he's liable to smell something fishy and turn off on you. Just a warning. But if you're patient with him, you might eventually get what you're looking for." He swept his arm toward building E. "He's over there. Can't exactly tell you where, but just look it up on the directory." He gave Gordy a small, conspiratorial wink. "I tend to not give out my name, by the way."

Gordy began to extend his hand, but not sensing a return movement, pulled it back. "Thanks, man. Nice chatting with you. I think I'll wait a day or two before I speak to 'The Situation.'"

"Suit yourself. Just don't come in too early in the morning or late at night. Too many knuckleheads wandering around at that time, too many for me to shut down." His chest briefly expanded.

"Okay. Later." Gordy turned, as an empty glass bottle exploded on the curb outside the grounds.

"Aw, man!" the voice behind him groaned. "Who do you think is the only one who will sweep that mess up? Me, that is me, only me...the man."

Gordy glanced back briefly, and lobbed over his shoulder, "Looks like we've both got some work cut out for us." Even though he was careful, his left shoe still crackled as his weight came down on a large shard of broken glass.

Four

To the writer, the blank page was dark at noon, transferring midnight to day before the unresponsive television screen flickered onto a sparkling commercial segment: A famous funk band was performing in wisps of bright scarves and faux-jewel encrusted, wide-brimmed hats. Cole turned the volume button to the right, and returned to his pad and pen. He thought about a movie scene involving a firebombing of the band members and audience on network television, then swiftly banished the thought. He felt jittery, because he and Gordy had already arranged a meeting later in the day to exchange ideas about the screenplay. He wondered how much "intelligence" Gordy had gathered thus far. "Should we just write an investigative journalism book?" he thought. "Like the Watergate scandal book? We might uncover all sorts of weird material, some of it even threatening our physical selves." He chided himself for the 'physical selves' part; it reminded him of an arrogant high school English teacher of his, who clearly resented not having attained tenure within the university ranks, who wielded language like a weapon over his students. "We could still shill it to the studios. Besides, neither of us really likes the screenplay format. And this way we can pack more research into the subject-Who or what bombed a Korean grocery and why?" Knowing Gordy, he might want a more provocative title along the lines of 'Blow Them Up: A True Account of the LAPD cover up of a Korean grocery bombing by Cole and Gordy X'?" On the television screen, the lead singer of the funk band was saying, "We are just about to set this house on fire. You dig?"

Cole turned off the dial and opened the blinds he had utilized to block out the sun during his unproductive writing session. The complex parking lot had a slightly ramshackle appearance, with old couches and tables with broken bases and legs, and various beer and liquor bottles strewn around, since it was one day before a major trash pickup. Cole turned on his heels and went to the kitchen, where he prepared an egg sandwich with a generous topping of ketchup. He wrestled internally with the parameters of the writing project, hardly satisfied when he mopped up the last of the egg with a piece of bread crust.

It was a prickling sensation at first, a crud that somehow seeped through his LA Rams windbreaker and clung with a subtle persistent itchiness, almost a second skin. Gordy's mind screamed, "What the?" as he deposited the required change into the bus box, his nose crinkling up. He grimaced, and looked toward the back, which drew some laughter from the five or six passengers. The woman bus driver waved her hand in front of her face and said, "The bum got off two stops ago, but the smell does linger. Damn." Gordy reconsidered his vow to not buy a personal car, even though he rarely ventured far outside his neighborhood, and could rely on Cole for longer travel. "Okay, alright," he exhaled. An older woman patted an empty seat next to her. She said, "Young fellow, the smell, uh, mess is worse back there. So why don't you take this here seat?"

"Thanks, ma'am, but, sure, okay." The bus headed east down Century Blvd., passing the burned out husk of the Korean grocery.

The police tape was still up, although it appeared to have been attacked in certain areas, the plastic jagged at the top.

She gestured with a gloved hand. "That's pure craziness, young man. Don't you think?" she asked with disdain. "Young dumb blacks act no different than white crackers. Makes me sick." She had a purple mark on her left cheek, which Gordy hoped was a birthmark, not a scarred over oven burn or a deep bruise suffered during a domestic dispute.

"Yeah. Little knuckleheads, no doubt." As if on cue, a young gangbanger "wearing his colors", with red bandanna and low slung jeans and black slippers, threw an empty 40oz bottle of beer onto the burned out grocery roof. A huge puff of dust rose from the impact. "Apocalyptic ghetto mushroom cloud," thought Gordy. "And here I'm sitting next to a frizzy, gray-haired old woman on a rank city bus. It's kind of a South Central war zone right now."

He hopped off at the nearest library, a typical generic rectangular box that despite its outer appearance housed a very good collection of African and African American texts. He was on familiar terms with the chief librarian-Mona Drew- who had been one of the first black women to graduate with a history degree from UCLA, and he always kept up-to-date with her work schedule. A small group of kids were playing cards outside the entrance, a few with large combs stuck in their prodigious afros. One briefly stood, detaching himself from the game briefly, but another said "Nah, man. Leave him alone. Looks like he doin' some serious business, be on some mission." Gordy interrupted their laughter as a slight dig about his research aims, the token nerdy brother in the 'hood, but also one who might be physically dangerous.

It struck Gordy that soft mustardy yellow was the standard color of that particular library branch, even bleeding into the immaculately kept index cards. Visually, he referenced it to a famous picture of the Watts riot of '65, of a middle-aged black man wearing green polyester pants and a tight, mustardy collared shirt, motioning toward cops with a menacing stick while flames licked the background.

As usual, he only nodded a greeting to the librarian on the way in, and went immediately to the non-fiction section. Although less comprehensive than the central library collection downtown, he usually found what he needed in the less crowded contours of this, the nearest library branch. Occasionally he visited the one downtown, in part to expose himself to the less controlled seediness of the area, where he could haggle over the price of ornate necklaces in the welter of Broadway stalls, and eat affordable Japanese buffet in Little Tokyo, and banter with groups of street poets hoping for liquor change thrown their way. To Gordy, despite the surfeit of bums and prostitutes there was a fluidity barely contained by the streets. "That is the key," he thought, "a sense of intense anarchy, yet one which is kept non-lethal by the boundary of strict walls." He studied the spines of books-*Anarchy in the 'hood is okay; Militants and monsters: Panthers, gangbangers, and the Quest for Racial Truth; LAPD and the Afro American community: The Price of Order.*

Mona had sidled up to his slightly turned shoulder. She was in her early sixties, with streaks of white in her otherwise jet black afro. Gordy used to joke that she looked like the Bride of Frankenstein. "The books you're looking at are fine, but if you want a real immersion in your topic see Dr. Warfield at Cal State LA, no, no relation to the actor, if that is what you're thinking. He keeps up with the Black Power movement. Word is that a flask of good whiskey loosens his tongue a bit. And, young man, you can tell him that I sent you."

Gordy smiled, and put the books under his arm.

He said, "I wish you were my age, you fine, intelligent sister. I don't suppose you know his office hours?"

"I do, indeed, Gordy. I'll, uh, bring your books up while you think about a way out."

Gordy thought, "Is that really what she said, 'A way out?'. What does that mean?" He nosed back to studying books on shelves, wondering if he and Mona might soon "collaborate" on something, afterall. "Why just collaborate with another writer on a book?" He thought about a bon mot for Mona to digest. "How many times have I told her she is a nice chocolate cake?" When he reached the check out desk Mona was busy stamping books, as well as answering calls on the phone. In fact, they only nodded to each other as she explained street directions to a patron while his books were cleared for removal from the premises. Gordy was pondering the maxim "Knowledge will set you free."

A few hours later, Cole turned to Gordy inside his car, where the wavering reception cut off the end of a rock song. Cole said "Now don't embarrass yourself by climbing onto the Bob's Big Boy fat ass slippery statue in front, all right? We both know you tried to climb it as a kid. You failed, and fell on your head. Predictably, you've never been the same since."

"Fuck you, white peckerwood." Gordy raised his bulky torso from his seat. "Don't be pissed because it's your turn to pay, and, yes, that does include dessert, my chocolate fudge served by a coffee colored honey is included."

Cole responded "That doesn't sound right," slamming his door. He waved off a street lady trying to slowly sneak toward him from the bus stop. Predictably, she gave him the finger, then threw a crushed can toward him for good measure.

One of the large, circular corner booths was available, thus they were able to spread out some notepads and books. Each attempted to combat an inner nervousness about the quality of what each had brought, and an initial burst of competitive fire. The waitress came with a pitcher of soda and glasses, and asked, with some charm in his raspy, blunt manner "The usual, guys?" She had on very bright velvet eye shadow.

"Yeah," Cole replied, "extra ranch sauce for the fries."

"As usual?" A slight smile creased her face. "You guys are hooked on the stuff, all right. Maybe you guys should take it to tv, you know, shill it and all."

Gordy returned "That's an excellent idea, Mavis. But I still crave the chocolate fudge sundae above all. Could you vouch for that?"

"Vouch?" Mavis began. "Oh, you're being cute, all right. Almost fresh, huh?" She winked and strode off.

"She's pretty cool," Cole said, pouring off the pitcher in a slightly cavalier manner, so that there was a slight splash which he quickly and dutifully wiped off the table.

"Yeah." Gordy was already thumbing through his books. "I bet she was some Hollywood line dancer back in the day. Probably blew a few directors, too." He felt Cole's stare in his forehead as he flipped through pages of selections. "But I shouldn't be talking shit about our Mavis. She's not a saltine cracker head, like-"

"Like me, you want to say, right?" piped in Cole. "Listen, I prefer white boy or honky to saltine cracker head, all right? I've always noticed how you kind of apologize when you introduce me to the 'cool brothers.' How do you think that makes me feel?" He was unable to keep a giveaway smile from teasing the corner of his mouth.

Gordy grimaced and said "Aw, come on, man. Sometimes I have to keep the peace with young hotheads in my hood. That's all. It's only a signal to them that, yeah, you're a white dude, but you're okay."

"Just okay?" Cole arose a bit on his elbows propped on the edge of the table. "Doesn't sound like much of a supportive attitude to me. Anyway, let's cut to the chase. I've got a Hollywood location, a bar to be exact, where a bartender let me know I'll probably find the right studio contact if I start coming in on a frequent basis. It's called the Rattlesnake."

"Alright," Gordy said. And I'm getting close to contacting someone who knows the person who witnessed the bombing. I've also started doing research that might lead to further leads. My thinking is that there could be a connection between militant separatist groups like the Black Panthers and its offspring with the Crips and Bloods."

Cole shook his head. "Man, you're on fire. But, remember, I've still got my part time painting duties on the side. Don't have the luxury of grandma's home-cooked meals to keep my ideas percolating."

"Right," Gordy parried, "but anyway, this thing is starting to take off. I think we might, if the intel comes thick and fast, consider just writing a non-fiction book about the police cover up. Leave it at that for the time being, then a movie contract later on."

Cole corrected "Or police lack of interest," immediately reaching for the burger. He put five or more fries into the bowl of ranch sauce to enrich their flavor.

Gordy said "I don't know exactly how it works, but if we keep it on the thin side, we could even base a screenplay directly from it."

Cole returned "Let's not get too fancy. Both of us should take notes each day, or even write out a list of our interviews every day. Then later we can shill it for tv or the movies. We'll look into legal issues later." He motioned toward the table. "But eat your food, or at least start in, why don't you. You eat too slowly, in case you haven't noticed. I don't want to be stuck here all day." At the same time he thought "I might be able to fit another Big Boy into my stomach."

Gordy had already started edging around his teeth with a toothpick, even though he was only a quarter of the way through his burger. This annoyed Cole. Gordy's shoulders tensed briefly, then sagged. "Hey, you can always speed read one of my books if you get too bored waiting. But, uh, remind me what kind of book we're writing?"

"Look, Gordy, let's keep it as simple as possible, all right? Just make sure you keep notes for later reference, and keep them in a safe place." Cole consciously slowed his eating pace, because he knew Gordy would never share his leftovers.

Gordy said "Safe place, huh? Maybe we should make Xeroxes for each other, and trade with each other whenever we meet up. That might be a wise and quick solution for now. I don't see either of us getting hurt, but at some point we might want to give each other detailed instructions. You know, like 'Go into top left corner of bedroom closet, near ceiling, punch out small secret compartment.'"

"Maybe you're right about that. We'll see," Cole returned a bit non-committedly. "Things have a way of moving toward the 'getting out of hand' area on their own anyway. Of course, if we don't stir anything up, no one will care about our book. We've got to find an audience, because I'm getting tired of house painting." His hands formed a kind of tent of temporary belief below his set mouth. He waved to Mavis and held up one of his empty plates, mouthing the word "fries," and she dutifully responded with the thumbs up signal.

Gordy piped in "Damn, you've got our gal Mavis on a string? And you're one upping me on the fries, too? Well, that's alright, I guess, even though you are a shameless white boy at times."

Cole said "And you're a, ah, I guess I'm going to not directly reply in kind, if you know what I mean, brother?" He shook his finger at

Mavis, who was spying him a bit from her beverage cart, pouring lemon sliced water from a metal pitcher. Then he pinched his own cheeks.

Gordy said "Hey, stop acting weird, man. That girl over there in the red dress is staring at you, she's starting to cry now." He smiled impishly.

"Where?"

"Got you, man! No little Red Riding Hood here for you. Come on, you're in the hood, brother," and the way Gordy spoke the word 'brother' operated in a way of saying "Don't worry yourself too much. I'm giving you the so-called slight umbrage because I think you're cool." Gordy subsequently drank his chocolate malt through a straw, with a grip on his slightly sugar-glazed spoon.

Cole said "Careful, man. Mavis knows I'm the one who leaves the generous tip. Otherwise I'll arrange it so your chocolate malt gets more and more chalky each time." Cole soaked his new batch of fries into the ranch dish.

Gordy smiled. "Ranch fry soup. I like it. Southern brothers have strange tastes, too. You heard? Some Mardi Gras revelers down in the Big Easy top off their excitement by chewing on fried alligator feet. Now that's what I call some serious toe jam."

"Sounds like my kind of place, Gordy. Say, when do you think we'll ever find our way down there?" He shifted in the booth a bit. "Seriously, we talk about making a story, the next day it starts writing itself. Little weird, right?"

Gordy was slowly eating half of an onion ring that he had dipped in ketchup, and as parts of greasy redness dripped onto the edges of the small plate, he simply nodded his head.

"Hey, the only thing is we could be sued for libel," Cole said in a tone a bit too casual for Gordy's taste. "You know, we've both done enough research papers to know how important it is to cite sources, all of that academic stuff." He was driving aggressively, as was his norm, accelerating at yellow lights and revving his engine whenever he was beside another muscle car.

Gordy replied "You can't seem to make up your mind. One minute it's a screenplay, the next it's an investigative piece."

Cole returned "Look, let's just start keeping notebooks, okay? We'll worry about the details later." It was only a few miles to Gordy's from Bob's, through an area of a race track, and the Fabulous Forum, where Gordy's beloved Lakers played. He was still piqued about Baylor, Chamberlain, and West retiring within a few years of each other.

Gordy said, "Fine. But you want me to trust you? Just make sure you keep your end of the bargain. Hey, every brother knows deep down white boys can't be trusted." He chuckled under his breath.

"Right." Cole accelerated between a Pinto and a Chevelle while changing lanes as his own form of punishment. The action jerked Gordy slightly to the side.

He said "Hey, you change directions like Andretti. But I'm really not in that much of a hurry to get home. I've got some weeding to do for granny, or I might not get that plate of pork chops I've been looking forward to. I like a light dusting of apple sauce on top, with those famous mashed potatoes, gravy..."

Cole said "You've made you point, Gordy. You get your home cooked meals, I go to Pat's Burgers of Juanito's. You've got me beat there. On the other hand, I get hit on by babes on Sunset Blvd. while you beg for attention at the bus stop."

Gordy guffawed. "I guess you got me there, smartass. But, hey, stop by the donut shop on the way back. I'm ready for dessert."

Cole had to brake hard in order to enter the lot. A man standing about ten yards away next to a bus stop bench shook his fist at him, even though it had hardly been a "close call."

Gordy said, "Don't stir up the brothers now. Or else I'll get the silent treatment for knowing you. And that will only hurt my chances for getting info about the bombing." He raised his hand over the large, sloping blue-gray dashboard. "And hey, man. You could use some detailing on your interior. You've got a light coating of dust here." Cole did not respond verbally. Instead he revved his engine to spur Gordy along.

Five

The bomber was sixteen years old, and lived three blocks north of Century Blvd. Between the house he shared with his mother and her parents were similarly small houses of off whites and yellows and browns. Most of the yards were well maintained, and random throw away cans and bottles were removed quickly. Gangs had yet to cause the noteworthy contagion of drive by shootings. But the underlying causes were already in motion, the ascension of cocaine over heroin, amphetamines, and marijuana, the diminishing blue collar jobs, the competing influx of Asians and Hispanics, and an overall declining economy. Also, the undertow of black nationalism was still strong, even after Malcolm X's assassination. The Black Panthers had directly challenged white authority, and had been pursued relentlessly by Hoover's FBI. Clearly, Martin Luther King, Jr. had been killed by yet another mediocre white southern cracker. Young blacks naturally wondered about the efficacy of toying with the rules of the white establishment. After all, Malcolm and Martin had both, through varying levels of militancy, tried to work within the system, and yet both had been erased. Thus the Black Panthers were battered into the margins. The bomber himself had grown up listening to his elders argue, sometimes over the supper table of mostly roast pork, fried chicken, biscuits, mashed potatoes, burgers, macaroni and cheese, and yams. Only his grandfather opted at times to retreat with his plate to watch his beloved Rams, opining, "This is supposed to be comfort food? I'm like ol' Satchel Paige, stress makes a mess of the stomach." His grandmother would invariably make a sucking sound through her front teeth, and say "Suit yourself."

The bomber warmed to the philosophical discussions, but for many years he saw sports as his future platform. Maybe become a Jim Brown, a Bill Russell, or a Henry Aaron or Kareem Abdul-Jabbar. He was confused as a boy when he first saw the baseball great Roberto Clemente, although culturally Hispanic, speaking Spanish, because his skin was as black as his. His mother told him "See? Black people speak different languages, son. Blacks were taken everywhere as slaves in centuries past. But that black man Clemente has pride written all over him. And class, too. That is the kind of person you should want to become."

"But I don't understand him. Even when he speaks English. I don't want to end up sounding like that."

His mother had laughed. "But you see that man beside him? He is translating for him. Sometimes, like now, you have to read the translation, the English, that is, on the television screen. Other times the man beside him will speak the words out loud."

Television, especially in the color era, had brought children a closer link to their sports idols. The bomber rarely watched other programs, because the people in them seemed plain, like his family members. His grandparents often told him he was smart enough to become a teacher, but he was uninterested in education as a potential career. As for athletics, his left knee was savaged while playing tackle football as a ten year old. He tried to become a power hitter in baseball, but he never developed enough to make the high school team, and running track would have further endangered already brittle knees. At one point he tried to commit to becoming a bodybuilder, but discovered that even a knee brace could not provide the level of stability he required. Afterward, he began devoting himself to books, devouring above all those examining the struggles of blacks and other minorities. His boxing training, however, prevented him from being teased much for his bookishness, and some of his teachers warmed to his goal of furthering his intellect.

The bomber kept separate notebooks, each with a different subject. #1 was sports, #2 leaders, and #3 styles. The third was one he wrote in when he felt light-minded, not in the mood to attach significance to a particular person or event. He hated the idea of a diary or journal, and felt he was already opening himself to enough opprobrium for being stubborn enough to think that writing was an honorable and wise choice for a career. In other words he was adjudged to be emulating certain "cracker nerds," such as the tenth grade teacher English teacher everyone called "Mr. Snore." There were rumors that Mr. Snodgrass was stiff in part because he had been fired from a community college over a romantic entanglement in the admissions office. This humiliating demotion accounted for some of his less than stellar classroom energy, and the despair written on his face when he had to thank a student for depositing an apple on his desk. Meanwhile his body language said "Leave me alone." In class the bomber was known as Mr. Willis, but Hitch on the streets, due to the fact that after his knee injury he always walked with a slight hitch/stutter in his step. At first, the nickname angered him, but over time he gravitated to it. Years later, the popular "pimp roll" mode of walking looked like a poor imitation of his original, jaunty stride.

"Ah man, you're just trying to be pimp cool. But don't let the fuzz see you walking down the street like that. Your ass will get arrested for it." Someone had made this statement in the high school cafeteria.

He had shouted "Who says? Come and show yourself," but the voice had issued from the back of the cafeteria line, out of his sight. He quickly gathered that abandoning his place in line between a Jeri curl weave and a balloon afro could not be rectified by an excuse or exception to the traditional rule of "losing your place." When some Jeri curl grease flicked off onto his Rams t shirt, he almost wrenched himself from his place in line to confront his heckler. Instead, he concentrated on the smells of spaghetti and garlic bread as best as he could to distract his anger. And he reminded himself that his upcoming militant action was only a few weeks away. Thus he could not afford any sophomoric nonsense. So he just muttered under his breath "No wannabe thug is going to take me off my focus. No one will crimp my style."

Hitch avoided his family the last few days before the bombing, taking notes, and memorizing the mental checks he had to make before he delivered the "package," as his superiors called it. Some late nights were spent with a flashlight under his bed covers, reading inspirational militant tracts. He distilled passages into his own language and recited them to the bathroom mirror while he anxiously watched for the first appearance of chin gristle. "Avenge your ancestors" was one. And others? "Brother, do you want to hurt individuals? If you do, don't. Instead, when at all possible destroy capitalist, fascistic institutions. Attacking the ruling white majority will gain you more enemies than allies. Sure, 'Off the Fuzz,' and 'Kill the vampin' pigs' appeals to your masculine pride, but, trust me, you will lose. Not only that, your brothers and sisters in the 'hood will be punished for your actions. That is not right. Be the fox, brother. I beg you. I'm not asking you to allow yourself to be physically beaten by a sick white cracker. No, in that case, be the lion. But don't go out to the corner and shout about killing honkies. Other militants will tell you that is the best way, and is the most honest. Be angry, but don't become an animal as a result of it. Dig? Killing white crackers is dumb. It's the men in the shadows, the ones Dylan talks about, who are the ones pulling the strings. You might go after them. But first you've got to draw them out. It might just be better to do something now. That will take time. You're a young and capable brother. You respect yourself and others. Make it your goal to compel others to respect you. Speak to someone older than yourself. But not just older. Wiser, brother. Feel each other out. If you trust him, and he trusts you, come up with a plan. But it has got to be just between the two of you. Tell him I told you to tell him it has to stay between the two of you. Be focused. Find the right project for you alone, brother. I assume you're not famous like Russell or Ali. So you can't use sports to enact change. Politically, man, Malcolm and Martin are gone, too. So where does that leave you? And where does that leave us as a people, brother? Determine your own destiny. Shape your own soul. You're hurt. You have scars. But do you want to be truly great, brother? That's what I'm asking you. Be great inside yourself first, then all will succeed after that choice. Do you have to hide these kinds of books from your family? (Hitch chuckled to himself). If you do, it is for a reason. Your family is conformist. They can't see, or they even refuse to see, which is worse in a way. They might humor your idea, brother, but they also might turn you in."

Hitch felt possessed. It was as if a part of him had been dead, as if an avenging spirit had spoken to him in tones forceful, yet more suggestive than commanding, to act. Mornings were the time when an inner voice of caution pestered him: "They could put you away with this shit for the rest of your life! And what does that Korean grocery have to do with the plight of you and your brothers? Leave it alone." On the other hand, he realized that not going through with the mission after committing to it could cause him personal danger. "At least be a man of your word," another voice counseled him.

Six

Slowly the slab of butter melted into the hotcakes. Gordy poured the maple syrup onto the stack and cut the breakfast sausage into small, bite-sized squares. Then he tipped the teapot and poured hot water into his hot cocoa seasoned cup, and dressed. His chest of drawers was organized from the previous night, when he had folded his new batch of laundry perfected by his favorite fabric softener. He removed his construction boots from the closet, because he felt he would be embarking on a serious mission, and they were a hallmark of such business. He rolled on his socks, placed the boots near the door, then sat down to eat his breakfast. He ate slowly, even methodically, chewing each piece at least five times. Halfway through, he heard the distant droning of a police siren, then the slight chattering of a police helicopter shortly thereafter. It struck him that there had been many flower bouquets placed in front of the destroyed Korean grocery. Briefly, he considered starting a tally within a notebook. He thought, "Am I getting a little crazy with this investigative journalism stuff?"

"Housing project, building E," he thought while he finished his breakfast, wiping the remaining sausage grease off his plate with the last scraps of hotcakes. Then he completed a quick set of push-ups, twenty in total. He wrote a reminder to himself to buy toothpaste and razors later in the day, then half-heartedly flipped through a few of the history texts he had checked out of the library. He was anxious to speak to "The Statement," the mysterious figure, about the bombing. Even though on the surface he and Cole were working the project together and simultaneously, he felt he would have to unearth the first actual facts about the case. "I've got to be the catalyst now," he thought.

The remains of the Korean grocery had begun to slump inside the destroyed exoskeleton. As Gordy passed it on the way to the government housing project he noted an inspector of some kind. He was sweating in a long white starched dress shirt adorned with a prominent pocket protector. He was posting some kind of notice. In fact, he was using a staple gun to attach it to a telephone pole, the red block letters boldly displayed. But Gordy was near-sighted, and as a result could not read it from a distance. He thought, "Probably just posting an official notice about the property being technically seized by local authorities." Another part of him was urging him to saunter over and ask the guy, "Pencil necked honkies shouldn't be in this 'hood, you know? Maybe you should get your cracker ass out of here as fast as possible." He chuckled to himself and entered the housing grounds. The de facto security guard was at his usual spot, crouched on the steps. But his back was briefly turned, as he was talking to a woman in a flimsy negligee on the second floor. Gordy thought she blinked once in his direction as he proceeded to building E. He thought "The brother doesn't look too interested in her, and I can't blame him."

Gordy examined the wall of mail boxes. He read mostly first initials and last names. One example: V Hodges. Most were printed on narrow white labels with various smudges of gray on them, others with scrawled-on asterisks and stars. Gordy quickly scanned it the first time, and peered back over his shoulder to make sure he was not being watched. The second time he saw what first appeared to be the initials I.S., but then he noticed that the top bar of the I had been penned in, very neatly, but still quite obvious. So it actually read TS. "Are you 'The Statement' brother?" he asked. "And do you have vital info?" The number of the apartment was 4F. Since he was leery of elevators in general, he passed the bank of lifts, and proceeded to the stairwell at the end of the hallway. He smelled marijuana at door IE, saw a potted plant in front of IG and a complex note warning the occupants to move out by a certain date, with a scent of patchouli emanating from it. "Must be some hippy chick," he thought. He kicked aside an empty Coke can at the first floor landing and spoke to himself under his breath. "Keep on an even keel, man." He recalled the talk he had with the de facto security guard downstairs, and wondered in what manner 'The Statement' was dangerous. It was already immaterial, because he was well up the steep steps of a slightly decrepit government housing project. His interior monologue described the snaking dust bunnies sheathing the stairwell window's sash. He thought while fingering one into a dust paste between the thumb and index finger, "This is kind of like a, uh, an insect's chrysalis."

The door 4F was bare on the outside. When his steps terminated in front of it, he was unnerved by the complete lack of noise in the hallway. One floor down, in comparison, was an almost continuous cacophony featuring hollow wood noises and the humming static of electronics. Here was an absence of all sounds altogether. He knocked lightly on the door. He heard a quick expostulation-"Awww!"-and the droning voice of a television newscaster. He heard a few footfalls advancing, but then they quickly disappeared, and he heard a faucet being turned on. At that moment Gordy wondered if he should start carrying a gun, because the setting reminded him of a police action from a certain suspense film. A moment before he considered knocking again, he heard the door lock turned. A loud clearing of a throat followed, before a spell of dead silence.

"Okay. This is how I work." The voice was calm and assured, but also slightly robotic in the vocal register, purged of normal intonations. "I have already heard about you and your interest in speaking to me. You are not allowed to ask me questions, nor will we speak face-to-face at such an early period in our contact." He paused, then continued. "I am momentarily going to recuse myself for a cup of hot coffee. Stand fast if you still want to proceed. Otherwise you'll have to go it alone."

Gordy's immediate instinct was to curse him and the mission, but he remained in place standing outside the door, silent. Part of him felt foolish, yet he knew that he had to abide by the control being exerted by 'The Statement.' At the same time he felt relieved that he had brought a small notepad and pen (the pen had almost speared his leg on the way over by slowly working its way through a thin pocket of cloth next to his thigh). Also, why had the lock been turned? Was it a test? In the event he tried to take advantage, would he be stabbed for illegal entry?

"You still there?" The voice trailed off, and a slapping noise quickly followed.

"Yes," Gordy responded in a flat tone. At the same time a door opened at the end of the hall, slammed shut, opened once more slowly, then slammed again.

"All right. My word is you're a pretty cool brother. Like me. I've asked around about you. Luckily for you, that word was on the solid side of things. Otherwise I would have refused to answer any of your questions. But this is where we start. I am going to make a statement for you. I want you to understand it is the best I can do for the time being. You are fishing for info. That's good. I am, too. Maybe down the line we can work together. But for now you're kind of on the first proving ground. I want to see how you will do."

Gordy was tempted to respond because there was a long pause. Then he heard 'The Statement' clearing his throat and sipping from his cup. It made a slightly slurping noise. He thought, "Cole wouldn't have patience for this. He would tell the freak he hoped he choked on his hot drink."

"You're still there," the voice continued. "You make a slight, creaking motion when you shift your weight from one foot to the other. You're a pretty heavy dude. Right?"

"Yeah, I'm about two-"

"No need to say more. I can tell by your voice that you're a brother, too. You've got a slight bebop beat in your vocal register. So listen here, I'm going to give you some info. He saw some of what went down the other night at the grocery. He's, uh, quiet, like us. You will follow the instructions I write on a piece of paper. If you follow everything to a "T" you will get further directives from me in the near future. I shouldn't have to tell you to keep it all on the hush hush, either. The back side of the paper will indicate when I will speak to you again. If you are the type that misplaces things, make sure you keep it in a safe place. That's all for now, then."

"But-"

"No 'but,' brother. This is it. You choose. This is the kind of shit a lot of people would rather leave alone, you know? The war over drugs is on. Too many cats won't do the military thing after 'Nam, and the manufacturing jobs are leaving.   Things will get worse, brother. Believe me there. Unfortunate, but all too true."

Gordy heard a slight crinkling of paper, then a neatly penned note, on Mead notebook paper, was shoved under the door.   "Okay, brother. 'Till next time." Gordy heard the footsteps quickly retreat behind the door.

Cole finished a small exterior job around eleven in the morning. It was only brush work, so he only had to clean the brushes in a container of turpentine before leaving. He deposited the supplies inside an outdoor closet and heard a band of squirrels snickering up in the trees. A voice of paranoia crept into his head, telling him the animals were chattering at him. "No, they're making fun of you, like you're a street derelict of some sort," the voice said over a thin, sharp wire pricking his brain. Even though he could not expect to be paid until Monday, he decided he could afford a meal at Juanita's on Fairfax. He thought "I haven't seen Rosie for quite a while." She was his favored young waitress, the one he had flirted with (and she with him) unabashedly for the past two years. Recently there had been times while she served his lunch plate (usually chile rellenos and cheese enchiladas) that their eyes had locked together in yearning and innocence. "Man, her eyes are like pools of water," he sometimes thought. He wondered what Gordy would say if he knew that his partner was "trolling for trim," as Gordy sometimes crudely termed the art of romantic pursuit.

In contrast, Cole considered himself a bit old fashioned, uncomfortable and unwilling to answer questions about past sexual escapades. Gordy sometimes tried to draw out a response by calling him a prude, which never achieved its desired result. Cole would simply retreat into philosophical musings about Door's lyrics, or debates about who had the better logo and uniforms, the Rams or Raiders. Gordy would say something to the effect of "You mention the Doors, the Lizard King himself, without mentioning all the chicks he got into the sack? That's really something, man."

Cole had not driven down Fairfax for months, even though it was only one mile east of where he lived as a youngster. Today, he made a point to pass the stretch of Jewish delis and Italian florists, which added such flavor to the otherwise dying embers of pure Angelenos Hippydom. Of course, the selfsame hippies would occasionally order a house soup in order to sit next to the old ladies and gents wearing their soft cream blouses and crisp brown suits. But people like Cole were not fooled. Hippies were caught between the molding tide of late sixties coolness and the nascent era of seventies sheikh, where people tended to dabble in only the more savory allure of the preceding generation; such as unrestrained sex and less mind altering drugs such as cocaine. In other words, the spirit of being high, but without experiences that might endanger developing careers. Thus only the most unthreatening hippies were invited to parties of the wealthy patrons of the arts, after passing an unwritten vetting process. He thought "When was the last time that Gordy and I attended a party that could also have been described as an event? Where people are really looking to connect spiritually, not just sexually?" As he drove past the row of restaurants and small shops, another internal voice piped in "Who cares? Now there are less dilettante writers out there to compete with Gordy and me."

Both were native Angelenos, which was sometimes a social lubricant in the city of angels. Gordy joked at times, "Why hasn't it opened more doors for us? Doors of perception and all that in the land of freaks and lizard people?"

Cole slowed to get a better look at the pedestrians and store windows, then agreeably stopped at a red light. He somehow felt like an interloper, or even an invader, as an old woman dutifully pushed her wire cart through the intersection. He felt foreign, as if he had unknowingly dropped in from outer space. He thought that he should maybe ditch his and Gordy's project, and instead write a screenplay with Rod Serling voice overtones, about a time travel tunnel located in the middle of Hollywood. "Great," he thought. "I'm already behind Gordy on our project, and now I start letting myself fantasize in other directions. I guess I'm becoming too reactive." He rolled down his window, and smelled a rich onion soup. It gave him a slight feeling of comfort, as unexpected as it was. He chuckled to himself. "Is that really a soup, because I hate most soups? Or is it really just the rich garlic aroma goading me?"

Juanito's lot was almost empty, because he was slightly ahead of the normal lunch crowd. He parked the Pontiac two spaces down from a Ford Fairmont, as he was always conscious of his car representing a trophy. "More security in numbers," he thought. He thought he would have to find a safe garage for it soon. The building's stucco exterior had recently been painted bright red. Rosie as usual was on her "perch" at the front, replacing the near empty salsa dishes at the front. She was wearing black jeans, and, as they had faded out a bit over time, her hair, feathered at the sides, appeared even darker. Her face was attractive, if a bit in a tomboy way, and a bit wide, with a prominent chin. Cole was only a few feet behind her when he said "Hello, bonita."

"Hola, Cole," she said, turning and almost brushing her shoulder against his as she walked to the back side of the counter. "You've been away long time."

Cole smiled. "Yeah, but now I'm back. So why don't you set me up with that quesadilla grande. You know, the one with beans, sour cream-"

She smiled back. "Sure. Quesadilla supreme." She scribbled on her pad and quickly tore it off and inserted it into the revolving order ring. Cole felt the amused eyes of the cook on them momentarily before the ticket was snatched off.

"Right. Give me a horchata, too. You know, something a little sweet like you. That's what I need."

"Aha. You still good at talking to the chicas, si?" she said, pouring off his drink into a large red cup. "But you're always so busy."

Cole smiled. "Yeah. All too true. But I've got to stay busy. Otherwise I go crazy. You know, loco. I'm starting a new project with Gordy. You remember him, right? Big black guy, sometimes loud, sometimes real quiet?"

"Si, si, el es negro. Yo recuerdo. Nice man. Like you. But what project?"

"Ah, I'll tell you about it next time. I think it is bad luck to talk about something too much before it happens."

"Okay." Briefly she looked awkward before heading back to the kitchen.

Cole thought "Do I always confuse people? Is that my way? Did she think I was warming up to ask her out? Or just playing with her?"

The booth was one he felt was a transplant from an old steak house. It had fancy dimpled brown leather cushions. And the table had a red-and-white oil cloth, the curlicue image on it slowly fading. On the walls were old black-and-whites of Hispanic performers. He thought "I should ask Rosie about who they are some day." He scooted to the back of the circular booth so he could have a closer view of his car. Rosie brought out his food, even though the normal procedure was for the patron to pick it up at the front counter. She said "Enjoy, Cole, and don't forget to say bye on the way out," and placed the plate down.

Cole wanted to say more, but simply replied "Thanks." He took care to spread the guacamole and sour cream equally atop the triangle shaped cheese and tortilla slices. He felt excitable and tired at the same time. Sleeping had been difficult for him to sustain in large uninterrupted portions since his visit to the Rattlesnake bar. In his subconscious was a warning that he and Gordy might uncover more sordidness than they could deal with. His more conscious mind informed him that deciding to dine in a quiet, familiar environment gave him some deserved comfort. He wondered if he had already begun to procrastinate about returning to the bar. Finally he thought "That's it. No indecision now. I'm going back tomorrow night. And every night until I get some answers." He returned his focus to his food, and glanced in Rosie's direction from time to time. He resolved to leave a generous tip in the front jar when he left. "But will I ever get her number?" he wondered.

Seven

Gordy kept himself in suspense until he reached home. Until then, the card inscribed by "The Statement" was kept in his pocket. As he sifted through his mail he wondered if he wanted to see The Statement's face. "Not yet," he thought. "Guy's a real jive ass, indeed." The note read: Julio Castroneves 3625 E Century Blvd. #D3. Phone number 262-3297. Call him 7-8pm Friday night. Do not confront him in person. Call him first. When he says he's given you enough information, do not press him. He thought "So I'm supposed to follow all these instructions closely? If so, I might be rewarded with further info sessions with Mr. Castroneves?" He wondered if he was prepared for a greater level of patience than he was accustomed to. His grandmother's favorite aphorism was "You won't get anywhere being in a constant hurry." His favorite rejoinder? "Won't get anywhere being slothful, either." At any rate, he would have to wait for the following evening, unless he was bold enough to believe he could ignore the commandments of The Statement. His mind arrested a picture of a man with wild eyes and quick hands. "When I see him face to face I'd better be careful," he thought. "But what of Mr. Castroneves? Should I try to pull up his background? But how? And what if The Statement catches wind of it? Would he abruptly end the arrangement when it has only barely started?"

Feeling the need to briefly escape his immediate environs, he caught a bus up Normandie. He was debating where to hop off for lunch when an argument erupted between the driver and a young woman. She looked vaguely familiar to Gordy. She was a light coffee color, short, and thin, with her large Afro accented by purple streaks.

Rumors circulated in the 'hood that she was an on and off again strawberry (prostitute).

"I've got the rest of the change, Uncle Tom. And can't you see I'm just as black as you?" She finally deposited the rest of her coins.

The driver cleared his throat loudly and she paused as she took the first open seat. "Yeah, just keep it up, Tommin'," she said. Her eyes darted around for looks of solidarity with her fellow riders. Most were intent on newsprint or stolidly staring outside the window at the slightly ramshackle appearance of many buildings, many in soft pastels of yellow and pink. Gordy sat in the rear, and she gave him a teasing smile, which he ignored. "Nothing but old bags and queers on this bus," she said under her breath before taking her seat. Gordy stared hard at the back of her head momentarily, then returned to gazing out the window. "Man, I hope this project works out one way or another," he thought. "Otherwise I will simply be wasting more precious time around here, just writing my stories inside of a bubble." His eyes feasted briefly on Gino's Pizza, then moved on. "I missed that stop anyway," he considered. But he realized the bus was bearing down on Badgro's Burgers, which featured a cheddar-and-onion double that he was craving. He pulled the cord beside the window, and walked to the exit door as silently as he could, not eager to further pique the ornery woman. Her shoulders were tensed, and she kept picking nervously at something near her left ear. The stop was only a few yards past the burger shack on the right. When he was a kid he and his buddies used to joke that it should be called Bad Brothers instead. Mr. Badgro was usually ensconced at a squat table near the back of the establishment, and taking over at the grille occasionally, his wiry, thatched hair a clump at the back of his unusually small head. He prided himself on his famous "pounders," ground beef patties that were flattened to and beyond the edges of their sesame seed buns. Cole himself had begun to copy the practice when he cooked for himself. Gordy appreciated the rustic brick décor, and the wide gray planks of the front porch seating area, also. He sat at the one in which as a teenager he had inscribed his initials-GB-with a sharp pen. More recently, someone had attempted to besmirch the letters by adding "ood" to the G and "utt" to the B with indelible ink but it was too close to the already marred surface of periodic varnish coats. So it appeared blurry above his enduring GB.

The burger had cheddar cheese, grilled onions, a special mayo with bacon bits, lettuce, tomato, and mustard. Ketchup was anathema to old man Badgro. "You've already got your tomato there, so why add some kind of sugar tomato extract?" he would banter with customers requesting the actual condiment. Eventually, he compromised, furnishing the condiments counter with ketchup packets. He swore by a common yellow mustard, "best tang for the buck," he told his assistants. "Why use that overpriced European sauce?" The front help was very brief with customers, but not unkind, either.

He was a short, beefy kid, with a cream polyester shirt tight across his thick shoulders and biceps. "That's odd," Gordy thought, noticing the initials JB on the right side of his chest (was he a nephew of old man Badgro?) "All right, brother, enjoy your Badgro," he said while waiting for the fizz to settle in the Styrofoam cup of soda. Gordy turned, brushing shoulders with one of the three in line. He was a tall and thin white guy wearing a Hawaiian shirt and a Dodgers cap.

Gordy's immediate hunch was that he was a lawyer of some stripe. Even with the casual attire, there was something martial in his character, which gave him added protection in a predominantly black neighborhood. It was already a catch phrase-"Street Smart"-the way people in potentially dangerous environments comported themselves. To Gordy, the lanky man, even as casually dressed as he was, exuded the same attitude. "Jimmy," he said, "get the usual, all right? But just tell Badgro to go light on the onions."

"I heard that, fancy pants lawyer. Just for that I'll add more cheese. Hah!" Badgro quickly turned his head and winced. But then he only motioned toward the grille, which was still manned by a rail thin teenager who had a silver transistor radio on low on a small shelf above him.

The lawyer sat at the large picnic table behind Gordy. He pulled out a baseball scorecard and a felt tip pen, and made some quick notations. Gordy glanced over briefly, unable to determine if he was actually writing in the names of players, or just utilizing it for scratch paper. Gordy ate his burger slowly, as was his custom, and wiped the greasy cheese off his plate with his fries. At one point the lawyer cursed under his breath-"fucking clients"-and ignored his burger for the time being. Momentarily, he added "wrong numbers." Suddenly, Gordy wondered if the lawyer was not only a Dodgers fan, but also a follower of numbers games. And his outer show of social ease did nothing to conceal some sort of wrenching inner knowledge. Gordy considered engaging the man in conversation, but reconsidered. He thought, "Don't I have enough suspense material already? Meanwhile Cole has done virtually nothing. I need to let this other stuff rest."

Once he reached home, he decided to write down his impressions of the past few days, then rest.

Until he was shoulder level in the ocean, Cole simply ducked under the waves. When he finally dove under a larger wave, his legs already had a leaden and slightly numb feel to them. He briefly admired a sailing vessel almost impinging on the series of buoys, then bodysurfed the first suitable wave back to shore. As he approached his towel, he saw forms of joggers and bicyclists on the snaking trail, toward the slowly crumbling palisades of Santa Monica. But at his depth from the ocean he only saw a few surfers hundreds of yards north surfside. It was quickly growing late. Cole had been planning an ocean swim for quite some time, but he had also been putting it off, until the early Fall chilly water rushed the process to a quick end.

He quickly dried off, then washed his chest and underarms quickly inside the men's public restroom. And before he maneuvered his GTO out of its parking space, he pulled a flask of whiskey out of the glove compartment and took one swig. "I need a bit of fire in my belly for the Rattlesnake," he thought. By the time he reached the bar, he had added a couple of Pink's chili dogs and fries to the mix.

It was a different bartender this time, a thirtyish redhead with freckles, her haired tied off in a ponytail at the back, with a clear and cutting Australian accent. Cole remembered the curt English bloke who had sized him up on his first visit to the bar. Presently it was 7:00 pm on a Thursday night. Her arms were sunk in the sink soap suds, plunging glasses. She said, without looking up, "Terry said you'd be coming."

"Whoah," Cole exhaled, and tentatively took a bar stool. At that juncture in the evening, there were only a couple of old-timers manning stools to his right, plunging hands into peanut bowls. He said "I guess word has got out."

"Meaning?" she replied, looking up with a teasing wink. "It's not like you just came in from the outback, mate. Relax. Just realize that good bartenders keep each other up to date. But before we continue, are you thirsty?"

Cole replied, "Yeah. Uh, just a Bud draft for now." He pulled a peanut dish within easy reach, and watched himself briefly in the bar mirror. "Got to look confident and assured," he thought.

"Right. You're a bit early for the action tonight, you know?" She frisbeeded a coaster in position in front of him, then set the mug down upon it. "But then, this girl will talk your ear off."

Cole smiled. "Cool. And I've never talked to an, uhm-"

"Aussie?" she said helpfully. "Okay. We're good minxes, that we definitely are. Hope that's an American verb?"

"Kind of." Cole fished into the peanut dish. "Fox is the word nowadays. Earlier on it was bombshell, broad, or-"

She leaned forward a bit teasingly and said "That's it?" She responded to one of the old timer's raised hand summons. She loped down and poured out of the bottle, straight into the glass, then returned. "Fox, huh? The English hunt those types."

Cole took one large gulp from his beer mug, then replied, "Yeah. Those English, for all their propriety, do some weird and cruel shit."

"By the way, my name's Kit." She started drying her batch of cleaned liquor glasses with a small towel. "And yours is?"

"Uh, yeah, sorry. It's Cole."

"Okay, Cole. Glad to meet ya. Terry told me about you a bit. Just so happens my cousin, the one who vouched for me to come up from down under, is a production assistant with Paramount." She paused to let the information sink in.

"No kidding." Cole tried to exude casualness, but was overcome by excitement. "I show up here the second time and already have a so-called 'in'?"

"Well, don't get carried away, mate." Without asking, she pulled his mug and refilled it. "But it could be the start of something."

Cole replied "Lately it is like things here have been connecting without me trying. It kind of, uh, I don't know. Lots of people in this town have Hollywood connections."

Kit said "You're surprised. End of story. Kidding aside, you seem like you're in a hurry of some sort."

Cole shrugged, for the first time catching the silky smoothness of her legs. "Well, my buddy and I are kind of in a race to make 'something' happen, if you catch my drift?"

Kit nodded her head. "That's what I both love and hate about this big town, on the make all the time. Luckily I'm forced home by the authorities once in a while to keep up my Visa. Otherwise I'd probably lose my mind."

Cole continued "Agreed. LA is the kind of place, when you're here, whether you want to be or not, it is best to try to do something big. Otherwise it's just better to leave altogether." Cole realized as he spoke that he had not set foot outside the city for five years.

Kit said "Sure, mate. But sometimes it's just better to pull back a stool and soak it all in, right? Because in three hours this place will be as hot as a barbie."

"Excuse me?"

"Barbie as in barbecue. Things will get hot. You strike me as actually being a bit on the quiet side. Am I right?" But her body language told him it was unnecessary for him to answer. She paused momentarily. "My cousin, even though he's just a production assistant, has gotten the ear a few times of the executive VP up there at Paramount. His name is Rod Owens. I'll tell him you might be stopping by-"

Cole replied "I don't know. I mean, isn't that a little too pushy? I don't want to get off on the wrong foot from the outset."

Kit laughed. "Don't worry about it. I'll tell him you'll be coming by. Me and him meet on his lunch break, which is a bit later than usual, about two to three. Just meet outside the security gate. I'll give him your description."

"And if it would help if I knew how he looks-" Cole said in a leading manner.

"Right. He's on the short side, stocky, and with curly and thick dark hair, in his early thirties. He's always said his parents named him after the great tennis player Rod Laver, because his nose appears more like the beak of a bird. I tease him about how the first time I poured him a whiskey I thought he would put his nose in first."

Cole shoved his empty mug across the bar top. "Well, you can see I don't nose around. Ready for another, I guess."

She spoke while she tapped it off, the suds spilling off the top. "You seem to be in a hurry for quick intoxication."

"Yeah. I've got to stain a back yard ramada tomorrow. It's a vacation property. The owners are arriving by noon, and don't want anyone around when they arrive. Then I'm meeting my buddy. We're going to discuss how the so-called project is progressing."

Kit tittered a little. "I like how you say 'project.' Makes it seem mysterious. And I don't like things explained too much, whether a book, a play, or a movie like in some films in a desert scene I don't care whether it is in Arabia or, hey, even Down Under, my backyard. I'd like to imagine where it is myself. Not that I care much for silent films, either. What about you?"

Cole replied "I guess I like a mix, but I always gravitate toward suspense. Like the French Connection. I guess I'm more into books." Cole felt a bit pedantic as he said it, but he still relayed the thought. "Besides, books come cheaper, and so do writing materials. My buddy

Gordy and I joke about not being able to afford to pursue any other art form, but it's true, actually."

"Self-fulfilling prophecy?" Kit said.

"Yeah, kind of like that." Cole squinted, because slivers of light from the opened bar door flashed in the corner of his eye. "Keep doing what you love, even if it brings you misery, too. I guess they all become clichés, the 'every blessing comes with a curse' kind of thing. I'll keep doing what I need to, no matter what." He started to stand.

Kit said "Don't forget now. His name's Rod Owens. Make sure you report back to me afterward. By the way, he can be very blunt. But don't let that discourage you."

Cole left a couple of one dollar bills on the bar top. "You've been too kind. Most chicks around here only have huge dollar signs in their eyes. They only give me notice sometimes when I drive my sports car."

Kit laughed. "Aw, don't get riled up about that, mate. Look at money or a fancy car as just a vehicle for a relationship. Get it?"

As he exited Cole was still smiling, with a warmth of beer comforting his stomach and the sun tanning his face.

He found himself smiling long into the night, until a thought struck him: "Did I rush out?"

Gordy had the personal info written on the back of an old business card: Julio Castroneves   3625 E Century Blvd.   262-3297   7-8pm.

Friday night. He had his small color television tuned into KCAL Nine. The Dodgers game was on. Their classic all white uniforms with blue lettering and red numbers on the canvass of bright Bermuda grass consoled him as he picked up his phone to make the appointed call at the exact, requested time. He thought to himself "I hope I'm not burying myself in a wack job cave." On the screen a Dodger outfielder speared a fly ball on the warning track, and he watched "Kissing Bandit Morganna" climbing down from her front seat porch down the right field line to embrace him, her prodigious bosom swaying back and forth, up and down. A shout of "Go girl!" emanated from next door. His grandmother was even more of a faithful Dodgers fan than him, sometimes canceling neighborhood card games to keep abreast of their progress.

Gordy pulled the telephone cord to its full length, and placed the phone in his lap. He tried to concentrate on the right approach to take for at least five minutes. He let himself be entertained a bit longer by Morganna's antics. He wondered if she was a failed actress from some part of her misspent youth. "But who am I to judge her?" he thought. He considered turning down the television volume, then started dialing on the rotary phone.

The voice was hoarse, even harsh. "Been expecting your call." Gordy heard a slight clicking/slushing sound, and thought that Julio was drinking his hard liquor from an ice-chilled glass. "And right on time, too. You follow directions well. But what's in it for me? I mean, man, I could use some dough."

Cole was thinking that the man was desperate, but still coherent (at least over the phone). "I could arrange some dough, sure, maybe some extras-"

"Like beer?" Julio's burp was just outside of clear reception in the earpiece.

"Absolutely beer, liquor if you want that, too. Look, I don't want the police to get involved in any way. This is more about research-"

"For what? Look, 'The Situation' seems to think you're on our side, the 'hood's. But we're not dumb. Everyone is on the make in this town."

Gordy overcame his desire to prolong his pause. "All right. Me and my buddy want to write a book about it, sell it to Hollywood and all that shit."

"Hah. Touche. Well, better you're honest up front. Don't know why you'd want to involve yourself with Hollywood douchebags, but I try to be forgiving."

Gordy tried to subdue the excitement in his voice. "All right."

"'All right'," parroted Julio. "Uh, never mind. I shouldn't be so hard on you. Look, as a gesture of goodwill, send me over a six pack of Molson's. I've got Mr. Long's number here in front of me. Write it down and call him as soon as I hang up. All right?"

Gordy felt a surge of anxiety, feeling that he might be duped, and so soon, too. "Never be the lamb, right?" an interior voice asked him.

But another one pointed out that a few dollars was worth the risk. "Okay. Now what's the number?"

"503-2985. Mr. Long shouldn't have to ask if it's to be delivered, but give him my full name. Julio Castroneves, and address, of course."

"I've still got that." Gordy was briefly plagued by indecision.

"Okay. Good man. Call me at the same time tomorrow night and I'll tell you about the guy I saw fucking with the grocery. Good enough?"

"Don't see why not."

"Okay. Good." Julio hung up without further comment.

Gordy did as instructed. Mr. Long had the voice of what he later described to Cole as a male stork. Mr. Long instructed Gordy that as long as an envelope with the cash was deposited in his mail slot the next morning, all would be fine. Of course, he could opt to deliver it in person, or use a credit card if he had one. Gordy mumbled that he might use it if he had one to begin with. Then Mr. Long read him his business address, and made Gordy repeat it back to him.

Gordy went to sleep soon thereafter, but not before consulting his legal pad to determine that he had to post grandmother's mail, shop for her cat Lovis, whose finicky tastes ran to canned sardines and oysters, buy a new spray bottle of weed eater, hand deliver payment for the monthly utility bill, purchase Martin's special breakfast burrito for granny, and water the lawn, and all before Cole picked him up for another Bob's Big Boy work session/discussion. As was his custom, he had one oatmeal cookie and a small glass of milk, and changed into his striped pajamas. He sat in the Barcalounger while he had his bed time snack.

At three pm the following day Gordy had accomplished all of the tasks, except one: He was unable to purchase Martin's breakfast burrito, because overnight someone had broken the storefront glass, even though it had a protective cage gate around it. Even though he knew the attack was not likely connected to the Korean grocery bombing, it still sparked an internal alarm. Only a very long rod or a perfectly sized rock thrown at extreme velocity would be able to crack the glass, in his estimation. Someone had a great deal of concentrated fury, indeed. But he decided there was enough to report to Cole without mentioning that detail.

Eight

In the gas station bathroom mirror, Cole noticed a small spray of red paint on his elbow. He rubbed soap and water into it but was only able to make it less bright; he could not completely eradicate it. But he had not used red paint that morning, so he wondered how long it had spent drying there. He remembered using red as corner trim in a Bell Air kitchen, but how long ago had it been? He studied his face through the spidery crack in the glass. When was the mirror invented? He thought he would like to look that fact up. Is that when people started killing themselves? When they could see how they appeared to others? He had read somewhere that knowing and caring exactly what everyone thought about you would lead that same person to immediate ruin. Cole paused a moment at the door, thinking that if he paused a moment longer he would have to once more clean the imaginary filth from his hands.

Gordy wearied of the wait, having been anticipating a Bob's burger for the greater part of the day. He hopped out of Cole's GTO and went inside the convenience store to buy a candy bar. He selected a Rocky Road, and had already eaten half of it by the time Cole sauntered back from the restroom.

Cole said "Man, what are you eating?"

"Nothing, okay. Just a snack. I'm starving."

"Yeah," Cole returned. "You're having your dessert early. But I'm driving. So I think you owe me at least one scoop of ice cream. And I'm the one with the real job. You hang around, pick up shit, do yard work. I do actual paid work."

Gordy raised his hands in a gesture of temporary surrender. "Ah man. Not that old number. Can't you give me a break for the time being?"

"Okay." Cole accelerated and the wide tires briefly caught on an oil slick, threatening to spin the muscle car out of control. It did cause an old woman to sprout a middle finger (obviously angry about being startled).

Gordy returned "Hey man, cool it. I have to come back here! I live here. You don't. Get it?" He almost punched Cole in the shoulder.

"Okay." Cole was out in a free lane, and accelerating again. "We're on our way, buddy. No doubt about it. But tell me again about 'The Statement,' the white dude who thinks he is black because he has dreadlocks."

"Slow down, man. I didn't even see his face. All right? He talked through his freaking door. He gave me the number for the guy who probably saw the bomber. Okay?"

Cole said "Wrong choice of words, buddy. But this is already epic, you know what I mean? Do we actually need all this, uh, preparation anymore?"

Gordy eyed him hard. "Are you high on something, man? I didn't know you did more than drink. And, really, slow down. Lucky the LAPD hasn't pulled us over yet. They'll assume we've got paraphernalia or whatever cop speak code words they use. You know how they call perpetrators of crimes 'perps' right? It's like another form of the word 'perv.'"

"I get the idea." Cole reluctantly let pressure off of the gas pedal. "We would be treated as very suspect. I realize that. But we're probably both cranky because we're hungry. I kind of wish I got a candy bar, too, when I had the chance."

Since Cole had slowed, Gordy adjusted to the extreme opposite. He wanted to ask Cole if he was beginning to travel too slowly. Afterall, cops might take it as a signal of nervousness on his part. Gordy distinctly remembered a since deceased uncle visiting his grandmother when Gordy was nine or ten. His uncle was fuming about "cracker cops," describing how they had hassled him about a cracked tail light. "Don't they understand I could fix it if I could afford it"" he railed. "Calm down now, Jerry, and tell me inside," his grandmother had responded, motioning for Gordy to go play in back. Later, Gordy called it her "swatting flies" motion.

Gordy spotted a young gangbanger "flying his colors" through display of a red bandanna and red sweatpants sauntering down the street. Gordy said "That's no good. Man. That young brother right there, Cole. Goes by some sort of nickname. I've heard he's been up to no good. I'd have the mind to set him straight, but he might be packing heat."

Cole braked softly. "Doesn't look too dangerous to me. Doesn't have a too obvious swagger in his step."

Gordy returned "Shit, I know his kind. All this anger toward white crackers, yet bullets killing his own. But you can't say anything to them either. Really, they hate the whole world, and crackers just happen to be a part of it. So they talk about things like insurrection, all this noble sounding stuff, then continue to do the same crap over and over again."

"I guess I don't need to hear what exactly you mean by 'crap.'" Cole signaled for the Bob's Big Boy parking lot. The young gangbanger was now almost one entire block behind them.

"Yeah, you're right. Pimping, robbing, extorting, informing, all the usual suspects. Vermin that's real difficult to scare off." Gordy twisted his neck to keep looking in the direction. "But the guy's name, it's, you know, almost on the tip of my tongue."

Cole parked, and was out of the car quickly. "Hey, come on, let's go. I'm ready for a chocolate malt, maybe two actually." As he traipsed past the rotund Big Boy statue in front he lobbed back over his shoulder "You look real eager to brag about what you've being doing. But I'm not far behind you, man."

Hitch, aka the young bomber, watched them go through the front doors. He recognized Gordy from the neighborhood. "Was it him or that other big guy who almost made it onto the Trojans football team?" he thought. He patted the fold of bills in his right pocket. Late last night he had stashed the rest of his cash into a square hole in the wall at the edge of his bedroom floor. He had refused his employer's offer to have it stored "more securely" in a more anonymous safe deposit box. He thought briefly about buying a 40oz. bottle of beer from a guy named Sales, an older guy who catered to the underage crowd. But Sales had an unpredictable temper, sometimes resulting in cops paying a visit to his ramshackle abode. Sales once joked with

Hitch that the sound of helicopters had become his indoor fan. And Hitch, so soon after his first, clear and violent action, felt especially sensitive to the proximity of law enforcement. "I'll just wait until later on. Someone is bound to collect a stash and head to the liquor store," he thought.

He passed a car wash, with all the workers in blue dungaress. He almost slipped on a smear of soap and water near the curb. He felt a pair of Hispanic eyes smiling at his awkward recovery, one hand almost reaching the concrete. A prick of rage prodded him, but then he had not brought along his gat (gun). It was not yet completely de rigueur on the street. Mostly only old school gangsters, with old Cadillacs in their driveways, carried them. Not cocky youngsters speeding toward early graves. Hitch had always despised guns, so he only carried one when he knew he would be outside after dark, or when he was preparing for his recent, dangerous mission.

Pat's Dogs had a drab exterior of mustardy yellow, and a great volume of barely numbered outdoor tables. There was not an interior dining area, so Hitch took a seat at furthest remove from a group of white men in white collar dress shirts. He instinctively identified them as lawyers, law enforcement, or some type of airport personnel. He thought he saw the glimmer of a badge peeking out of the pocket of one. He quickly ate the two chili dogs and fries that were alongside them. He mopped up the remaining chili that had escaped through the edges of buns. Hitch could not have explained why suddenly he wanted nothing better than going home and drinking heavily with the shades drawn.

Cole visually scanned the gleaming car door, because he thought he saw a small edge of a cut in the paint near the door handle. Yet he was able to insert the key and open the door before Gordy could criticize his suspicion.

Once inside, Gordy revived their dinner talk. "So watch your step around the Australian dude."

"They call themselves Aussies," Cole responded as he turned out of the parking lot. "Just saying, man." He turned the radio dial to the soulful wailings of Al Green.

"All I know is those dudes are the weirdest. When they drink enough they will wrestle alligators and box kangaroos. That's pretty extreme in my book."

"Hah. Well, I admit some of that is probably true. But that bar chick seems pretty cool. But you're not trying to deflect-"

"'Deflect'"? Gordy's voice went up in pitch.

"Yeah. You've got a lot on your plate, balancing some nut job without a real name and some radical professor. You're overwhelming yourself as far as I'm concerned. Man, it's not like you. No offense, but you usually don't strike people as someone in a hurry to get anywhere. I mean, I've never known it to take so long for anyone to eat one fudge sundae. Man, no one but you savors each bite like that. You probably noticed that I did most of the talking. I hope you know that you are somehow unable to flirt with the waitresses when dessert time arrives?" Cole sped around a supped up Trans Am, which contained a group of gangbangers with flowing head scarves. One raised his forty ounce malt liquor bottle in a slightly menacing gesture toward Gordy.

"Hey man, lay off a bit when you're around the fools," Gordy said. "They're just as likely to take my head off as yours."

"You're saying mine should be the one to come off in that case?" Cole remonstrated.

"Damn right. Acting like a cracker, that's what. There is change in the air out here. One new credo is 'Kill for sport,' in case you haven't heard it yet."

Cole responded "Well, I guess you've been trying to convince me of that for a while. Just seems weird to me, people taking potshots at each other over nothing. At least they could fight over meaningful things, like-"

Gordy chortled "Yeah. Like whose name will go on the book first. We'll probably have to flip a coin or something, because if our story takes, I don't know about you, but I'm definitely looking for first name place on the book cover over you. Hey, remember to keep the speed down here."

Cole did indeed slow around the corner from Gordy's house, as he studied store fronts. Even before he hopped out of the car he starting creating a picture of Rod Owens, the Paramount Pictures employee. Kit, the female bartender, had given him the following: "short, stocky, with red hair."

Nine

Rod Owens saw Cole first, in his freshly waxed GTO nosing up to the handicapped zone only twenty or so feet from the sidewalk entrance to Paramount Studios. Rod had only been outside for the matter of ten or more seconds, and his face was quickly annoyed by the midday sun, because he had sustained too much exposure at the beach the previous day, where he windsurfed throughout the morning. He was from Adelaide, a large beach town on the Gold Coast. He thought immediately "nice rod there, mate," as Cole flourished one more slight roar to the engine before shutting it down and ambling over to meet him. Rod extended his hand first, and said "Nice ride. For sale?" smiling widely with what Cole later thought was true Aussie bonhomie. Cole also noticed how the sun overexposure had kind of seared the pattern of freckles into his cheeks and forehead.

"No, sorry, no sale...Rod, right?"

"Right, mate. And you're Cole. Kit told me a bit about you. She has a good sense about people, makes friends much faster than anyone I know. But I can always trust her judgment."

Cole nodded his head. "Nice gal....but she'd rather talk about you and your movie exploits."

"If you can call them 'movie exploits.' Anyway, let's chat while we stroll down for a burger.   There's a good place just up here a ways. I can get away with an extended break once in a while." Rod pointed the way to the corner, and they turned left, heading north a few blocks. Rod was at least a couple of inches shorter than Cole. His step was jaunty and bouncy, like that of a bantam rooster. Cole noted the perfectly tailored lawns along the way and the Cadillacs and Buicks in the driveways of the cottage-like houses.

Cole began "So I gather Kit has already filled you in a bit about me and my buddy's project. We think it's got real potential but, ah, I hate trying to sound like a salesman. But I figure, and Kit, too, by the way, that it might be a project that could be salable to the studios."

Rod returned "Slow down a bit there, bud. I think we need to take this business as slowly as possible. Hunches can lead to good things, like my idea to come stateside. But then I had to be patient, and use Kit as my own conduit, if you catch my drift, mate?"

Cole replied "Uh, huh. Well, I think outsiders often have the best perspective on a particular place. And, often, they can translate their ideas to action more quickly. My buddy Gordy and I were born here, and we've done all sorts of things to support ourselves, but only now are we starting to get motivated about making inroads in the entertainment industry, as it likes to be called."

Rod chuckled. "Yeah, you've got it right there. A bunch of stuffed suits behind the scenes. I hear the rumors all the time, how an old fossil producer wants, no, get this, demands the next disaster film. Behind the scenes it turns into a farce, directors and producers storming around behind the scenes, pushing the too rushed film to completion before it's damn well ready." He stopped briefly, then rubbed the fin of a Cadillac jutting out of a driveway. "This point reminds me of the sharks back home. Anyway, let's keep going. We don't want to miss the closing of the lunch special."

Cole chimed in "Yeah, that would be regrettable, I guess. Anyway, I've noticed something about disaster films. They look backward. No, listen. They claim to see trouble in the future, but they're looking backward, with ingrained fear. Tearing down skyscrapers through film, for instance. One might imply they never should have been built in the first place. It's almost a paradox of some sort. Perhaps an ingrained guilt scenario?"

Rod opened the greasy spoon diner door. "Man, have you ever thought about being a movie critic?"

"No," Cole replied, following the waitress to a corner table. "I think the best thing to do is to insert criticism within the film itself." He picked up a menu, and gestured for Rod to sit. "Like Altman's Nashville, for instance."

"Seen it. Liked it. Thought it quite clever, mate. But I go more toward pure drama and suspense. Not cop movies or slashers. Thoughtful studies of character within place. Barry Lyndon, for example." He had his hands above his elbows momentarily.

"Absolutely." Cole moved his left elbow slightly to more easily allow for the water pitcher and glass. "My thinking with my project, and Gordy's, of course, is to suggest that things all come together in the end, the writer, the story of the movie, and the actual reality the movie is based upon. It all can then coalesce. So gangs, cops, lawyers, movie execs, starving writers like myself, combine-"

"Okay, yes." Rod responded to the waitress, "Ready, listo, whatever. I'm going to make an assumption. So two deluxe burgers, all the trimmings and fries and, of course, onion rings. And two draft beers, unless there's any resistance from the chap here."

"No, none." Cole could not help but smile. "And I trust the special burger is the right pick."

"Oh, you'll love it, alright. But to cut to the chase, when I'm around the movie execs I have opportunities at times to shill ideas. Once I have a better idea of your and, er, Gordy's project, I'll put in my words. It reminds me of what Kit tells me-'Don't worry if they don't like you. All they can really do is sack you.'"

Cole replied "Well, nothing is without some risks, right? My buddy Gordy is trying to ingratiate himself with Black Power groups, amongst others. That could be a dangerous mission." He nodded his head as their food was dropped off. He took one look at the burger, which had, at the minimum, grilled cheese, onions, avocado, and bacon, and said "Excuse me, Rod, you'll have to excuse my manners. I've got to do the mashing routine, this thing is too thick."

Rod smiled. "No prob," he said, and moved the fries and onion rings to a common center spot in the middle of the table. "This town, even in comparison to my home, is somewhat wide open. It's like there is a message behind what everyone says, that, as long as one is willing to be responsible for one's safety, just about anything is dished out. Almost like some people consider themselves above the law."

Cole chewed more quickly, because he realized his turn had approached. "Great burger. Uh, yeah, the cops, the winos down in the bowery, something about a big city unleashes the right of people to engage in extremes of behavior about, you know, trying to grasp the old American Dream?"

Rod had surprised him by dispatching his burger so quickly, one reason he was nicknamed "Shark" by movie set crew mates. "Yeah, I guess that's the idea. Grease the wheels any way you can. I haven't gotten far yet doing it, but, still, I find myself in a picture studio. Sometimes I gather it's the outsiders that get some lucky breaks. Kit is a great gal, don't get me wrong, but she's holding out on a musician, actor, or maybe even a painter or writer." He smiled. "No offense, but people here have the ocean and mountains, but they're not satisfied with that. I always figure to buy a beach shack at some point, so that if I tire of the fuss, I can escape to a comfy retirement. Have a fine miss along, and a couple of children."

"If I could afford kids I might have some," Cole returned. "Know it sounds blunt, even callous, but there it is."

Rod flinched a bit when a nearby patron's dark arm accidentally brushed his shoulder. Cole noticed the tattoo of a panther on the fairly bulging tricep muscle as the man's swishing gold chain fluttered at the thick base of his neck. "I like your project a lot. It's my kind of story. Creative but with a down-in-the-trenches vibe to it."

The first bus was crowded, the second less so, and the third almost bare by the time it reached the end of its line. Gordy rubbed elbows through the south central corridors and the spate of down-and-out types further east toward the 'burbs. He had to awaken early in order to do his trash and yard duties for his grandmother. He had yet to speak to Professor Dr. Warfield, the one recommended as a receptacle of some knowledge about Black Power groups by his local librarian. But he had been told his office hours by the friendly departmental assistant over the phone. It was a significant block of time on Wednesday afternoon-1-4pm. His final bus took him through the heart of Boyle Heights, past scores of lowriders, and cholos wearing chinos and black felt slippers. "I get it," Gordy thought to himself, a bit amused. "You all are just chilling, no need to wear real shoes, because no one is going to be running from anything." A few noticed him watching, and made violent, throat-cutting gestures, but he figured being on a city bus, especially one during the day, gave him some level of protection. At the same time, he appreciated how generally peaceful the streets appeared through the foggy bus window.

Gordy strolled through the main campus lawn, admiring the paisley dresses teasing uncovered and tanned calves and ankles, and the white stucco buildings free of graffiti. "Man, "I've got to get out more often," he thought, chuckling to himself. Instead of asking for specific information, he decided to stroll until he found the history department building. He found himself comfortable among the mostly sterile looking structures. From his time at LACC, which gave him a solid sense of how most campuses are laid out, he was quickly able to navigate past the science and sociology and philosophy buildings to finally, the history building, a squat two story structure. Gordy found Warfield's office in a small recess along the back hall at furthest remove from the history administrative offices. He only paused momentarily before knocking on the half open door. The professor removed his reading glasses and looked up. He had a salt and pepper goatee, and a slightly freckled face of dark cream. Gordy judged his age between fifty and sixty.

"Well, come in, young man. And how can I help you?" Gordy later recalled how he had turned over a book he had been perusing, a very thick volume in black.

"Professor Warfield, I come by way of a certain female librarian in south central. She-"

"Wait." Warfield's brow crunched up with seeming chagrin. "You just stroll on in here...but then, ah, God bless that woman. Is she still looking as good as ever?"

"Yes, indeed, sir," Gordy returned with a slightly clipped accent. "She is. She found me browsing for books on militant brothers. And it didn't take her long to bring your name up."

Warfield spoke quickly, and only later did Gordy sense that there was a certain rehearsed quality to it. "Ah, she did, didn't she? Well, tell me a little about yourself. I can't start loaning out books from my personal stash here without at least having some grasp of your character. The books you need are elemental, harsh, direct, confrontational, and sometimes a bit flighty and intellectual. I like to mix it up, historically and otherwise. Everything from Douglass to Styron's Confessions of Nat Turner to Soul on Ice to Malcolm X to Toni Morrison. I see you nodding your head to all of those. So you're already at a certain level of understanding. So now is just the time to keep digging, and see what you can come up with."

Gordy replied "Sounds right to me. To cut to the chase, I want to dig into mostly recent black militant stuff. Black Panthers, to be more specific."

"Well, if you want to do that, I suggest you still do a quick review of what you've already digested. That way you will have a firm footing, to buffer the most extreme Panther precepts. But may I ask about your academic background?"

Gordy rubbed his palms together. "Typical south central high school, mostly writing courses at LACC. I mostly write poetry and short stories, but lately I finally started a novel. It probably won't be a long one, but still..."

Warfield formed a small tent atop his desk with his hands. "Don't sound apologetic about it. Even though I'm a professor, I've always had inner doubts about academia. But, of course, I have to be careful about who I speak to about such feelings. Some might even advise me against speaking to public people such as yourself. There's a trend for academics to have so-called 'moles' in their employ, who can act as spies to a degree."

"Interesting," Gordy returned. "But you've got to know that people like myself are squarely on your side. I've been wanting to stick it to the man for quite a while. Don't get me wrong, professor. Nothing violent or illegal in my proposed actions. It's just that I sense already, after the changes of late, that people are starting to get a little too complacent again about things."

Warfield grimaced. "Things? Yeah, I'd say so. People without health insurance, nothing to fall back on, 'hoods starting to be torn apart by drugs and violence. People adopted some positive attitudes from black militants but, suddenly, young gangs jumped in, upping the ante, so to speak, with idiotic drive by shootings, so it's kind of like a bunch of armed camps springing up. Even Native American tribes had trouble with hot-headed young warriors, though. South Central has been desperate for respect, even self-control, but it's starting to spiral out of control again."

Gordy sighed. "My buddy and I want to write a story, with a kind of journalistic flavor to it, based on recent history. Of course, if you want to be involved in some way with the project, we're all for it." He paused, in part because he had not exactly been given permission by Cole.

"That's pretty bold, which I like, by the way. But read up over the next week, then catch up with me later, and let me know how your project is coming along. At that point I'll have done some research here on the academic level. You can tell our mutual friend, the lady librarian, though, that I might have to take her out to dinner in the near future. Yeah, tell Mona I'm still spry." Warfield stood.

Gordy promptly shook his hand. "Okay. I think I'll pass on your library for the time being. I've got a lot already working 'upstairs,' if you know what I mean. Thanks, professor."

Warfield smiled broadly. "Okay. Suit yourself, young man. But keep in touch. And try not to stir up too many hornet nests in the meantime. And even if you normally pack heat, try to avoid it as much as possible. Some of my contacts forecast a high spike in misdemeanor drug possession and unlicensed firearms busts."

Garfield chuckled, because Gordy was partially frozen in the doorway. "Don't ask me who that contact is, however. Let's just say I've got all my communication and radar tentacles out, fully extended."

Gordy was surprised by the quality of the university's cafeteria food. He returned with his tray for another slab of meatloaf and mashed potatoes slavered in gravy. He was half-expecting to be carded for school identification at the entrance, but there was not anyone to check. The walls were a light brown color, and the plastic chairs a dark cream. It was far from full, in part because it was past the normal lunchtime hour. Gordy's table, which could accommodate up to ten, was free for him alone, and he had free reign over the large salt and pepper shakers. He thought the meeting with Warfield abrupt but also substantive in quality. "He's comfortable, but also a bit bored here," he thought. "Maybe this business with Cole has sparked his interest somehow." He reached for the pepper shaker again, tipping it over for a solid second. "Well, I guess we're on our way..."

His step was energized, taking him back to his bus stop quickly. The adrenaline of purpose had saturated his body and mind. Finally, he thought, he would shake off the lethargy of his living situation. If he had been pressed at that moment, he would have admitted that he was sometimes addicted to adventure. And, further back, he had been a bit captivated by the formation of the Crips as an organized gang, when street rules were still enforced by fists instead of guns. He thought "After all, I might start packing heat myself."

Ten

Later, he thought he had been influenced unduly by Blacula. As was his custom, he attended the matinee of most films in the last two weeks of its run. In this way he could avoid all the vampire freak brothers and sisters stuffing popcorn between painted on red lips, and unruly viewers making comments such as "Now that's a fine sister. She should be sucking on something else." He would never admit it to anyone in his south central neighborhood, but he fancied within himself a slightly elitist attitude, culled from such intelligentsia as Kafka and Jim Morrison, so that he was slightly abashed about seeing a Blaxploitation film. He felt lassitude as soon as he made his way home from the bus stop, after his campus visit with Warfield, and decided to lie down temporarily.

The dream opened with him peering into the living room of a small house Cole was in the process of painting. As he approached an outside living room window his arm was slightly scratched by the tentacle of a tall, spiny cactus. One moment the places it had contacted his flesh was slightly pimpled, the next the ridges had almost become sickening looking pustules. They were breaking out, bleeding until his forearms were slick with the red stickiness. But he was determined to force his way inside, so he pulled the window up from its lower edge and put his hands onto the ledge, preparatory to lifting himself up. Then his hands were essentially glued to the window sill. He noticed a kind of suctioning when he tried to pull his hand away. It was cold, but when he finally pulled it away, and turned the hand over, he noticed the palm was covered with a thick glaze of blood.

Cole sat on the couch near the open window of his apartment. More specifically, he pivoted on his butt so that his legs were splayed out in front of him. In this way he only had to turn his head slightly to the left to admire the bathing beauties. The tan flesh erupted a demon on his shoulder. "Go down there, Cole. Go down there now. But once you get there, stay cool on the outside. Don't ogle too much, but don't look uninterested either." Sun was slanting acutely, so that he began to perspire. But he felt that opening the window would pry his head open completely, leaving him even more vulnerable to the shoulder-perched demon's thoughts: "Look there. That ebony goddess. You're always wanted to try one out. Or over there. That Asian princess. After a night with her, you'll dream of exotic females forever." He found himself staring at the overhead fan as sweat began to trickle down his flanks. Then he gazed out again longingly to the pool area, now of a brighter banana yellow color since its recent repainting. Finally, he realized that all of the pool deck furniture had been replaced. He gazed back at the ceiling fan, shrugged, stood up, and turned it on. The demon came up through the cartilage in his shoulder, and surfaced through the thick skin: "Hey, are you worried about your pasty white boy skin?" Cole spoke aloud, "Now it's Gordy talking. You're just jealous because I have an ebony goddess in my sights." Another cautious voice intervened: "They'll be there next week, too. So take your shower and prepare to pick up Gordy."

He left his GTO in its assigned spaced in the lot, opting for his less conspicuous Ford pick-up. Because Gordy had suggested they do some explorations of South Central instead of the traditional Venice beach cruise in the shiny GTO. Both agreed that it was wise to start keeping a lower profile. The demon erupted out of his shoulder again to declaim, "Okay. Save your muscle car for the ladies. But don't waste too much time, either."

Cole decided to take the "scenic route", which entailed driving west to Lincoln Blvd., then heading south toward the airport. He almost stopped in route for a breakfast burrito at an Asian owned hotel. Surprisingly, they seemed to serve the best arterial clogging morning fare. He appreciated how the Asian variation added mashed potatoes and gravy to the usual sides of bacon and sausage links. He relented, in part because he knew that Gordy would have an eatery or two in mind for them to visit in short order. As Lincoln headed south it passed a lengthy stretch of vacant weed-infested lots. He noticed some leaning shanty-like structures removed from the street. A stooped figure with dreadlocks stood with arms upraised, taunting the traffic with mysterious hand gestures. Cole figured that it being early Fall the former hordes had abandoned their summer encampments. Seagulls, with their gray-white feathers, lulled on an ocean breeze. Momentarily distracted, he almost failed to press his brake pedal when a produce truck stopped suddenly on a change to yellow. He briefly laid down on his horn, and some hovering birds cawed with fury.

Near the turn to Century there was a line of wino and hobo types holding up crudely stenciled signs. Some were wearing the dark green of Army jackets, others had pots with peace signs painted on the sides, perched on their heads like strange bird plumage. Cole quickly relived the day. Under the threat of a possibly long layoff from his painting business employer, he had sauntered down to the entrance to the nearest armed forces recruitment center, then stood for a couple of minutes before moving on. In retrospect, he had been infected with a strain of adventurism. Later, he called it "Jack London's disease," a potentially disastrous addiction to drama. People like Gordy liked to chafe him by saying that he was trying to be a swashbuckler from an old Hollywood silent film.

He glanced at the Bob's Big Boy, wondering, even after a meal at a competing burger establishment, if Gordy would try to direct them there later that afternoon for a dessert. It had almost become a tradition for the two of them to bring a close to a particular day's events by saturating their palates with sugar. Often Cole attempted to appease the craving with only a scoop or two off Gordy's chocolate ice cream dish. Luckily, Gordy never followed through on the threat to impale his hand with a fork as punishment. "You must've been one of those kids that smeared Bob's fat mug with fudge when you were a kid," Cole said.

The old pick-up labored a bit up a long, shallow rise of a hill. A gray primed Camaro paused a second beside him, and out of his peripheral vision he noticed three Hispanic men motioning toward him/and or his vehicle with some animation. A few yards before the next intersection and light, it accelerated away in a flood of the newly sprung red light. Cole briefly glanced at his baseball cap on the right side of the dash, thinking "No, I'm not that afraid. I can deal with this fine." He thought that concealing his ethnicity might even backfire on him. "If someone thinks I'm a cholo they might figure it easier to get away with taking a pot shot at me. Then it would only be yet another gangbanger hit reported in the papers, if at all."

"I've been doing quite a bit of research." As soon as Gordy said it, Cole was a bit bewildered. He thought "What hasn't he been doing lately?" He noted the maniacal grin on his friend's face as he put the truck in drive, and pulled away from the curb. Over the following ten minutes, as they headed north toward the university district of USC, Cole was hardly able to interject anything. They headed toward a large food court that housed many varieties of affordable chow.

Gordy was saying "I have started a list. A good one. It is filled with current and former black militants. Not just Black Panthers, but anyone associated with even just the concept of armed opposition to the ruling white power structure. Of course, Oakland is considered the epicenter of it all, where it started, per se, but there are many other, uh, iterations. I believe one sociology professor put it. You might call it a splintering effect. I know how you like things put in a real descriptive manner, so there you have it. Before I go on, my impression is that after the decade of revolution, of Vietnam, assassinations of public figures, and the civil rights movement, most people have found it no longer sells. You dig? Television, movies, and the press all contributed to making it universal. Now? Nowadays, with Watergate, no one seems to trust anything or anyone. So no one wants to acknowledge many of the same people are still very active politically. It has slowed, granted, because many see no way to combat rampant capitalism, which, if left unchecked, tends to bury the already downtrodden. I see you smirking a bit, but you need to understand that it's never too late to engineer a mass movement. Of course, every movement requires a spark. I was reading one tract in particular, and it struck me. Sometimes the spark has to be brought to light, kind of a paradox in terms of language, but there it is. We could create a screenplay to expose, no, even magnify the symbolism of a Korean grocery bombed by a black militant, or at least by an agent of black militants. We could light a spark, and-"

Cole cut in "You're so agitated I think part of it is that you're hungry, and you have been talking to too many people in a short period of time." On one hand he was alarmed. On the other, he was eager to hear more.

"Hear me out, Cole. We have nothing to lose. Okay. Maybe we could be in some trouble for this down the road at some point. But we don't have families to protect or provide for. We've kind of got boring lives actually."

Cole grimaced. "Maybe. But I also like it that way. Look. I'm just thinking that this could get complicated very quickly. And down the road, maybe legally dangerous. It's not getting shot I'm worried about. I'm thinking about legal matters. Honestly, man. And you know I've read speeches of Malcom, Martin, Carmichael, and others, and read quite bit myself on black militants. Something seems, uh-"

Gordy coughed. "Dirty, right? You read all kinds of elegant arguments and philosophies, but find crude graffiti and even some stark racism against Asians? Hey, a lot of brothers despise the Koreans, believe they only want to take our money. You know, they're both right and wrong on that score. Some are kind, some aren't, that's all. So they aren't better or worse than any other group of people."

Cole revved the engine a bit at the next light. "Hear that? It's my blood pressure spiking. But, seriously, we are already kind of projecting our picture on the screen. My contact is an open-minded Aussie, but I don't know how eager he will be about taking on such incendiary material."

Gordy answered, "Hey, man, I really dig that word, I might have to poach it for one of my new poems. But slow down here. University police have real tight asses, and they'd like nothing better than to show off to their superiors by collaring us. They'd suspect us of running drugs, strawberries, or stolen merchandise. Otherwise, in their minds we must be freaks of some sort, maybe sexual predators. But I've gotten off track. You've studied history as much as I have. There are such moments in time-like The Shot Heard Round the World-but the point is, if people don't see and pivot on timely events, change is contained."

Cole took a right turn, and immediately had to stop for a young girl, in the crimson and gold USC sweater. "I think you're trying to expand our reach when we don't need to yet. If we're going to act like investigators, we need to start from the most obvious. You haven't filled me in much yet about the bombing, but I believe that we should keep focused on the local area for now."

Gordy noticed how crammed all the lots were, and hoped they could still make it inside in time for the public cafeteria buffet hour. "Yeah, you're probably right about that. It's just that all the researching I've been doing has given me lots of ideas."

Cole smiled. "That is good, and not so good, at the same time, for a writer. Let's stay focused. We are in danger of running on different wavelengths. Okay. It's a bit of hippie talk. I'm adventurous, too. But I'm thinking more along the lines of revisiting the bomb site and seeing if we can uncover some evidence."

Gordy whistled. "So I gather that you want to wait to uncover evidence which might actually implicate someone and for something specific. You realize that's opening a proverbial can of worms, don't you?"

"Just one," Cole interjected, maneuvering into an open space. "Maybe a big one, but still. You know, each time we talk about the project a little, it changes a bit. And I like that. Keeps it fresh. Don't you think? And I've already got a night kit behind the seat here. Maybe we should take a long peek at the burned out grocery together."

Gordy laughed. "Man, now you're talking. But neither of us wants to go to jail, that's for sure. Let's make a list over lunch and make sure we're geared up the right way. Neither of us has a lawyer, so I sure hope we're not seen." Outside the truck, they were greeted by the smells of garlic, ground beef, and tomatoes. "You'll have to be patient with me this time. Real patient, because not only am I a slow eater, I also have a lot to think about."

Eleven

Gordy waited until Cole parked the pick-up in the gloaming awning of a 7-11 convenience store before he opened the old gray Army duffel bag, and quickly identified the key items: flashlights; ski masks; utility knives; plastic, elastic gloves. "Whoah, hey, pretty slickster stuff, man," he said under his breath. Meanwhile he still pondered the list of potentially valuable contacts that was folded in a square and flattened against the social security card inside a flap of his wallet. He thought, "Well, I've been leading the charge up to this point. I'll let him have his little adventure tonight before I regain control of the reins." He felt the material of a glove, and felt that a person's fingerprints could actually bleed through, since they were thin to an extreme. "Couldn't you have added nice black leather gloves to the mix, and black berets?" he said aloud, watching Cole's back over the front register inside the store, his right arm crooked in to hold a pile of snacks. Earlier he had forced Gordy to leave the buffet without partaking of a dessert. "Coming down off a sugar high will affect you concentration level," he had said while already setting down enough cash for both the main items and a tip. A few minutes before the last stop/snack both had grown quiet, a collective condition that rarely struck them. Each was anxiously struggling to control his high level of adrenaline. Gordy found himself wringing his hands together when Cole backed out of the parking lot. As the truck nosed across the first intersection, Gordy said "Watch your mirrors. We need to start knowing when we are being followed."

"Well, as you can see, buddy, you've got a good chunk of mirror on your side, too. So don't hesitate to help me out."

Gordy had already opened a package of salted cashews, more than a couple which had spilled onto the floorboards. "Oh, you don't have to worry about that. If I see a black-and-white, you'll know right away. Hell, if our asses get put in jail, my granny will never let you hear the end of it. I can promise you that. She'll make me promise her to never pass on her biscuits and gravy to you."

Cole replied "I don't have any warrants out on me, so I'll be okay regardless. As for you-"

"Come on, man. I've told you how I used to be chided with cries of "Professor, come over here so I can copy the homework assignment.' In a way they were right. I was usually too busy reading to get into any trouble." As the numbers of the street signs went up heading south, he wondered how he had been so quickly convinced about undertaking such a risky mission. It occurred to him that they could find alternative routes to a story, one that did not directly involve the recent bombing. He said "This thing is kind of taking on a life of its own."

Cole smiled mischievously. "Yeah, what I've been thinking, too. And that's what we want. Isn't it? I mean, it is kind of like we'll be starring in our own movie." As if on cue, he turned on the truck's headlights in the gathering, grayish dusk. With a temporary lull in traffic, and the yellow orbs of the streetlights lining each side, it was akin to traveling through a long tunnel. Or, perhaps, being inserted into a motion picture scene. "Scene Five: The Gauntlet," Cole thought. "Two protagonists must safely breach the outskirts in order to safely invade the fortress." He leaned back, putting weight through his hips, and felt the handle of the .38 snub nosed pistol poking the small of his back reassuringly. It was cached inside the folds of an old spattered painter's shirt. He pressed back, and his spine popped in a slight adjustment. His eyes shone more brightly on their periphery, catching a glimpse of Gordy. But there was no seeming reaction of any kind. Thus he returned his entire attention to the road, the yellow middle stripe of the lane divider growing brighter each minute, his pulse slowly increasing, until he caught his foot overzealous on the gas pedal. Gordy gave him a long look when he sped ahead of a supercharged El Camino from standing position at a stoplight. Cole imagined the driver revving his engine in challenge, but it was a minor delusion. The misguided thought faded within the bleeding taillights of other cars.

"We'll park close by," Cole finally said to break the awkward silence. "We don't want to have to run far in case of an emergency. On the other hand, the further away from the place the less connection there will be. So we'll cut it down the middle."

"Yeah we will." Gordy turned briefly toward Cole, and his eyes appeared a bit glassy, as if he had been nipping off a liquor flask. "I'd say five or six blocks cuts it down the middle, so to speak."

"Right." By the time they found a space under a widely spread oak tree, the gray gloaming had almost turned to solid black interrupted by the halos of hazy streetlights. A child of about ten peeked through living room curtains from across the way, and duly reported his findings to the nearest adult, who was lying in bed with a six pack watching the Dodgers coast to another win. A few minutes later the man put on a trench coat over his bathrobe, donned his black slippers, and walked out to write down the license plate number of the mystery car for future reference.

Most of the yellow police tape had been slashed, and was fluttering on the ground, mixed in with gravel and torn candy wrappers. Cole said, in an almost absent tone "Hmm, not any Rocky Roads or Three Musketeers-my favorites," then motioned to Gordy and crouched half-running toward the scorched backside of the former grocery. In the darkness Gordy could not see the slight puffs of dust stirred up by his feet. He lowered his head and caught himself before he could yell "Wait up!" He surprised himself with how quickly he moved for the large man that he was. In his neighborhood, of course, it was deemed unseemly to be seen running, as if even joggers were trying to outrun bullets. "Don't draw undue attention to yourself out on the streets," his grandmother recently told him. "These new hoodlums on the streets, they want to be gangsters. And they don't fight fair. Don't make me visit you on life support, okay?" The words filtered through his mind as he gave Cole a boost to crawl through a partially open window. "Follow me in," Cole said as he gained traction inside, sliding spilled boxes to either side as he did so.

"You sure?" Gordy responded, looking back over his shoulder.

"Yeah. It's better for both of us to be inside. At least that's how I figure it. Although being blind about who might be outside isn't good. We'll need to operate inside as quietly as possible."

Gordy hopped down off the ledge, causing a few soup cans to roll to either side of his feet on the floor. "Okay. I'll take the back end.

You go toward the front. But only use the flashlight if you have to. We don't want any five o interrupting our treasure hunt, right?"

Cole gave a small grunt of approval, and moved immediately to the front. It was darker than he had anticipated, because a layer of plywood was now on the front. In fact, the only natural light was provided by a marginal flash of moonlight flowing in through the window in the back. "Not much danger in using light on my side, G," he said, and yet he still crouched when he turned on the flashlight, and did an awkward crab walk. Through the dust on the floor and a slight mist in his mind came a distinct thought-"What am I doing? What are we doing here?" His hands splashed through the clutter on the ground. Meanwhile he held the flashlight between his teeth. Briefly he half stood, and as he scanned across the floor he noticed a particular red-and-black card, repeating itself in dusty glory. He knelt again and picked up one while he heard Gordy's muttered curses from the other end of the blackened shelves, then a loud sneezing fit. A police siren approached. They briefly froze, but it continued onward. Just as Cole mouthed the card's message, Gordy spoke it aloud: "Long live righteous brothers!" Then he held up his own card and compared them. "Yeah, they look the same alright," he finally said after a final inspection. "But, man, this place is a wreck. And no bodies, guns, or cut off fingers lying around. Let's get the hell out."

Cole remained silent for a moment, returning to a study of the floor. He spoke out of the side of his mouth. "Well, I guess we could. We've got something there in that card. We might be able to trace it back to someone or something. We could take it around to the guys you want to talk to and question."

Gordy rapped him once on the back of his shoulder. "Let's discuss this outside, all right? Every moment we stay in here increases the chance of us getting caught. And this 'hood wouldn't care too much for a honky and a brother hanging out together. I hate to be abrupt, but right now we need to scoot out of here."

Cole shrugged. "All right. Just one more minute. I want to take one last look around here." It occurred to him that at some point he should have been able to find traces of, or actual, outright blood. But already, reality and cinema were competing for space in his head. "Did a young Korean kid die in the blast? Or a black kid? Did the authorities decide to keep that part of the story quiet?" Momentarily, he thought that beneath a broken sack of rice rested a large glob of gelled blood. Of course, when he took one last look with the aid of a flashlight, he discovered that it was actually a broken bottle of ketchup.

"Let's go!" Gordy half-rapped, half-pulled at Cole's shoulder, and Cole finally let himself be led away. When he went over the window ledge the second time, his windbreaker caught on a small shard of glass, which tore a section from elbow to wrist. "Come on, Cole. It's only a jacket. It was probably already ruined by the fire ash crushed into it."

Cole did not look or feel for the damage. Instead, he sped his pace in order to catch up with Gordy. "Okay. We're getting out of here. But, you know, we didn't exactly come up empty. There's an address on the back of the Black Panthers card."

Gordy said "Yeah, we can read that fine print," and almost tripped over an intact beer bottle. He was encouraged to see Cole already pulling his truck keys out of his pocket. The loud chattering of a police helicopter only startled him a little, because they were already three blocks north of Century Blvd., the constant flight path artery for the LAPD. Even aggressive dogs apt to sniff out and growl at potential intruders barely raised their heads to regard the large, foreign object. Gordy recalled that when he was a boy they were often called Big Birds. "But not friendly ones, either," he thought.

As the pick-up pulled away from the curb the same man who had written down the license plate number inched his way up the seat of his large two door Buick, started the engine, and put it into gear. He had extensive experience tailing vehicles, a gift he had discovered when following police patrols suspected of targeting black militant leaders. In essence he had motivated law enforcement from a safe distance. He had prepared to take photos in the event of an overzealous officer or two abusing his(their) power. He waited until Cole had made the first turn before activating his headlights. He was very curious. He thought "What is a honky doing in the hood with a brother?" After only a few miles he saw the truck enter the parking lot of Don's Burgers, which had a bleak, faded out apricot color on its heavy, weathered exterior. "Don" was a faded kind of Jack-in-the-Box imitation with a rotund Caucasian head surmounted incongruously by a giant sombrero. "Hmm. I'm still kind of hungry," he thought. So he rolled past Cole and Gordy slowing climbing out of the truck, who were dining inside. While waiting in the drive thru window he wondered what could have taken the two only a few minutes to complete in his neighborhood. "Drugs the obvious calling card," he thought. "But what would they be so worried about to make them park purposely so far away? Unless they know the narcs are already on their tail." He chuckled under his breath when the drive thru help, a black girl with an afro crushed by a paper sombrero, handed him his order. "Come on back to Don's," she said, and flashed an embarrassed smile. He pulled over a half block north of the restaurant and started eating his large order of onion rings. He was able to adjust his rearview mirror so he could see the outlines of Cole and Gordy's heads.

Halfway through the greasy bag of onion rings he decided to change his approach. Unwrapping his cheeseburger he topped it with the remaining large onion ring. "Carl's Junior style," he said aloud. A few inches from his right hip there was a specially created compartment for a small pistol. A tool he had yet to use, but not because of any fear, either. Over the years part of his pride stemmed from his ability to negotiate dangerous situations, and remain unscathed. He was part marijuana dealer, part curious poet. One of his most dubious claims was that Muhammad Ali had once asked him for advice on how to self-promote through brilliant spoken poetry.

When he was finishing his burger Cole and Gordy exited. He was a bit surprised to see them turn left instead of continuing north. This required him to execute a quick U turn, and accelerate quickly while fumbling for the headlights. His back tires skidded a bit, but did not screech. When the truck pulled into the house one block south of Century, he wondered if he should wait around for another pursuit. But then he promised to note the location of the house when he reached home, then immediately go to sleep. Another instinct suggested he loosen his pistol's grip with the front seat, and allow himself to exhale some of his demons into the night air. "Bullets, that is," he said aloud. But he was distracted by the wind in the trees. He drove home, thinking "My little look out did a good job for me. I'd better let him go to the ice cream truck tomorrow."

Cole and Gordy sat directly across from each other, with a recently unfolded card table between them. Through glances they indicated relief that they had not been confronted while sifting through the shop's debris. Their virtual silence had begun after they left the fast food establishment, where they had joked over their sombrero sandwiches, which were actually beef tortas inside burger buns.

"Something doesn't add up with those black power cards, man," Gordy finally said. "They don't look legit to me."

Cole chuckled. "You're right about that. What if it was a feint? On one hand, someone could've attached them to the bomb package."

"What the-"

Cole resumed "You know what I'm getting at." He leaned forward. "These cards were to lead people to believe it was somehow Black Panther related. Rock comes crashing through with cards attached, bomb explodes, cards scatter."

Gordy responded, "Okay, man. What we could do is ask around at city printers, and ask them if they recall doing a small size printing for a black power message. They might not want to admit it, because they might be worried about the police asking too many questions." Gordy reached into his bag of fries.

Cole shook his head. "Yeah. It's a bid weird, isn't it? What if the Korean store owner agreed to stock the cards on his counter top for free? There are all sorts of variables. Or maybe someone wanted to play a prank, went into a militant bookstore, stole some cards, then stashed them somewhere inside either before or after the bombing. But all of this material will be valuable to us in some way."

Gordy replied "If we use it right, that is. Listen, I think we should go back to square one. Journalism, you know what I'm saying? At least get the story into the Times or the Herald. I'm not saying we should drop the whole screenplay/movie angle. But that might be more in the offing later on."

"Wait there," Cole responded. "We could have a short film made outside the blasted building. I could get Rod to do the actual filming, then we could go to a newscast with it."

Gordy shook his head. "That might be moving too quickly, and either news channels and/or the paper might insist on some sort of-"

Cole folded his hands into the shape of a pith helmet. "Non - disclosure form signed? Well, maybe. I don't know about the legal end, but we could ask around. Maybe I can come up with a lawyer who knows the ins and outs of this sort of thing."

The momentum of talk lapsed once more. Gordy paced around the space, and periodically shut the slightly ajar door, thinking he would have to repair it in the near future. He watched a bright bougainvillea bloom slide across his floor, and glanced half-heartedly toward his broom propped against his microwave. "My stuff," he thought with a half-mischievous grin on his face. Meanwhile Cole was gazing off into a small private space bounded by the slightly greasy kitchenette wall. Finally he said "So we're really moving now. You will be talking to some of your contacts, and I'll try to fire up my entertainment industry connection. We're alive and free. Hey, what more could we ask for?"

Gordy replied "Yeah, man. Let's just use some caution. It's not naturally in either of our styles, but it might be crucial. Granny likes to say 'No health insurance around here. And no money either, boy. So if you act foolish, you'll have to scrape yourself off the street.'" At first, the laughter came as through an extremely tight spigot. Then, as the spittle reached the corners of his mouth, the mirth spilled out in a burst. "By the way, man. You've been looking a little pale. We might need to get back to the beach before you become the marshmallow man again."

Cole scanned his arms. "Well, I guess it's my face, and I don't carry around a vanity mirror. That's the issue. I've thought about getting a tattoo of an anchor. You know, like an old Popeye? Anyway, we might be on tv at some point, you know? Competing with the KTLA weather girls. So looking a little rough around the edges can't hurt in my mind."

It was not a particularly intense moment, but later Cole would return to it. He supposed it was partially due to the pregnancy of the time, the sense that they were creating something, fleeting or otherwise. They were devising one story alongside each other, and he had to wonder when and if they might intersect.

Twelve

Cole stubbed his right big toe on the bulky edge of the shower tub. As he stood under the water jet he rested his right leg's weight on the outside and back of the heel in order to avoid the most exceeding pressure, causing shooting pain up the back of his leg. It was like a hot, quivering wire trying to reach the primary pulse of his brain. Over the course of the afternoon, after he closed the curtains so he would not be distracted by the nude bather in the pool area, he watched the inflamed toe change from an initial shy red to a deep, purple bruise, its color approximating that of the tub that had caused it. "How many times have I done this?" he thought. "Half asleep stumbling into the shower?"

After an hour, he made an ice pack out of plastic bags and cube ice, hoping that the inflammation would subside enough through the course of the afternoon in order for him to meet Kit and Rod for an early dinner. He realized that the more prudent course would be to cancel, because his boss had locked him into a large painting job in Brentwood, which he also insisted he review in person with Cole the following morning. "Unless my toe swells up to the size of an orange," he thought.

The pain appeared to encourage his appetite, because he had three salami and cheese sandwiches with liberal doses of mayonnaise and mustard. He turned on his television and watched an old cowboys and Indians film featuring US Cavalry, with their immaculate blue uniforms and flowing yellow scarves. "Man, even after a terrible battle most look ready for the photo studio," he thought. "Of course, most if not all of the 'Indians' in these films are actually white men, also." He wondered if such historical airbrushing was one of the chief reasons he had dropped out of school at an early age; he had been appalled by the liberal whitewashing of unseemly historical incidents and his mother, as sensitive and as intellectually astute as she was, had encouraged his rebellion.

About ten minutes after resolving to put pen to paper he fell into a lengthy nap on the couch. When he finally awoke he resolved to take another shower to properly awaken himself once more. "I've got to be sharp with the Aussies tonight," he thought. "And even aggravating my stubbed toe is better than being half asleep. What's that about pain focusing energy?"

The restaurant was slightly outside the perimeter of Little Tokyo proper, and as a result was not quite as generic in exterior and interior styling points. It featured some old framed news clippings of a Noguchi sculpture installation, and Mickey Mouse t shirts with Japanese characters, as well as brightly colored furniture. Cole had chosen it, in part because, according to Rod, neither he nor Kit had ever eaten there, although they had gone many times to an upscale establishment across the way, which featured expensive sushi and sashimi. Cole arrived first, and ordered a few appetizers: sashimi and California rolls, admitting to himself that he hoped only one of the two liked raw fish, because he was a huge aficionado, and could easily finish off one platter on his own. He relished putting as much of the green wasabi sauce mixed in with soy sauce as he could stand. Kit and Rod entered while he was stirring the wasabi paste into a small white saucer. They looked approvingly at the large bottle of Asahi beer in the middle of the table, water beading down its stem, which was surrounded by three glasses.

Rod said "You American chaps know how to treat us Aussies, that's for sure," and winked at Kit, who was making a last minute adjustment to her ponytail secured by a simple large black rubber band. They were both were wearing white pants, which clashed a bit with Rod's Hawaiian print shirt and Kit's almost sheer layer of silk red blouse. Cole kept himself from making a verbal jab about them trying to look like housepainters.

"Welcome, amigos," he said in return, and nodded toward the California roll platter. "You guys might get started on that while I prepare to have a few pieces of this sushi platter on my side. And, no, you will not be allowed to 'pitch in' for these special goodies. It's my way of showing appreciation for getting my concept into a movie producer's sights."

"Yeah, right," Kit returned, and elbowed Rod in the shoulder. "You might have an inflated view of the power of our connections." She sat down and repositioned herself a couple of times before she was satisfied about her seat. "We're happy to oblige you, that's for sure. But we are not high on the totem pole. You might have to take your idea on your own at a certain point and, uh-"

"Run with it, right?" Rod interjected, spearing a roll with his fork. He quickly noted the two other occupied tables, and the couples seated at them. "Well, we all know that having more than two people in a collaboration can quickly cause friction. I've learned that the hard way in the past, and, no, you are not allowed to ask me specifics about them. People move, change their ideas about the project and each other at inconvenient times. And get this: By its very nature, one person has to broach the idea to the other, and, unfortunately, I found that that same person seemed to feel more 'ownership' in the project. Just the way it works. At any rate I am fascinated by the whole black militant movement. But I'm not like you, Cole. You actually have the balls to befriend a black person and visit him in his less than-"

"Sorry, there," Cole interjected, "and no offense intended, but right there my buddy Gordy would be a little insulted. When you say 'befriend' it is almost like I am patronizing him, and that I am doing it with almost a martyr complex. Don't look at me like that, Kit. I'm just telling you guys up front that people like my buddy Gordy are hypersensitive about how white people talk about them. Don't get me wrong here, either. At times I get frustrated myself. People in his neighborhood probably assume I'm either an undercover cop or some kind of weird religious proselytizer. Hey, I considered Gordy coming along with me today, but I felt that I needed to kind of prime you guys for it. He is a very intelligent guy, very well read, but he definitely has that 'most whites are devils' attitude about him. I think it has been an ongoing challenge for both of us to reveal ourselves to the other." He picked another piece of sushi and subtly nudged the dish further to the center of the table.

Kit had a habit of either leaning in or back when she was concentrating, so that at times Cole had an almost overpowering whiff of her apricot scented perfume. And he noticed just how cute her small, button nose was. She responded "I've had similar experiences in the past with Aborigines. In a way, though, because their lifestyles are so primitive in comparison to American blacks, there is a wider gulf between the two peoples. So in a way it makes it a bit easier to engage them. In other words, there is not the scent of competition like here."

Rod almost choked on his first piece of sushi, and Cole could not tell if it was due to strangled laughter. "Wow. You two are really quite the philosophical blokes, aren't you? I guess I'm more straightforward. I think we need to start figuring just what kind of parameters for your project, uh, you know, make it more specific. You and your buddy have a nice, tentative idea, but it needs the heft of actual events and such. Next time I propose that the four of us discuss that. I will put out more 'feelers' within my studio, and Kit and I will strategize."

Kit smiled. "Sounds fair enough to me. What do you think, Cole?"

"Yeah, I guess it is time to take it to the 'next phase.' Seems to be happening very quickly now. I'm pretty amazed about that part of it. That's for sure. But let's dig into this food. Really no need to hurry, however. There is and will be plenty of beer to wash it down with." At that moment the waitress arrived to take their entrée orders, and placed another chilled bottle of beer in front of them. Kit looked a bit abashed, as if she was drinking too quickly, but Cole appreciated how her slightly freckled face had a slight, natural blush to it.

"How can I say this properly?" Rod said, putting down his black and gold menu. "I guess I'll just say it directly. I am not a cops and robbers kind of guy. And this whole business feels as if it might get a bit tricky. So, uh, I'd like it if you give Kit and myself a little leeway to say when and where, and who we meet in the future. Your buddy Gordy will be fine, I'm sure, but I'm unsure about how others will fit in. But I'm getting ahead of myself already. It might not be too bad altogether."

Kit said "You guys chow down. There are still a few bites left of our appetizers. I guess I'll take care of them as long as no one objects. But I'm with Rod, Cole. Even open-minded Aussies like us cannot dive in all at once without some reservations. Don't get me wrong, I like some extra excitement, but, as it is often said, there are always limits to ambition. I'm not about to bed any sleazy director for a small part in a film, that's for sure."

Cole smiled. "Well, you know I respect that. But, hey, you still might want to have a bite of my shrimp tempura. It is flaky, and when you dip it into the sauce it comes out just right. You can trust me on that."

Gordy picked up the phone, and dialed Julio Castroneves. At the third ring, he started feeling anxious, that he had purchased beer for his so-called contact for no other reason than to be made to look foolish. "So I trusted an alcoholic over the phone," he thought, shaking his head. "I guess it goes to show how eager I am to get info about the bomber." His eyes were fixed on the blue and white striped wallpaper of the kitchen. At the sixth ring, he heard the line click, then a quick burst of coughing. Finally the voice chimed in, "Not a minute too late. Or were you supposed to call last night? I forgot. Now listen, I might be able to get a name for you later, for a price, of course, everything has a price, but for now all I can tell you is the guy you're looking for is definitely black, is short and stocky, wears a red bandanna and gang get up, if you know what I mean, and limps like an old man."

Gordy waited, but apparently Julio had nothing else to disclose. "That's all? Well, it is a start. But, uh, do you remember which way he ran?"

Julio cursed under his breath. "Oh yeah, sorry, man. He headed north, right around the corner. Doesn't mean he necessarily lives up that way, though, you know?"

Gordy thought it a bit strange that Julio's tone was suddenly a bit apologetic, but later ascribed it to a nervous condition related to the man's alcoholism. "Okay. I appreciate it. If you find out anything else in the near future, here is my number..."

After he hung up the phone, Gordy make a few notes on his pad, then went to his kitchen to warm up a few slices of pizza. He heard the distinctive spitting of the next door neighbor's sprinkler system being turned on, and the hollowed out cadences of loud voices, no doubt part of a domestic disturbance, assailing him from about a one block distance. He returned to the kitchen and retrieved a small bottle of Tabasco sauce. He folded the pizza in half lengthwise and allowed five drops of the red sauce to saturate the bubbly cheese; then he had to wait until it was sufficiently cooled to eat. He thought, "I am never angrier than when the top of my mouth bubbles from a steaming slice." It struck him that he could never upbraid a pizza man for producing a delicious slice too quickly, when the aromas would not allow him to wait for a safer eating temperature.

He let himself sink further into the old couch. It surprised him that he had not heard an overhead chopper for at least an hour; it was an anomaly in his mind. "Well, the long days of Summer have finally gone, so action might not be quite as hot." He closed his eyes and started meditating on the description of the bomber. He thought "Sounds like he is a bit thick, athletically built, kind of like a fire hydrant, a smaller version of me. But with a limp? I know I've seen someone like that, but it will be hard to recall a face."

He thought of the two as his quarry; it recalled him to stalking the LAPD during the Watts riots a decade ago. At the time he was able to master his drinking just enough to safely follow the police cruisers at a distance, keeping the small flask of whiskey in a brown paper bag under the large space beneath his front seat. When his car hit bumps the bottle inside the bag thumped against the Colt .45 he kept in reserve as a final defensive mechanism; in the event the police decided on chancing an updated version of an old-fashioned lynching, he would have a quick answer. "If you have to go down for good," he thought, "go down swinging."

He sat in his car across the street from Gordy's, a few doors down. Optimally he hoped for the appearance of Gordy's white friend at some point that evening. It was only a hunch, but he was pretty confident. Another voice advised him "Maybe you are just anxious to confront both of them. Yeah, maybe you want to punish them for....what?" He played with the idea in his head for a while, trying hard to ignore the loud calls of children racing each other on their bikes down the street. One loudly complained about someone's discarded lollipop almost causing him to crash into the side of a car, another pulled out his own large earlobes to their extreme width with mock pain stitched across his face.

But towards dark the warmth of the whiskey had migrated to his head, and he felt himself nodding off as the children went inside their respective houses. "Shit," he thought, "this has definitely been enough for one day." He eagerly anticipated arriving home in time to see the first pitch of the Dodgers game, to once again immerse himself in the glorious greenery of the baseball diamond.

Two nights later: cigarette butts were crushed under black boots, and the crinkling sound of leather followed as men climbed into an old Ford Fairlane and a Chevy van. Black leather gloves were passed around, as well as ski masks. The driver was older than the rest, and not a full-fledged member of the group. But he had provided such valuable intelligence over the past couple of days that he was enlisted on a kind of temporary basis. His driving skills were impeccable, and on his suggestion both he and the other driver following in the van were equipped with walkie talkies. The group had gathered at a safe house in the Pico district of town, then driven down together in a van to pick up the driver.

Talk was limited. They only knew each other on a first name basis; but then these were so-called "code names." It was being treated as an initial "dry run," an action that could be studied by current and future operatives. Indisputably, though, they all wondered what a straight white dude could be doing in the neighborhood of a brother. One posited that he was an undercover cop; another maintained that he was just a drug addled fool that was looking for attention; another proclaimed that the two just happened to be working together.

Finally, they pulled up a half block down from Gordy's. The driver, the one who had first espied the two from his porch, walked down the rest of the way to confirm that both were home. He confirmed the make and model of the old truck the part time painter drove. He took his time walking back, slowly dragging on a cigarette, hoping that no one would be killed during the operation. He thought "Young fools don't necessarily deserve to die."

Thirteen

Later, Gordy recalled that it had been 11:13 pm when the door was opened. Cole was standing at the kitchen counter with his back turned, struggling to separate a sausage pizza slice from its twin. Granny was known to play occasional pranks, so Gordy was only partly alarmed when the door swung inward. When Cole turned with the paper plate in his hands, a beam of moonlight spilled onto a space on the floor. They quickly exchanged glances, "Who opened the door? And why hasn't anyone announced themselves?" Cole quickly set his plate back on the counter and approached the open space. He leaned out cautiously, and a heavy blow from a blackjack rendered him unconscious before he hit the ground.

A very thin and tall figure took one large step across the threshold, a gun at the end of a long arm, his face obscured by a black ski mask. He said "Stay calm, brother. You notice the silencer at the end of this barrel, right? So just sit still while I talk. I'm not a robber, and I don't represent robbers either. You and your friend here on the ground will see tomorrow as long as you're straight with us. We want to know what you've been doing snooping around lately. Okay? Alright. Now I'm going to put this gun away. Just don't think about making a move or making any loud sounds either. And someone will revive your buddy in a few minutes, but not until he is firmly under our control in the back of a van. You looked scared enough, but not too scared, either. So you should still have your head on straight. We've done some quick homework on you two. You're not undercover fuzz, that's for sure. I want us to have a talk at a more remote place, though."

The promised van pulled into the driveway, and two men emerged to load Cole into the back. The tall, thin man with the long barreled silencer gun simply motioned by jerking his head to one side, "Let's go, big guy." Gordy inwardly shouted at himself to remain calm, even though his legs were shaking slightly. At the same time, he was straining to recognize something in the tall man with the slightly reedy voice. One thought that immediately came to mind was "He sounds kind of old." When he preceded the tall, thin man out of the door, he faced the open side of the van, and the men in back did not have to tell him that his proper place was near the back doors next to his friend. Cole's face was partially wet, and his head lolled a bit groggily, but there were no signs of blood, and his eyes were open, if still blinking a bit in disorientation from the head blow. His right hand was a rigid claw on the brown shag carpeting of the van's bed. Cole finally nodded his head and said "Hey" in a small whisper. Gordy replied "All right man. Now just stay cool," and patted him on the shoulder. Until that moment he had been considering trying to overwhelm the three masked men himself, such was his rage at seeing his friend hurt.

A partition was leaned up between the van's driver cab and the back of the van, so that Gordy and Cole would not be able to track their movements within town. The van backed out. The man said "No small talk now. That goes for both of you. This won't be a long ride. Once we reach our destination everyone will hear from both sides." He leaned back with a small revolver crossed over his left arm. At the same time the man next to him pulled a long bladed knife out of a scabbard on his leather belt. He also turned on a large type of floodlight, causing both Gordy and Cole to turn their heads aside. The muffled radio noise seeped into the back, a pumping funk beat. Cole was beginning to understand the extent of their predicament, and was recovering pieces of the recent past. At first, the only image he received was a cropped back picture of the last piece of pizza on his plate. Then it slowly morphed into a glob of blood, then a short burst of a red flower in bloom across the driveway, before everything became black. He began to ask a question, but it was prematurely cut off, all that came out was "Who are they?" in a choked whisper. At one point he felt a large hand gingerly wading through the back of his scalp, and he slowly realized that it was Gordy making sure his head had not sustained severe damage. When the van hit bumps a slight swelling that would later become the size of a golf ball had a kind of crinkling effect, and made his eyes water a bit. He was also experiencing a serious case of dry mouth, lolling his tongue around in vain in an attempt to acquire moisture. And his tongue felt queerly fuzzy, as if he could identify each individual taste bud on top of it. At the same time he felt the recent pizza slice threatening to rise in his throat. "Stay calm, man," Gordy told him periodically while they continued to bump over rough stretches of road, to the point where it was clear to Gordy that they were not traveling on the freeway. But he counted off the minutes in his head, and estimated it took them about twenty minutes to reach their destination. Gordy wondered if his grandmother had seen their abduction, but reasoned regretfully that it was well past her usual bedtime, and he had not seen the kitchen light on either. Moreover, it was rare for her to indulge in midnight snacks; only during Holidays would she occasionally have an extra sweet item such as a slice of apple pie or a cookie.

"I could use a candy bar right about now," one of the two masked men chuckled under his breath. "Now that would really feel like a reward."

His partner was testing the sharpness of his blade gingerly, running an index finger slowly across it. "Yeah, I could use some chocolate thunder on my woman later. I feel like some kind of freak mummy in this mask. Man, we should've taken the freeway-"

"Yeah, but it is better to be cautious, brother. There are actually not many freeway exits. So later these two could replay from the time we were off the freeway, from the slowing down and breaking at the exit, then already have a good idea of where the safe house is located. Alright, you two. Listen here. We can't be too far off now. We will be backing right into a safehouse. That way you won't get any fresh and dangerous ideas about calling attention to yourselves. You're probably thinking, the way I talk, that I'm Minister of Information or something. But I'm not. I just try to be as polite as possible."

His partner made a few short, jerky motions, then was still. It was as if he had suddenly become discomfited by the flow of words within the tight, and slightly musty space. And he felt a smile of derision cross his face when he gave his full attention to Cole. "Does this honky cat think he's the Lone Ranger or something?" he thought. "Comes into a brother's hood thinking some cool vibes will rub off on him or what?"

As promised, after the van backed into the garage there was not even a sliver of a strobe light to illuminate them, and give Cole and

Gordy actual hope of being seen. They were allowed to step out on their own once the garage door closed. Immediately they were assailed by the smells of gasoline and grease while they tried to restore circulation to their legs. Through a slightly ajar door on the left they saw faint glimmers of a color television screen, and what appeared to be large, billowing sheets, or even carpets hung from the walls. On the extreme edge of the garage on their side was a line of bright tool boxes. The thin, tall man, the one who had held the gun on Gordy, advanced a few steps ahead of his colleagues. Meanwhile the driver, the one who had espied them from his porch, quietly slid through the space into the next room and pulled the door quietly shut.

"Relax here momentarily," the tall one said. "They have to make sure everything is prepared for you. And don't worry, we've got an icebox, so we can treat that bump upside your head. At least there should be one unless you came back from Nam with a metal plate on the side of your skull."

Gordy and Cole darted each other a few looks, but it was clear that they would not be left alone even temporarily. It was dawning on both that their abductors were working on a fairly high plane of criminality, one that might be the purest representation of what they were investigating. But both did not welcome the shock of being thrust into the middle of a plot so quickly; they had surrendered any pretense to initiative. Gordy thought "Maybe the pen is mightier than the sword, indeed. But if so, will I survive to wield it tomorrow, and the next day?" In a kind of blurry haze of consciousness Cole wondered why the two of them, the two chief actors in a kind of play, were being kept behind curtains, where their talent would remain unseen. Of course, in reality the curtain he and Gordy were behind was, in fact, an actual door, albeit a rather flimsy looking one.

After being escorted into the larger room they were pointed to a moldy looking dark cream couch along the far wall. The walls were completely bare, which was very clear from the strong band of fluorescent lights bathing the space. Cole's head was sore, but he felt close to being on his way toward a full recovery from the concussive blow he had received. Gordy leaned forward slightly, as if to shield Cole from another strike. The tall, thin man straddled an old, legs rusted kitchen chair while the remaining three filled a couple of small, squat tables along the far wall. "Disciplined," Gordy thought, "no booze or smoking. And effective. These brothers are serious." That thought gave him confidence that they were not recklessly violent, but at the same time convinced him that, when needed, aggression would come swiftly and hard.

"You two I'm assuming are at least fairly intelligent. So you've probably come close to determining who we represent. But don't automatically be so concerned about us. We do not care to bother you too much about your own interests and activities. We just want to ensure you are not outright in league with the 'other side,' as we call it, or a type of double agent. No reaction? Okay. Good. And we'll be giving you two some chow in a while. Don't worry about that."

"Our group does not call cops 'pigs' or ladies 'bitches.' But we also do not care much if someone happens to eat pork, prays while facing Mecca, or not. We have some who do, some who don't. We don't organize marches, we don't write incendiary literature. We act. That's it. Some might call us pseudo terrorists. You see, we have figured out that the so-called 'discipline of gangs' is overrated. Besides, we are past the age of Gandhi and Dr. King. We are willing to sacrifice time, but not our physical selves. So some of us hate whites? Of course, but that's beside the point. We are crafty, sly, and intent on winning the game, see? We don't have time for integration versus exclusion versus some mix with a fancy philosophy thrown into the mix. Our threads go back to the Amistad and Nat Turner. Our group is small, but because our message is direct, it appeals to all colors. We are master thieves, former bankers, even lawyers, but also intellectuals and athletes. None of us knows where the others live, what places they like to visit, family relations, all of that crap. Right now we are just doing probes around the city, gauging how the city reacts. Of course, they are made to look random. People want recognition too much. They can't help it. And then guilt comes in, too. So if we can stay away from fatalities, even better. But realize this is only the beginning. And the spark? That's easy. U.S. racism and imperialism, killing of Malcolm, Martin, and Vietnam. Boomerang effect, in a nutshell."

"Okay, and did you guys arrange to have the Korean grocery bombed?" Gordy asked, watching the man squirm a bit while straddling his chair.

"Of course we did, brother. But bear with me. People are too obsessed about killing people. Sure, there are some people I'd gladly take out if I had the perfect opportunity, but what's the point? They are figureheads. It is better to attack the symbols, the corporations and banks and such."

Cole broke in. "And then they rebuild." Gordy shook his head in chagrin.

"All right. The token white guy has a point here. Right, brothers?" He looked back toward those at the wall, who were clearly shocked by the boldness of the statement. He briefly pointed to the tip of his knife, towards Cole's chest. "Okay. They rebuild. Clearly. Then we hit them again and again. You dig? Every man, no matter how powerful, can become mentally beaten down. We won't see it, but we will feel it. Maybe some old gum flappers will pee themselves, or worse, when they see or hear how their stocks went down. That thought makes me happy. Because their assets are what they really care about, not other people. You see, you can't hope to replace them. That is fantastic nonsense. Why did the American Revolution succeed? Because other countries became involved, and there was not a huge centralized power structure at that time like there is today. It will take chipping away slowly at it. No doubt about that. You guys look shocked. I'm a true autodidact. Self-taught. I don't go for academic hokum. It's while looking with a wide lens that one finds truth. Complexity is the order of the day. But what advantages do us moderns have? Most importantly television. Print goes only so far to expose wrongs. Imagine if during slavery there had been actual video footage? Not just the scarred over evidence of abuse through early photography? See what I'm getting at?"

Gordy felt some tension loosen from his shoulders. "You are making sense, all right. And me and my buddy here might be able to realize your goal."

"We definitely won't get in your way," Cole added. He could hardly believe it, but it appeared they might not be beaten, tortured, or forced to give information with a gun to their heads. As if reading his mind, one of the two at the back pointed his knife toward him once more. Gordy was almost inclined to ask if he could have a drink.

The leader continued, "Excuse our lack of tact. But we get a little nervous when we see a, uh, some white dude hanging out with a brother while snooping around one of our hoods. But listen, if you tell me the truth no harm will come to either of you. I promise you that. Still, you might never see any of us without our masks on, for both our protection and yours, too. So let's hear it brother. What have you two cats been up to?"

Gordy cleared his throat. "We've been investigating the bombing of the Korean grocery. Seems like the LAPD doesn't want it reported for some reason. We have an idea to possibly write an investigative series about it, or even use a Hollywood connection to have a film based on it." Gordy tried to gauge from a non- verbal reaction if he had said enough.

"Okay...okay," the rail thin man paced back and forth momentarily. "I see your pal is in agreement. And you've probably already noticed that I haven't asked for your names. Take that for what it is worth. So you're a couple of creative types. I respect that. Crossing racial borders, too. So this is how we'll play it. Someone will call you from a pay phone at about the same time of the night as when we detained you. We will then arrange another meeting. For both of our protection we will not use your place or ours for business meetings. Also in case you haven't already noticed, this place is practically bare. So the sooner we release you, the sooner you will be able to eat. So on our way back, let us know if you have a particular place in mind. Sorry to be curt, but this is it for now. As long as you two do not cross us you will live."

Fourteen

Cole was later kidded for recommending, "Our favorite joint Bob's Big Boy." His tongue still felt a bit heavy, but he reassured himself that with a mere splash of cold water on his face he would be able to enjoy a meal without fear of his stomach rebelling. They were, indeed, dropped off at their favored Big Boys location on Century Blvd, still pumped full of adrenaline, and relieved to still be breathing. A few minutes later they found themselves eating two burgers apiece, as well as onion rings and milkshakes. Cole found himself smiling while admiring the glare of the traffic lights on the outdoor pavement, and the purple neon glow of the Century Roadhouse motel across the street. Gordy thought he might not be chided (for the first time) for indulging in two large dessert items. They maintained an almost absolute silence through the entire meal, each wanting to internally arrest their recent spike in anxiety before slowly and safely releasing it in speech. Cole daubed at his damp face with a small kerchief, in hopes of tamping down the obvious signal of a recently intensified pulse.

Finally Cole spoke. "I think my head is okay. Guy was effective with the blow, but I think I will see straight tomorrow."

Gordy wolfed down an entire onion ring with one bite. "Well, we're on a road now we can't get off of. But, hey, it looks like the waitresses are trying to close up shop. Maybe we should get out of here. We don't want to miss the last bus of the night."

Cole fumbled inside his pocket, half-panicked. He wondered "Did someone rifle my wallet?" But it was still present and financially intact.

His hearing was a bit tinny one moment, a bit muffled (as if underwater) the next, although he had always had a bit of the swimmer's ear complex. "Yeah, we shouldn't push our luck any more tonight."

But they only felt secure once they were within the comforting shell of the bus hutch, even with its faint hint of urine and tobacco with soggy cigarette butts surrounding it, and an old sun-bleached movie poster inside a scratched frame.

Gordy was wondering how directly connected to the militant group the young bomber was while he breathed in the cool night air. Despite his misgivings about the mission he was still encouraged. Meanwhile an undercurrent of fear still pricked at the back of his skull, making him itch and wave over it as if flies were trying to nest their eggs underneath the skin of his scalp. "You should crash at my place tonight," he said with a mumbling out of the side of his mouth. "And with that knock on the head, you'll probably sleep like a log. As for myself, I'll probably stay up late writing as usual."

Cole did, indeed, fall asleep while hearing the rustling of Gordy's notebook pages, as well as the chopping rotors of the hovering police helicopter. After a few hours of rest, he awoke from a dream in which he was hanging from a rope dangling from the underside of the chopper, with spiked extrusions that tore into the palms of his hands. When he jolted awake he was in the process of freeing each hand at one time, painstakingly pushing the flesh away from the small spikes. But his blunt return to reality was punctuated by the realization that no matter how heroically he tried to extricate himself, one of his two hands would always be caught by one of the rope's teeth. He felt a kind of humming vibration within his skull, accompanied by the slight swelling, yet he was still able to enter another long phase of sleep.

Gordy refilled his tea cup about once every other hour, his writing hand becoming nervier as the night wore on. He nibbled on a blueberry muffin, and at one point he became entranced by a small piece of the muffin finding a place in the dark space of spilled over tea within the tea saucer. "We are being pulled around," he thought, "and it feels strange to be swirled around, too." He felt sparked by the touch of a night lunatic's creative burst. Only when the diffuse dawn light started seeping through one of his narrow windows did he pull out his rarely used murphy bed in the corner. As exhausted as he was, he thought that setting his alarm clock was a cautious way to ensure he did not sleep too long. He was assailed by questions: Should I tell Mavis or Dr. Winfield what happened? How much more notice will women pay me in the event I become famous? Should I write a series of stories based on what is happening? Should Cole adapt it to a screenplay, even work alongside me as the book develops?" He heard a thud, then a cyclonic note of cats hissing and crying out as they fought for territory behind his guest house. Then they scuffled alongside and up against the stucco wall on the outside near his bed, causing him to fold his pillow over his ears for a dose of protective sleep. In his dreams he found himself on a futuristic highway of the night, tunneling through cities and hills streaked by a lurid purple light. He had a steering wheel, but it moved on its own. He kept wondering why it was necessary, since it was clearly only a frustrating anomaly, not allowing him to have any control over it.

Policemen passed on three wheeled motorcycles, their onyx black heads devoid of ears and eyes, the purple reflection shimmering off the darkness in patterns of amoeba-like birthmarks. He awoke with a cheek creased by the impress of his pillow.

Cole left a terse note: "Had to go, be in motion. Feel the wind on my face. Talk to you later." His use of the gearshift was halting, even jerky, and he looked in his rearview mirror with abnormal frequency. There was a slight tic in the corner of his left eye. He sped down Century Blvd. through Centinela, only stopping himself briefly to purchase a six pack of beer. While his car idled in the parking lot of the convenience store he opened and drank most of the contents of one can, a bit of overflow dribbling down his chin. Then he prepped each can by placing each in individual brown bags. He thought "Do I have a problem or what?" Since it was a Fall workday there were not too many people about, only a handful of beachcombers with wide brimmed hats and metal detectors patiently scouring for buried treasure under the loamy sand. A slight tremor in his hands dissolved after the second beer, which he had deposited in his jacket pocket. He returned to the truck once more to retrieve two more, and drank more slowly as he watched the waves curl into the wet, brown sand, the white froth on the wave tips similar in shape to the frothy head on the top of his can. He sat with legs crossed, hoping to dampen the fierce glow of the head blow he had recently suffered. He ran his hand through his scalp and found a light scabbing near his ear. He said aloud "Honorable war scar."

An offshoot of the Black Panthers? A lethal, chaotic brew of anti-nationalism, militancy, and native intelligentsia? Gordy played these questions over and over in his mind. While his stomach resented quick abandonment after one lonely piece of buttered cinnamon toast. He brewed a pot of tea and prepared to write a synopsis of the characters and events of the previous week. His goal was to have a completed document by the evening, when he would pass it on to Cole who would, presumably, then forward it to Rod Owens of the picture studio. Because although they had not been explicitly threatened, they both sensed a subtly powerful message that they should proceed with the project as quickly as possible. Or else the group's wrath might revisit them. The greatest germinating thought was that he and Cole could tell others that their story, the abduction writ large, should be treated as fiction by Hollywood. In other words, telling their story without changing it one iota, yet passing it off as the glorious fantasy of their intellect. At the same time he wondered if he should reserve the right to submit their story as a testament to their fidelity to historical truth. The hours passed quickly, and he was startled by the car when it arrived.

The GTO almost skidded to a halt, then slowed to a crawl, shadowing Rod Owens as he turned his shoulder in response to the sound. Cole hesitated briefly then pulled ahead to reveal himself. He was already forming a proper explanation for Rod when a shout spared him a lengthy interior monologue: "Damn! It's Cole!" The pattering of Rod's sneakers briefly interrupted an old woman watering her sunflowers. From Cole's vantage point it looked like she briefly head butted them while leaning forward archly. But her white visor barely touched a cluster of yellow petals. Cole braked and before he could reach to pull the inner handle of the passenger door, Rod had snatched open the outer lever, and plopped into the passenger seat.

"Good show, mate. I wasn't expecting to see you again so soon, but here we are. Kit insists the four of us have to get together within the next week or so, by the way. We can't have her thinking we've abandoned her. Trust me. She can become a tiger shark quickly."

Cole asked "Did you say 'shock'?" He took a turn toward a Greek café he had recently discovered.

"Shark, I said. The one that bites. You understand me all right, even with the accent. And I guess we'll be dining at a place of your choosing this time."

"Yeah, there is a place that has a great falafel, and it's rarely packed. So we should be able to have a nice spread, if you follow?"

Rod nodded his head. "Sounds good. Never heard of a falafel but I've eaten shark, and I'm always willing to branch out."

Cole turned on his radio but kept the static of rock and roll on low. "I've got an idea for at least a couple of scenes for a movie. Wild, man. I've even written down the first couple of scenes. I'll give it to you after we eat."

Rod answered "Cool. Our director is looking for something that he likes to say 'hits it out of the park,' so I think we'll get his juices going. And he is always talking about using 'insiders' and such. Even 'people who do not give a damn' he says. I figure he fancies himself a new Orson Welles or something."

Cole turned into the lot. "Okay. I'm encouraged." He wanted to be more expansive, but he was briefly struck by a pang of guilt about having to be less than fully honest in his disclosure. "Your director sounds like just what is needed, as long as he can get the producer aboard. You know, a guy who wants to be known for discovering new talent."

Rod pulled open his door before responding "Things could be blown wide open. Believe me. But let's get our food so we can sit down. Then I can hear your story of adventure, and as quickly as possible. I guess I'm still adjusting to the fast-paced Hollywood attitude. Don't get me wrong, I don't plan on becoming another burned out coke head. Kit tells me she's starting to see people who sniff too much while seated at the bar, but they never actually sneeze into a handkerchief. And the muscles in their jaws jut out. It's as if they've turned into cannibals, yet they're only hungry for more of the white powder." Rod made a final, quick step to open the door for Cole, whose face grimaced in the temporary reflection of the front glass, as if he had sensed the permeability of his body to outside forces.

Cole passed off the abduction story as a primal and cinematic portrayal of the stirring of racial and political movements. Rod interrupted occasionally, but was more interested in the assortment of sharp flavors within the falafel. Finally he said "Sounds fascinating, mate. Mysterious figure, almost vampire-like. Some sinister guys holding knives in the corner. You've got a knack for this kind of thing,

I can tell. What is great, though, is the dark haziness surrounding the whole scene, or maybe I should say 'work of art.' A film noir actually. That's what I've been hinting at. And, you know, it's probably better that you imagine something like this rather than live through it. I kind of have a picture in my head of Aussie Aborigines, their faces white."

Cole opened his second Budweiser can, then speared a large piece of tomato out of his salad. "Yeah," he began, noticing that the red on the label of the beer can closely matched the tone of the tomato. "Gordy and I are kind of just riffing on militancy in our own way. Using the pieces we can, just expanding the shape and size of each."

Rod paused briefly and when he spoke the words began cavalcade like, gathering momentum with each passing moment. "You know, a tall, thin black militant wearing a cape. You get what I'm after?   Not a vampire exactly, but like one. But you aren't called names, either. Are you planning to stress certain things, you know, uh to-"

"Sensationalize?" Cole chuckled. "You know, you might have a good point. Make the main point, yet lightly clothe it in something else. But how did we get here? Maybe we should adopt a slower pace, you know, you pass what I've written to your director, then we see where it's at."

Rod scratched his large, freckled forearm, which had an old scar where he was accidentally speared by a diving pal on the Great Barrier Reef in Australia. He had been trying to spear a fish, and he had almost drowned after swallowing too much water when he yelled underwater. At the time he was wondering how he could have let himself be caught unawares by a barracuda, or some other malignant fish bursting from a shallow coral shelf, before realizing he had been accidentally shot by his friend. "Okay, mate. That should work for me. But I'll have to get back to you about what the director thinks. Of course, he will have to get final approval from the executive producer and president of the studio."

Cole disliked the formal business implications of what he had prepared to say, but still took a large gulp from his beer to steel his nerves. "Okay. Just talk to him first about the story before actually handing it over. My buddy and I don't expect a contract offer right away, but it would still be better for us to have a verbal, I guess that's what they call it." He only half-nodded as their check was placed on the table.

"Oh, no problem there. If we get a bite on the old bait, you'll know when we all meet up. But we'll have to come back to this place at some point. I like it. If it comes down to it, we should have a scene or two set here."

Cole set the bill down and said "It's on me. I'll try to force the next one on Gordy, but he pushes back when he is feeling stubborn." He glanced at his watch. "I should be getting you back. I realize you've got other projects going on."

"Yeah," Rod replied, waving to the counter help before exiting. His hand scraped out a few chocolate mints from a white ceramic bowl shaped like a turtle. "The hundredth Western. I'd rather work on something contemporary, like your story. I can even see faces back in the shadows picking at teeth with small blades."

"Uh huh." Cole swiped off a pink flyer of a new adult store opening on Hollywood Blvd. from the clutch of his windshield wiper. "Danger can be attractive."

Fifteen

The cat ducked under the rock and virtually flew into the protection of the slightly gnarly hedge toward the back end of the yard, where his grandmother stored old furniture. "Don't come back, moocher!" Gordy hissed. He was excited and anxious about the upcoming meeting with Rod and Kit. He thought "When is the last time I spoke at any length with white people besides Cole?" dropping a rock he had held in reserve for the offensive cat. "Well, they're not Americans, so they might not have such arrogant attitudes." He encountered an immobility within himself, one which kept him from venturing past his yard for a couple of days. Even the sun was an enemy, piercing the false cloak of security. He rationalized that he was simply tired from a couple of hectic days. He thought "I'm trying to keep my wits while being threatened, which is not my forte." He sensed a clawing toward the back again, and picked up the rock he had recently dropped once more, and stalked the property's dividing line, raking along the hedge with the top of his hand. But the cat did not burst out again with frustrated ire. "He must have thought caution the better form of valor. He keeps thinking me or granny will leave the lid off the trash can so he can get at some bones." In his nervy state he wondered if granny was secretly leaving out snacks for the furry moocher.

Hours passed with him wandering around his driveway and backyard, more attuned to the wind and the chattering of helicopters and the droning of sirens than he normally would have been. As objective as he could be, he wrote his impressions down inside his kitchen, eating the last of the loaf of bread thinly spread with peanut butter and jelly, and conserving his rapidly dwindling tea bag supply in order to avoid immediate shopping. He still had a half gallon of milk and a large box of Cheerios, as well as a small box of vanilla wafer cookies, which he sometimes dipped into his cup of heavily milked and sugared tea. Once every two days he was able to direct his steps to the donut shop, where he bought an assorted box of one dozen and nibbled them at home while he pondered such questions as "Why don't more people still use old fashioned quills and ink bottles and wax for writing and sealing letters?" He judged it yet another way in which modern writers of all stripes were deprived of a certain aesthetic pleasure, namely a sound, the tracing scratch of the quill end on a piece of parchment.

Although he allowed that there was hardly any preparation required for a simple meeting, his hands still felt slightly tingly, and there was a faint pressure under his ribs. In addition his breath felt shallow. He laid down for long stretches of time, immersing himself in a monologue about himself. "I'll tell them I'm militant but peaceful, kind of like Gandhi," he thought. "And joke about how some brothers still call me Professor."

His motivation, more than any other, was to avoid noise, people, and anything else that might distract him from his concentration on recovering from the shock of having a gun pointed at his head. To a degree he thought he would never be the same. He thought "I guess I could write a cheesy poem or two about it." He napped liberally, whenever he had the inclination, but when he awoke from his brief slumbers he was slightly panicked. Each time he resorted to eating a couple of donuts, telling himself that they would calm his nerves.

When it became dark he welcomed climbing into bed without any reservations. He thought "Now I can sleep without guilt." Only once, in fact, was his sleep disturbed in any extended manner, by the hovering police chopper. He awoke to a bright blue sky, to the harrowing responsibility of being alive. Even the chirping of birds seemed like a thin wire threatening to find its way into his auditory nerve. He sat anxiously waiting for his phone to ring.

The cat did not return.

Cole spent some time in his pool area, but did not encounter the nude female bather again. He wondered if, all along, she was simply staying with a friend, or if she had been behind, or at least a part of, the temporary destruction of the pool area. "Well, at any rate she's a wild one. I'm pretty sure of that." Marco the maintenance guy came out periodically and did the clean-up in what could rightfully be called short phases: 1. Major trash pick up; 2. Removal of trash bags; 3. Repositioning pool furniture; 4. Sweeping area; 5. Skimming leaves off the top of the pool with a net; 6. Hosing down entire area; 7. Backwashing pool; 8. Checking pool chemicals. Cole was able to convince Marco that he would not be a hindrance in any way to his patient but thorough process. Cole's rapidly thinning scalp allowed some rays to contact the slightly scabbed over pattern of his scalp that had already been struck too much by rays. He monitored the development of a pinkish scar that was slightly inflamed by exposure to the sun. By the end of the second full day in the pool area he was wearing a baseball cap. He happened to find a small bottle of suntan lotion within a small bush behind the diving board and kneaded globs of it into his scalp.

At night he was able to settle in quite easily, watching his beloved Rams and Dodgers. Both appeared to be heading to the playoffs. His headache had subsided to a gentle pressure, and he slept soundly. At the same time he wondered if he had made a subconscious decision to sleep more in order for his waking time to pass more quickly. He awoke at odd hours to take long showers, and drink tall glasses of chilled chocolate milk. Or he pulled his blinds back to regard the swimming pool quivering in the moonlight. He had a brief vision of lying in the pool face down, although he floated back to the surface for the time being instead of sinking outright. His mind's fancy was to submerge itself into such a dizzying array of competing images that it would not have to confront the idea that he and Gordy were no longer masters of their project.

It was a Japanese restaurant at the top of a curving drive in the middle of Hollywood Hills. Recently the menu had been expanded into a larger blend of Asian spices. As Cole's GTO wound its way upward, Gordy noticed a few isolated couples, wearing the creams and browns of bellbottoms and wide-collared shirts and hairspray plastered coifs, playfully nudging shoulders and gently cuddling chins under manicured hands. Gordy's window was down, allowing for a dusky breeze to waft in some of the perfume and cologne scents. "Man, Cole, Rod says he will be able to write off this meal at tax time, 'cause this place is already looking pretty rich. Sure smells rich," he added, rolling his window up.

"He'll be good to his word," Cole replied, veering around yet another couple, hand-in-hand, walking down the wrong side of the road. The young woman smiled, and briefly held up the small flame of her lighter. The sharp light enhanced her pink lipstick and her mouth into a kind of bubblegum donut.

It was a valet parking situation. Gordy hesitated after getting out of the car, then waited for Cole at the front door, which was so smoothly lacquered in black that it appeared to be granite. Rod had reserved a table near the front, so he simply waved at them when they were through the scrum of people around the waiting area of lava lamps and plaid couches.

"Sit down, mates. Kit is running a bit late, her relief at the bar jerks her chain at times, and her boss won't put him in his place. She gets upset, but she can't really do anything about it." He motioned to the two chairs directly opposite to him. "It's good to finally meet you, Gordy."

Gordy replied "Nice to meet you, too. But, now, you know how to treat your clients. This place is something else. I wouldn't be surprised to see Bruce Lee himself-"

"I wouldn't either," Cole finished. "Has the look of old and new Hollywood at the same time."

Rod smiled a bit wolfishly. "Explain yourself, mate. Is this some kind of philosophy?"

Cole replied "No. What it means is, the owners want the place to look older than it actually is. But that means they have to do renovations in present time."

"Fuck man," Gordy chuckled. "Are you a bullshitting wiseass or what? Anyway, I'm the expert on martial arts films. Not you."

Cole returned his attention to Rod, who had thrown menus down in front of each. "Here, take this envelope. It is just a short sketch of what I've already told you about. Oh, and here comes Kit." She wore an apricot scarf around her tanned neck, and a peach skirt and white sneakers. "I hope someone here knows for certain where this is all headed," she thought. "Gentlemen," she said, and began to lower her posterior, then reconsidered. "Ah, you must be Gordy. Nice to meet ya. I'm Kit."

Gordy controlled the slight catch in his voice and replied "The pleasure is mine." Meanwhile he reminded himself "Don't act like too much of the polished gentleman, because you're not." Her appearance and scent had them all briefly intoxicated.

Rod resumed "Now where were we at before we were so, uh, graciously interrupted?" He winked at Kit. "This gal has wrestled kangaroos when she was but a little lass. I keep telling her she could be the next big thing in movies but she just waves me off."

Gordy lurched into momentary silence, unsure if he had acted preemptively. "I guess Hollywood directors can order exactly what they want."

"Hah," Kit started a chain of laughter. "A la carte for all movie studios. Sushi this way and that. I guess it is hard to condemn though."

Cole added "Too much power in small heads," as much as to hear the sound of his own voice.

Rod said "Well, let's cut to the chase. I like to concentrate on eating during the dining hour. Kit can attest to that. So I guess I can be a bit of a tyrant." He nodded toward the menus. "Let's make that the reward for getting our business done."

Gordy piped in "Let's put it this way, we've had a shock to our systems. Don't look at me like that, Cole, they would quickly catch wind of the truth regardless of our hints. At least so far, our story can go directly to the big screen."

Rod coughed and took a sip from his water glass. "I had been wondering, honestly. But this is fantastic. Reminds me of the whole 'truth is stranger than fiction' saying. I mean, you guys have balls-"

"Remember," Cole rejoined, "we didn't think this was going to develop such momentum so fast. Call it bad luck or whatever else you want to call it, but it happened."

Kit resumed "I like it. It's a bit dangerous I think but then I don't think militants would threaten an established picture studio."

"Can never be sure one way or another," Rod rejoined. "But I think we can all look forward to an adventure." The festive mood continued throughout the dinner.

Sixteen

Cole replayed the dinner in his mind after he dropped off Gordy later that night. He was stunned by how savory the food was, and the high quality of general conversation. Perhaps the highlight was the shitake mushroom soup, punctuating the sticky rice and the usual staples such as chicken teriyaki and pork dumplings dipped in a sweet and sour sauce with a hint of spicy peanuts thrown in. It took a while, but he finally settled on a cinematic analogy: It was as if he and Gordy had been given a homecoming feast after a lengthy prison stint. The opposite view, of it being a type of Final Meal, also struck him, as did the ravishing presence of Kit.

Rod had assayed to steer along most of the conversational flow, and had put on a black restaurant hat he had purchased up front at the gift shop, a baseball cap with the restaurant's shrimp logo. Kit later joked that he had "put on his salesman's cap." Cole, loosening up with his third beer, had joked that if she continued to carry on like that, he would have to hug her. Gordy sipped carefully, "almost daintily," Cole joked.

Rod began "Man, getting smacked behind the ear."

"It was more on the side of the head," Cole corrected.

"Alright, but being hit on the head in a dark alley-"

"It was actually Gordy's driveway," Cole again corrected.

"Okay, but dark out, and you get hit, Bam! Out of nowhere by a big brother-"

"Only blacks call each other brother, Rod," Gordy cut in, with his handkerchief wiping off a bit of beer dribbling down his chin. "No offense, especially to the lady amongst us, but the way you describe it might give people the wrong idea. It's the context. Saying brother to another person is always cool, but when you refer to another person the way you do, it doesn't ring the right bell."

Cole drafted in "'The lady amongst us'? Huh? More surprises from you tonight. Have you been reading Romantic literature lately or what? Anyway, I'll spare you a lecture. Anything that comes even close to 'big black buck' is not received warmly by blacks. 'Negro' is outmoded. 'Jigaboo, spade, and monkey' don't work. Don't laugh, Kit. Your sides might split."

Rod grimaced. "Gee, you guys here in the states are more uptight that I imagined. It's like putting a bloody finger in a shark tank. But it's good to clear the air now, amongst us, instead of trying to deal with a heavy hand at the studios."

Kit piped in "On that subject, gents, we might have to draw up a no liability contract in case someone ever has the idea to come after us legally."

"Okay, but then we're essentially dealing with criminals." Cole leaned in. "How would they ever be able to press a suit?"

"Understand," Kit responded. "It's just a formality, really. But Rod could be sunk otherwise."

Rod piped in "She's right on this, guys. Look, we need to expect the unexpected. I can't afford to be deported over some nonsense.

We are talking about a screen version of an, uh, a screen version of a documentary I guess. Where is the precedent for it?" He plopped a dumpling into his mouth.

Gordy replied, "Well, there's a rumor that the bestseller about Nixon's fall is slated to be shot for the big screen pretty soon. But technically the movie will be the second version, after the book. We might do the exact opposite, from film to book."

"Hmmm," Kit murmured, "Uh, let's not get too ahead of ourselves at this time. Maybe we should return to how the first project will work."

"Right, right you are, K," Rod returned. "I will give a rough treatment to the studio. If they are willing to shoot it in small installments, which is unlikely, we'll go that way. If not, I suggest you guys figure out where the story goes from here."

Cole said "I see. You're saying it will either be bought outright or not, that it could be shot now or in the near future or much later. No objections here. What about you, Gordy? Any more surprises up your sleeve?"

Gordy was momentarily distracted by the tuxedoed bus boy reaching over to refill his water glass. "Not that I can see. I guess we're on our way. Just hope we don't run afoul of law enforcement."

"Well, I guess looking at it another way, you could be rescued at some point. Right?" asked Kit. "It could go a number of ways, I'd say. But your story is already more entertaining than anything I ever hear at the bar."

Rod poured from a fresh bottle of beer, and wiped an appreciative finger through some beaded condensation. "I could tell my spear fishing story-"

"No, not again, please." Kit raised her hands in mock horror.

"Again, I could tell my spear fishing story, but you guys have me beaten squarely with your yarn. It is dark. Ah, hope that word is enough. I am going to push it to the hilt, your story, that is. So let's fill glasses and make a toast to, well, us..."

Still under the alcoholic influence, Gordy picked up the phone as soon as Cole dropped him off. It was about 9:30, much past Dr. Winfield's office hours, and even in his hazy state Gordy realized after about the fifth ring that it was much too late when a female voice, more of a drone, in fact, spoke after a loud click: "Dr. Winfield is not available. Please speak your name and number slowly and clearly after the third beep, and he will get back to you." While he dealt with the slight shock of dealing with his first answering machine, it make three distinct beeps, then was silent. After he finished, he felt he rambled on too long; later, however, he reasoned that it was better to be expansive rather than the opposite. Unbeknownst to him, the tape machine, working on two spools, was in the possession of LAPD Detective Logan Mankins, who had taken over the case after the untimely demise of O'Dool, a man of almost legendary status within the department, known for his steely instincts. O'Dool had been killed by a sniper. Mankins, a short burly man with a mop of red hair, which he always styled with a military bowl cut, had searched for the killer for months, even though higher ranking detectives had already been assigned to the case. Later, he liked to say in his blunt, clipped manner "I took care of him." Later it was found that delivering six fatal bullets to the sniper's midsection was an act of self- defense. It was Mankins himself who had requested, and received, authorization to tap Dr. Winfield's phone.

Mankins did not have knowledge of the firebombing of the Korean grocery, but he always had hunches which uncovered criminal activity. Dr. Warfield had written a series of articles for the Los Angeles Sentinel, in which he warned of a forthcoming crisis, in which disaffected black youth would heed a call for militant spirit, and prepare themselves in terrorist activity. Warfield had also written a series of short stories in which a wide range of non-black owned businesses were targeted. Although far from an avid reader Mankins had an almost fanatical devotion to Los Angeles daily newspapers. He trained himself to speed read, engineering the velocity through constant practice, and copious amounts of coffee. With a glue stick and scissors he pasted headlines into a spiral binder before doing a portion of his daily push up regimen. He winced from time to time, because of a bullet that had nicked/shaved the underside of his left collarbone near the shoulder while serving in Vietnam. Although no longer a rookie, a few seasoned cops had joked "Look at young Mankins. All that pride, like a young virgin. Then he goes and gets his cherry popped, getting his hands dirty like the rest."

Mankins, as impatient of an interrogator as he could be with suspects, had, on the other side, a highly refined strain of patience that went beyond his newspaper clipping collecting. In the jungles of Vietnam he had been called Killer Buddha, because he could sit and wait for the enemy as long as was required with a constantly changing calculus composed of weather, topography, and jungle thickness. Other men would be spooked by animals in the undergrowth and sudden gusts of wind. Not Mankins. To his enemies he was a black panther, merciless and extremely efficient with a kill. He used to perch in a tree as his favored lair, descending to ground only when he was assured of nearby human prey. At the outset he had mistaken animals for men, but over time he had adjusted his hearing to a better frequency. As a boy he had been a precocious hunter, as well as a star running back throughout high school, which lent him the strength and agility of an animal.

He had not hesitated when his name came up on the draft list.

When he heard the tape of Gordy's voice the first time, he thought "Okay. I've waited long enough on this one."

Seventeen

Cole expected a knock on his door or an unexpected visit at his job site. The mental stress added to the physical toll of his labor; he watched his mirrors closely while on the road. Once home he placed his gun in a kitchen drawer next to a garlic press which he utilized to make his clam sauce, butter-and-garlic, and Italian sausage pastas. "The nude bather hasn't returned or been on my mind in general" he thought to himself. He took longer showers and naps and made notes of impressions he hoped to turn into poems. But his form of rest only lasted two days.

Gordy's voice was a bit scratchy over the phone line. "We've been requested to meet with the hoods again."

"Requested?" Cole cut off a burst of nervous laughter. "I'd prefer to wait a week or so." He turned his vertical blinds to the closed position.

Gordy said "Right, smartass. Well, it's happening later tonight. They want you at my place by eleven pm. Then we're to wait for instructions, over the phone, that is."

Cole grimaced. "Man, that's not much notice. But I guess I shouldn't complain. My head is completely healed by now, and I don't have a hangover."

Gordy laughed briefly. "Good. Why don't you come over a bit after ten then. That way we can make sure we've got our story straight."

"Okay. I might get another plate of pasta in the meantime. Later." Cole hung up and immediately walked over to the kitchen and opened the drawer containing his gun.

But he left it there and only occasionally peeked out of his blinds to scan the pool area leading toward the parking lot a few times over the course of the following three hours. He carved the remnants of garlic cloves out of the press with his small knife, then pasted them onto a piece of buttered toast. Because he was distracted, there were small pieces of garlic pasted to the corners of his mouth when he left his apartment.

Gordy closed his door and Cole heard the click of the lock going into the strike as he padded over to the couch. He swept aside the sports section splayed across both cushions and said "Now you lock the door, when it probably won't serve its purpose." He started scanning the baseball box scores while Gordy put leftover pizza into the oven. In a delayed response he lobbed back over his shoulder "I'm pretty sure of certain things, like that you won't beg for a slice once the pie is warmed up. But I can't be sure either, you know?"

Cole replied "For all we know this hood might already be under the threat of retaliation should we be bothered. Still you're right. I might have a slice when it is up and ready, once on a roll with Italian food it's easy to keep shoveling it in." From quick perusal he established that Gordy had also been indoors a lot, because there was hardly any evidence of dust. He said "Thanks for cleaning up for my visit."

Gordy replied "Right, smartass," suppressing a chuckle. "Keep joking. You're the token white boy in the crowd. So you can act like a hippie and be alright. But as for myself, I have to worry about being labeled a traitor to the brothers. I would say 'my brothers' but you'd give me shit about it."

"Yeah, I probably would," Cole replied. "But all we have to do is tell them half of the truth, that their story is on a director's or producer's desk, and that it has been told truthfully."

Gordy dusted some crushed red pepper onto the pizza, then closed the oven door. "I guess we don't have any other options. At least for now. So let's try to make it as painless as possible tonight, and not promise too much. My guess is they won't come here again. We'll probably be directed to a specific place."

Cole creased the paper, accidentally tearing the upper edge. "Makes sense to me. They should continue to be cautious. I'm just a little worried that they might get impatient waiting to hear the final word from the studio."

Gordy put a teapot on the range to boil. "Don't worry too much. They've got to realize they don't have direct control. Let's chill with a few cups of tea. They will be calling soon enough I'm sure."

The phone rang about an hour later. Cole watched Gordy pace back and forth, taking the phone cord to its limit, nodding his head and blurting out continual expressions of agreement: "Sure; okay; no problem; count on it, brother; Peace to you, too." When Cole started to stand, he waved him back, saying "No rush. We can leave in about a half hour. But let's not drink too much tea. We want to be alert alright, but not jittery."

Cole just nodded his head, thinking "Well, I'm going to be the midnight driver, so I'll decide how much caffeine my system can take." He said "So how far do we have to go? Don't tell me they want to meet in Bellflower or something."

"Nah. More like a downtown warehouse." Gordy fished into his cupboard for a couple of tea bags. "Sounds like it is next to the LA River. But don't be surprised if the final meeting is somewhere completely different."

Cole was wondering if he should have brought his gun. "Well, it's sounding a little sketchy, man," he said. "I don't need to get assaulted again, that's for sure. My skull might not be able to stand up to more punishment."

The freeway was light with traffic. Cole reminded himself to look beyond the red gleam of taillights so that his eyes were not hypnotized by the blur. He kept the radio off, although both remained largely silent, counting off the exit signs as they neared their destination. At the last moment Cole switched one lane to the left to get on the Harbor Freeway, where an old Volkswagen bus had been pulled over by the CHP. The motorcycle cop, with tall, shiny black boots and space-like helmet, was cautiously looking under the chassis near the back bumper, and the two occupants of the cab wearing headbands had their hands splayed over the dashboard. Cole cursed under his breath because the cop had placed a flare within the far left lane, and he had to center it under his truck in order to not crush it. "What's he trying to do, make someone crash?" he said aloud. Gordy remained silent, admiring the twinkling lights of the Bonaventure Hotel. After a short stretch on the 101 they exited, the truck's right front tire crushing an empty beer bottle underneath near the first stoplight. Gordy quipped "Hope that's not a bad sign for us." Cole's eyes darted to the left and right, because he half-expected another bottle to follow in short order, but one more focused by the sharp malice of someone hoping the bottle smacked into the truck's body after a targeted throw.

The corner gas station parking lot was alive with bikers, at least ten milled inside the convenience store while one stood post outside, sitting on his "hog" motorcycle drinking straight from the bottle. Although it was a windy night he only wore cutoff Levi shorts and a tank top. "Looks like a Mongrel gang member" Cole said. "They are kind of an offshoot of the Hell's Angels, but maybe not as disciplined." As if in direct response, the biker emptied his bottle and smashed it on the ground.

"Brothers picked a real nice neighborhood, didn't they?" Gordy asked. "Man, even most cops probably do their best to avoid this area so late at night." He slid slightly on the seat as Cole took a corner a bit too quickly. "Okay, halfway down the black slow to a stop. We should get a flash of headlights, then the van should appear. It will circle around, then we're to follow it."

"Where to?" Cole asked, his left foot tapping the floorboards.

"Not sure. But somewhere very close by. That's all I was told over the phone." As soon as the truck slowed the van did, indeed, appear ahead, turning left to pass them closely on their left on the narrow, dark street. Then a three point turn was executed and the van passed them and the headlights came on, illuminating the scrawl of graffiti on the façade of the three story, block long brick building. One looked like a mix of Asian and Spanish writing, a few characters forming the sharp edge of a knife.

The van led them alongside the LA canal, aka The River, at times going off the road to push up dust clouds next to storage sheds and dumpsters. They proceeded underneath a couple of freeway overpasses, where some homeless were gathered around barrels with fires blazing within. A few shouted toward the van, and one began to lope toward it, then thought better of it. He did make a quick, throwing motion toward Cole's truck, however, even though his hand was empty. After a couple of miles the van went through an opening in the fence, and went down the concrete edge to the bottom of the canal, where there were only a few inches of water. "Well, man, at least they can't bury us down there," Cole said and, after pausing momentarily at the top, put the truck in gear and descended slowly.

Gordy quipped "Hope your brakes are okay. Cause if they give out we're dead men." Once the truck stopped, four figures emerged from the van once more, none carrying guns, but each face was still covered by a mask. The tall, thin one presented himself last. Gordy and Cole moved slowly as they climbed out of the truck, and approached the small group of men.

"You put your lights out already. Good times all around," the leader began. "This meeting is really just a check in of sorts. We don't like being caught much over phone lines. And excuse the masks, brothers. We wouldn't in any way want cops to stop more brothers than necessary if they had so much as even general descriptions of us."

Gordy said "You sure they wouldn't stop every last damn single one of us regardless? Every chucklehead, gangbanger, and jock?"

"Damn right" one of the three behind the leader burst out. He had his hands in his pockets because the chilly breeze was too strong for his thin, cut off Raiders sweatshirt. "The old five o is getting nastier by the day."

His colleague standing to his left shoved his shoulder roughly. "Yeah, uh huh, you tell it like it is," he said. "But give it a rest now."

The leader coughed to cover up his laughter. "You're wise on that point alright." He looked directly at Cole. "And how is your connect going? I'd like to hear this project going ahead as quickly as possible."

Cole walked forward a few steps. "Within the week I should be hearing back from my contact-"

"And you're confident your 'connect' is the dependable kind?" He grinned wolfishly, rolled his shoulders back, and kicked a jagged piece of glass in Cole's general direction.

Cole stood rigidly. "Yeah. He seems determined to get it pushed through. Gordy and I should be talking to the Hollywood group over the next week or so." He told himself to keep his eyes pointed firmly ahead while a train hummed, screeched, and clattered overhead just to the south of them over a concrete bridge. The lamp of the engine car briefly resembled the strobe light of a police cruiser.

"Okay" the tall man replied. "I'm good with that. And I'd like us to have input on the movie title also, when that comes around. 'Righteous' kind of strikes me, has a nice ring to it, but a bit too commonplace, even boring, I guess."

Gordy took a half step in front of Cole. "The people working for us, and I mean all of us, don't want to make trouble. I assure you of that. And no one in Hollywood likes cops."

"Damn!" one of the three at the back declared. "This guy shoots it straight. No bull. We like that, and-"

"All right." The leader half-turned and held out an upturned palm. "One of my sources by the way feels that the Korean grocer is preparing a lawsuit against the city for not investigating the bomb. You dig? So don't even think about going to the scene again. Alright? It's getting hot. This is good for my group, maybe not so much for yours."

One of his men choked off a chuckle, then a kind of high pitched scream emanated from the burning barrel homeless area. Quick glances shared the same thought: "Was someone's hand put in the fire?" Cole noticed one of the three rubbing his eyes and thought "Is he still adjusting to the LA smog? Or does he have a cold? If I was a detective I might draw the conclusion that he is from somewhere else, maybe out of state altogether." When they started hugging their own arms to retain heat, the leader said "Let's get out of here now. If a bum is getting roasted alive over there the cops might be coming. I suggest you two get going also. But don't follow us when you reach the top of the berm, okay? Turn left, then look for a red storage shed. Behind it you'll find a gap in the fence large enough to drive through. You'll be out quickly."

Once they were in the truck Gordy said "You hear that? They're going to take the quickest route out of here, and make us take the longer, more dangerous one."

Cole revved the engine. "Makes sense to me. Hey, they might share skin color with you, but they're definitely not your friends. I'm sure of that." By the time they reached the top of the rise the van was nowhere in sight. Once they reached a paved street they noticed a cop car directly ahead at the next stoplight, facing them. There was one alleyway halfway down the block, but Cole figured it would appear suspicious to the police cruiser if they turned there. As soon as he passed the mouth of the opening the police flashers went on. Gordy could almost see the faces of the two cops, and saw the one on the passenger pull the radio to call dispatch. As the truck approached the intersection the radio was waved at the end of its long cord. To Gordy it was clear they were being pointed out as the target. Cole felt blood rush to his head.

But the cruiser turned to the right and sped away.

Cole exhaled when they were free to head home once more. "Well, we weren't attacked by bums, cops or dead cats" he deadpanned. "And since I wasn't hit again my skull thanks me."

Gordy said "I was relieved they were a bit more casual this time."

"Yeah," Cole returned. "That seems about right, but people can be killed 'casually' just as much as angrily. So I wouldn't get too comfortable."

"You know what I'm saying, man. But anyway, we are both still in one piece, and we've got a kind of rap established between us." Gordy watched the downtown skyscraper lights with an enhanced appreciation, thinking "We weren't close to death, but why does it feel that way?" He continued "Man, I haven't thought much about my folks over the years, but with all this happening I guess the possibility of, well, you know, I guess it makes me realize watching movies about hoods is one thing, trying to deal with their crazy asses is another."

Cole laughed. "'crazy asses' huh? I like that. You're not giving them every break in the book just because they're black. It's progress, you've got to admit that."

Gordy responded brusquely. "You saying I can't look at my people objectively? What kind of garbage is that? I know there are all sorts of blacks, just like whites-"

Cole replied "Okay, okay. I'm just saying you have a habit of stargazing, trying to find some heavenly spark. As if you're just waiting for it all to come crashing down."

Gordy said "Man, are you suggesting I believe is some form of deliverance or something? Cause I don't. I don't believe in people saving themselves, that's for sure. Call me pessimistic if you must, but I'm trying to keep it on the level with you. Both of us have been tweaked, that's for sure. Some might say-"

"Don't" Cole offered, his left foot beginning to tap on the floor next to the brake pedal. For a moment he thought he smelled fumes permeating the truck's cab. "We're both a little off, maybe jaundiced in our blood a little-"

"Are you all right, man?" Gordy chuckled. "Cause you're sounding a bit crazy now. I go into something, then you tear down all the walls to make your point."

Cole felt a hair on the back of his neck bristling, reminding him how vulnerable he was to resentment about anyone questioning his wisdom. "How did two blood brothers like us ever find each other?" he thought. "And why does it feel like a serpent has curled up just above my groin, spitting venom slowly into my navel?" He had to reposition his ambition about the project, align it with a more primal part of himself, a part that might perhaps in other contexts be called spiritual; a spirituality that requires a complete admission of pain. He thought that if he wrote this scene into a movie he would streak the sooty streets with rain.

Gordy felt temporarily defeated, as if the mere fact that Cole was driving instead of him led to the definite conclusion that he was no longer directing his own life. He thought "What are we sensing now?"

Eighteen

On his worst days Detective Mankins had to leave the city behind, and drive up into the mountains. There he could shout himself hoarse, sometimes scaring small birds from their perches on the wispy branches of trees. He marveled how, once sure of their safety, the birds reformed ranks in sharp geometric patterns; reminding him of the manner in which seasoned Vietnam patrols could reform ranks after an ambush. Because it did not matter who was the aggressor, the end result was the same back stateside: wrenching screams of pain. On his worst days even his pasting of news clippings did not bring him relief, and then the lure of a cold midday bar was almost an implacable lure. His Vet buddies would have chided him for his introspection, but he realized one thing: Despite having a reputation for allowing patrons to "come as they were" even cave-like, slightly grungy bars had their particular cares. Because, even in the ultimate escape of imbibing large quantities of alcohol, and the solace of equally inebriated patrons, chaos is only one arch glance or unappreciated comment away. Mankins drank alone in most cases, and when his rage was threatening to burst its bounds, he added the disciplined exertion of weightlifting. Other cops chided him, saying things such as "If you like flexing your muscles so much, why don't you go down to Muscle Beach?" His equipment was in a driveway shed alongside his washer and dryer.

On his work desk in the morning was a virtual order for him to use at least two of his accrued vacation days at some point that week. He grimaced, because he was notorious for claiming he could never coordinate a vacation in the proper manner. Mankins thought that it would have been less annoying if the specific days were selected for him. At the same time he reflected that if he allowed the days to expire he might hear from his fellow officers, because it was expected of everyone to take advantage of the increasingly generous package of benefits that officers both past and present had fought for. He sighed to himself. "Departmental brass just has to lump me in with the rest, don't they?" "Hey Mankins, loosen up a little. Go away and give yourself and your buddies a break." This note was affixed to the edge of his desk with a small piece of chewing gum. He shrugged, thinking "I'll let it rest overnight," and pocketed the memo. He only felt the eyes of a rookie detective from the far corner, and was sure that he had been instructed as his first task of the morning to catch a violent reaction from Mankins. Of course, from his corner desk the callow cop could not see the cords standing out on Mankins' neck, or the cracking knuckles of his scarred hands. Since receiving the phone tap message on Dr. Warfield's phone, he had been anxious to begin surveillance. "Well, at least an occasional tail," he thought.

He drove his Dodge Avenger to his flat on a sloping hill in Silverlake, then switched over to his Chevy pickup, which he maintained himself, using an empty bay of a mechanic friend's shop in Burbank. On the way due east he stopped at an IHOP and ate two heaping plates of waffles slavered in whipped cream and syrup, one plate piled high with sausage, and three hard-boiled eggs, along with a glass of milk and a soda. He was already debating whether he should honor the enforced time off at the beginning of the week, or wait until the end. Of course, he could secretly work during his time off, but he would not have access to police records. Unusually for him, he had skipped shaving in the morning, wondering "Could I be another mountain man? One shunned by society more than I already have been?"

His ascent to the mountains was his own psychological return to the highlands of Vietnam. In the first few months he had been assigned to a supply air base on the coast, which was encircled by slowly ascending hills. It did strike him that perhaps his mountain ventures were a way to assimilate the topography of Vietnam. Clearly it was solitude that he hoped to find in the mountains behind Pasadena, not Vietcong soldiers; not strange succulents with edges that could razor easily through your flesh, but softer strains of pine needles; not impaling spikes carved out of bamboo, but friendly trailhead signs; not leeches stuck into the squishiness between boot and foot, but the cold, dry treatment of mountain air. In his mind he sensed a coming escalation in the Korean grocery bombing case, owing partly to him, of course, just as he had been in Vietnam when the escalation in troops occurred. Even though he was only thirty when he returned to the states, the intensity of his experience in military terms equated to a slew of higher degrees. In Vietnam, through years of an almost constant stream of commendations he had only begrudgingly accepted the merits of ascending the ranks of officialdom. His psychology inclined him to separate himself, and remain as free from the higher ups as possible, and ingratiate himself with the men who he more and more eclipsed within the narrow corridors of ranking. Mankins became the expert on artillery positioning, rifle protection, leech removal, storing of foodstuffs, and minimization of glare, which could alert the enemy. Other officers joked about Mankins' own brand of fanatical preparation before leading patrols into the jungle: "You act like you're all preparing them for actual auditions," a foil named Sergeant Charles said. "You don't have to be all washed up to be fucked by the gooks." Mankins kept warning himself to not lose his temper and stomp Charles into unconsciousness, because Charles was a virulent racist, telling his crude jokes with doses of unschooled language.

As a recreational hiker back in the states, Mankins was prone to veer off the trails when they shadowed streams. He would hop from one partially submerged rock to another and revel in the slight crackling of pebbles bumping into each other as a light breeze wafted the hair on his forearms. It took him a while to stop pondering what sort of business a certain Dr. Winfield was wrapped up in, and begin to see the silver, scaly sides of trout rippling the water of the mountain creek.

Cole was thinking that money was essentially demonic, but, on the other hand, that the lack of it often produced demonic acts. Although far from a student of history, he sometimes wondered about his links with ancient peasants who, like him, tended to finish a day's work in fading sunset light. He rinsed off his paint brushes in the patch of dried out weeds poking out of the square in the far corner of the driveway. He had begrudgingly put on his first long sleeved plaid shirt of the season, already paint speckled from the previous year's work. At the end of the week he would have to drive to his boss' house with a scribbled invoice for "his lord."

Gordy had called once to confirm the next meeting place and time with Kit and Rod, but otherwise they kept their own counsel. Cole had a thought, that they were, indeed, fulfilling their roles in a movie of sorts, only coming out at the director's whim. It was as if to a degree even their physical presences had been diminished through exposure to a giant production. "Will our lives be sacrificed for the cohesion of a greater narrative?" he thought as he climbed into his truck's cab, throwing his tool bag on the passenger side, which had a wrapped taco in a greasy white bag. He opened it and quickly ate it while driving home, although he almost choked on the first bite because he failed to remember that he had smothered it in Uncle Tso's hot sauce.

There had been a minor argument about where to dine next, but in the end Cole's argument held sway: "I know the best Mexican place which means that at the very least it has the best enchiladas in town, not too watery, not too dry, either. You see, enchiladas set the bar in Mexican places, everything is always good after the immaculate enchilada." Kit had laughed, put down her cocktail glass on the bar, and said "Well, we're following you then." Cole turned to Rod and said "I'll try not to outspeed you, but then my GTO is probably not too much faster than your supped up Chevy."

Rod patted him on the back and took one last handful from the peanut dish. "Don't be too big for your britches now mate. Even crocs get out of the way when I floor it."

Cole did not give much notice to the police cruiser as he exited. Its lights were on in the gathering darkness but not with its flashers pulsing, and it did not slow as it passed him. The passenger cop glanced over briefly. That was all. Rod, Kit, and Cole had already turned into the parking lot, so he had to assume they had not noticed the cops. He wondered briefly if he should inform them, and thought not. "Besides," he thought, "no one is being completely truthful with each other. No one is."

Sitting next to him, Gordy was in a pensive mood. Long ago he had realized that he would never hear about why his folks had left him when he was still a child. But he suspected his grandmother was reserving the future truth for, perhaps, his future edification. His meditation continued while he watched the taillights of the police cruiser until they disappeared around a curve.

It was called Maria's. "Couldn't they have put at least a little more thought into the name?" Gordy asked as they rolled into the parking lot behind Rod's Chevy. The lot was almost completely full.

Cole answered "It's a perfect enough name as far as I'm concerned. It's sentimental, man. Probably named for a deceased grandmother. And now I'm going to give you some advice."

"Really?"

"Yeah. In case you haven't heard, women are sentimental creatures. They like to believe love can overcome everything."

"Right."

Gordy chuckled. "Hey. I don't entirely agree with that either, but you've got to give them the room to believe what they want to believe." Cole draped his arm over the back rest and turned off the engine.

Gordy said "You know, you don't do so well in the ladies department yourself. I think you're saying this because you're just hoping having a better handle on females will help your writing. And I think you're wrong on that score."

Cole watched for Rod and Kit, but apparently they were also delayed. "Right. Be hard, brother. Don't show emotion about anything like an inner city stoic. Trying to harden what is injured. Let it heal first, man."

Gordy answered "Don't psychoanalyze me. Please. Don't talk about things like 'psychic scars.' Anyway anger can be connected positively to motivation. Gets me off my ass instead of dwelling on the people who have left me."

Cole unlatched the seat belt because Rod and Kit had begun to walk in their direction, Rod feigning to brush her hair with brotherly affection. "We are artists, man. Or at least we purport to be. So I think we should be a bit more open-minded in general."

Cole caught up with Rod and Kit at the entry, and waved them on. Clearly he had built up a rapport with the staff because he escorted them back to a large red corner booth, and only had to nod at a young busboy to announce their presence. The crowd was thin, what both Cole and Gordy called "dinner prelims" and Cole had timed their dining to coincide with a fresh batch of tortilla chips being produced. And chiefly, to Cole's thinking they did not have to worry about the invasion of a mariachi band, because Maria's only allowed them during private parties. The low light and the lack of a television over the bar imbued the dining area with tranquility. Kit scooted into the booth first and positioned herself in the middle. Her predominant thought was how dark, even ruby red and hazy, the restaurant interior was. It reminded her of an old fashioned steak house in a hotel off Wilshire Boulevard, where the waiters had such patience and reserve, where white pristine towels were draped over arms and one half-expected to see mobsters with steely glances and sport coats pulled from shoulders with exceeding care. But here it could be assumed that, at worst, switchblade knives were concealed in chino pockets. Maria's had, in fact, experienced a scandal four years previous. A melee had broken out on the sidewalk involving two gangs, and had spilled into the restaurant's waiting area, where someone had suffered a knife gash to the leg, and had bled out staggering out to the parking lot. Incidentally, according to a series of LA Times investigative pieces the incorporated town of Boyle Heights of East LA was trying to siphon more police off the LA city government budget. Regardless, the incident did not, as expected, result in a drawn out gang war.

Gordy and Cole took the two outside positions at the booth. Cole gave him a mock salute and Gordy returned a middle finger, although, as was his wont, he twirled in in the air while he made the motion. "Senora and senores," their waiter introduced himself briefly, bowing in his immaculate white double-breasted suit. "My name is Ernesto. Can I get you all started with some refreshments?" With only a slight nod of his head he commandeered a tray of chips and salsa to the center of the table. Kit slapped hands away and sunk her hand into the chip's bowl while saying "Coronas all around, unless-"

"Nah, nah," Gordy piped in. "Dos Equis here."

"And here." Cole raised his hand.

"Ah. I've got to go with the girl here. So count me in on a Corona," Rod offered, over his shoulder straining to admire a painting of a manolete skewering the already bloody spine of a bull. "Very well, amigos y amiga," the waiter said, and retreated to the kitchen.

Rod cleared his throat after washing down a clump of chips. "We've got the old traction, gents. The studio wants to go ahead with your concept. But they want my input, meaning we might need to spice it up a bit."

Gordy shook his head. "Isn't this enough? Here we are with a concept, about two guys who sell a story to a movie studio, except they don't know it is the actual truth. And the studio can do with it as they want."

Rod jumped in. "Look, you're dealing with huge Hollywood egos here. They will do what they will with that they've been given, within reason."

"And the contract?" Cole was trying to appear casual by concentrating on the tortilla chip basket again.

"Ah, the contract" Rod continued. "They have high-powered lawyers. You don't. They know how to manipulate the truth to make their case look stronger. Look, I'll do what I can to have it made the way you'd like it to be, but obviously I can't make any guarantees."

"Come on guys," Kit said. "I sense a lot of tension. But this is a collaboration, okay? So let's treat it that way. It's all, uh, frankly, a bit confusing right now, as I see it."

"Confusing?" Cole parroted. "Yeah, I guess so, but then sometimes debts have to be made to art. It's the message that's the most important, not the form. Like as a writer, you start off with an image, and go from there."

Gordy chuckled. "Speak for yourself. I make sketches of characters first, and make story boards, too, when the mood strikes me. It's where you end up that's the most important." He winked at Kit, who smiled back.

"Philosophy aside," Rod resumed, "they want to meet you guys at the studio, maybe even establish a contract. Might not be the long term, finalized version, but still it's a start."

"I'd rather sign the finalized one, or none at all," Cole said, nodding to Gordy. "It would be better to be clear cut on at least that detail." He raised a finger toward the approaching waiter, signaling for more time.

"Okay, I'll work on my end to effect that." Rod picked up his menu and the rest followed his example.

Kit said "Hey, let's eat before we discuss more of this. I think everyone is a bit cranky because of hunger. It makes us all have issues."

"Dr. Shrinker?" Cole joked, and felt less for the effort. "Uh, we're tight on all that. But let's order like Kit here suggests. Enchiladas con crema is a great choice, so is the chili verde meal."

Gordy felt he had to have the last word. "I just hope if things get real heated down the road, that, being black myself, people might defer a bit to me. Because I know what 'will fly' in the 'hood, if you know what I mean."

Rod half-shrugged, Cole shook his head, and Kit arched her eyebrows questioningly. Before the awkward silence extended much further their waiter returned to puncture the tension. "You all look serious, but after your meal you will have smiles. I assure you of that."

"The chili rellenos were very good but the chicken enchiladas were even better," Kit remarked before taking the last sip from her beer mug. "I might have to mention this place to my bar pals."

Rod returned "They would ruin it."

"What? Anyway, thanks for the suggestion. I'm glad we agreed to it alright. Maybe we should set a scene here-"

"Here?" Rod parroted. "Slow down. Our pal Gordy just mentioned he'd like us to hear him out when at all possible."

Gordy was smiling back in approbation, and Cole was already fishing into his wallet for cash. Kit said "It's how dark and cool it is in here contrasting perfectly with the hot, delicious food. That's the great contrast in my mind. It might be an, uh, kind of quiet scene between intense action episodes."

Rod dropped cash in the middle of the table and said "That should definitely cover my part. But now I've got to go to the loo." His first step was almost a hop, because one toe had briefly caught on the edge of a Spanish tile.

"Whoa, Nelly!" Kit called after him. "Look how eager he is. Don't be surprised, gents, if he gets us a meeting with the picture execs within a couple of days."

Gordy thought he saw the glimmer of a tear through her purple eyeliner. "Is she in love with him? Or was she reminded of a profound old grief? But let Cole think about that. I just want to get back home and work on my poetry."

Nineteen

Once he decided to take the police department's enforced two days off, Mankins used a bit of legerdemain to keep working. The result was a rookie cop named Stevens spending early mornings at the police records building downtown. Police brass did not expect such a strategy from Mankins, so the clerks at the office were not forewarned. Stevens was a bit doughy in the face, but carried himself well. When asked he told the clerk that he was simply looking into some misdemeanor traffic violations which might have some bearing on a current gambling ring with ties to Las Vegas. Stevens was proud that he did not have to ask Mankins for a pretext about files relating to Gordy Redding and Julius Winfield of Cal State LA. Mankins told Stevens to give him a brief report on each day, which turned out to be inconclusive. Gordy had a sealed juvenile record and there was nothing concerning Dr. Winfield. Mankins cooked himself steak and macaroni and cheese meals with large salads of oil and vinegar dressings and did his news clippings work a little bit later than usual, at some point during the late afternoon. His hope was that his habit might uncover some previously unrevealed connections. Mankins roamed through his large home in Silverlake scanning through his files, some of which were in the study, the spare bedroom, or the den. He had inherited the house from a wealthy uncle who had made a small fortune from helping perfect the modern rubberization of tires and had been contracted to car racing teams throughout the country. Only a few months before Mankins had removed all of the carpet from the house before refinishing the wood underneath, at times cutting through with slashes of a razor knife, and finishing his days with extended workouts on the workbench. He bought slabs of roast beef and cheddar cheese, sometimes making sandwiches, at other times simply dousing the roast beef with pepper and vinegar, and wrapping them around slices of cheese. He carved with the same knife he had used to slit the throats of young Vietnamese soldiers. To him it was his sole, solitary concession to the war, and what he had brought back, a way to transform the experience in a unique manner. Over the course of two days he felt he had adopted the role of a commanding general while Stevens operated as his sergeant, scanning for intelligence in the jungle(office) of every underground bunker(police officialdom).

Mankins sweated at night, anxious. Like the way he had perspired heavily in Vietnam, a constant sticky sheen attracting mosquitoes, flies and other indescribably aggressive flying insects, and even gigantic ants in pursuit of moist passages to exploit. So that at times he had wondered to himself "What comes first, the moisture and heat, or my sweat?" Some nights he held icy bottles to his head in a slight trance inside his kitchen, as if preparing himself for yet another daytime jungle patrol. When in reality he only had to put on a collar shirt of slightly understated style, and flatten his unruly hair with a coating of gel. And instead of checking his daily grenade ration he cleaned a small pistol.

Sunlight filtering through a gap in his blinds provided him with enough light to spread news clippings on the carpet- stripped floor. He pasted racially motivated homicides next to militant disturbances, illegal smuggling stings above forced migrations through the holds of container ships. At the top he posted mug shots of various convicts and in the top right corner a university black-and-white of Professor

Winfield. He traced Gordy's call and discovered that he, Gordy, lived in close proximity to the Korean grocery bombing.

Cole worked the next week with anticipation of an unannounced visit or two. But despite his concern, when his Italian sausage and clam pasta meals were ready he was able to enjoy them in peace. Solitude came easily to him. After the recent flurry of activity he felt a bit drained, and was indisposed toward heavy interactions with people. "Even the nude bather hasn't returned," he thought wryly. He kept his pistol in the kitchen drawer next to the garlic press. It bemused him that he could be   industrious in the kitchen without the pressure of a partner spurring him on. He also ate in larger quantities than was his norm.

Although Rod had indicated that they would quickly receive copies of the motion picture contract, they were similarly surprised to see it within three days. Both were relieved that it was fairly brief, only three double-spaced pages in length. Each hesitated to pick up the phone to consult the other about the document and both resolved to allow twenty four hours to expire before contacting the other. Cole rolled out paint on the walls of a guest house in Bel Air, and Gordy immersed himself in a philosophical tract or two, returning to the contract every couple hours or so, refilling his Big Gulp cup with ice and soda while Cole cut into ceiling corners with his paint brush. He purchased a few grocery items for his grandmother. After storing away the items while she sneezed in front of the television he picked up rocks along the driveway and scared off the feral cats nesting at the back fence, the rocks spitting through the canopy of weeds. He thought he would have to urge his grandmother to call out a landscaping crew because being a writer he believed that he should be spared humiliating physical labor, a characteristic he inherited from his deceased parents, who were bohemians to the core. One of his earliest memories was of them dancing across the living room floor to a jaunty cadence of bebop, and the rattling of the screen porch door during a brisk night breeze. His young mind was captivated by the periodic appearance of a eucalyptus tree branch swaying beyond his parents and the door.

At seven the next morning Gordy's phone rang.

"Hey, Gordy. Thought I'd check in before another long day. Have you read the contract yet?" Cole asked.

Gordy answered, "Yeah. Seems pretty straightforward to me. But we might want to chat with Rod a bit before our meeting with the Hollywood mogul."

Cole said "Alright. I'll stop by after work. But it will probably be a long day. So we might just order in pizza for your place. It think my boss will not have as much work for me next week, by the way, so we can concentrate on our writing and such."

Gordy said "Okay. I'm down with that. I wonder if we should get more money up front though. You know what I mean? Even though we're starting out, and unproven, I think we might still be able to get a larger audience on the project."

Cole pulled his telephone cord to its extreme so that he could turn down the heat on his pot of oatmeal. "Yeah. I'm going to call Rod. We'll discuss that, then fill you in later."

"Sure," Gordy replied, "see you later," and hung up the phone. He was struck by how their fortunes had changed through an unlikely chain of events, and he was anxious about capitalizing on an event. "We're kind of ambulance chasers," he thought. "If slightly more refined ones. Banking on a crime through Hollywood. Well, at least we're not selling drugs to kids...and so what if I'm started to feel a bit put upon having to do yardwork."

Cole gashed his hand open on a jutting piece of metal on the rim of a paint bucket and had to cover it in layers of masking tape in order to keep blood from smearing a living room wall. He pulled off the sticky red mess of tape, rinsed it off quickly in the kitchen sink, then reapplied another glob of tape, encouraged to see quickly notice a blood clot. He refrained from bandaging it after work, opting to head to Gordy's first. He stopped at a Pizza Hut and purchased two large supreme pies, then filled up his truck's tank. He reflected that he might have cut himself due to the distraction of the studio contract. "Calm down" he counseled himself. "It is too early to be projecting too much." Yet the white envelope on the passenger truck cab mocked him slightly, attesting to a symbolic weight. He half-expected it to be swept away by a freakish gust of wind yet it remained, all the way to Gordy's.

Both were famished, so they ate without comment, only making satisfied smacking noises from time to time. Their eyebrows arched once in reply to the omnipresent, overflying police helicopter.

Gordy spoke first. "The contract looks solid to me. I even jetted down to the library to get a quick opinion from my library lady, and she was supportive, said it should not prove to be a big trouble for us. She handed me a guide to business contracts, and I didn't see anything alarming or out of the ordinary when I compared the two."

Cole said "You surprise me a bit Gordy, being on top of the issue like that. I thought along those lines a couple of days ago, but of course I could not tear myself away to do any kind of fruitful research. I've had to entertain myself with my own questions and answers. Good news is I haven't had a headache for a couple of days, and I don't see spots either."

Gordy chuckled. "Good to hear. So your brains won't be scrambled when we talk to the Hollywood muck-a-mucks. And slow down, man. Just 'cause you bought this time doesn't mean you get to wolf all of the food down yourself."

Cole replied "Well, I worked hard today. Give me a break. I've been burning the candle at both ends lately." Cole pulled off one more slice from the box and sat on the couch. He massaged his cut hand, and wondered if they were adequately prepared to discuss a contract. According to his mother, his long absent father had been a mediocre lawyer specializing in legal writs until a freak diving accident had rendered him largely unemployable, and unavailable to the small boy Cole. He often lamented that he had not developed through the guidance of a responsible adult. "Well, at least Mom tried," he thought. "But as hooked on tranquilizers as she was before she finally succumbed to her demons her happy moments rang a bit artificial to me. There was something forced and unreal about them."

Gordy remained sitting at the card table in the corner, the one his grandmother had been pestering him to use before she added it her own burgeoning pile of junk. It had old Cracker Jack and Snickers bar wrappers glued to it, along with some carved in initials. Gordy guessed it had migrated from the back room of a bar deep in Louisiana, where it had been taking on grease spots from fried alligators' feet and po' boys, been briefly matriculated in a wino's train yard card game, and eventually appropriated by an itinerant junk salesman spending the last of his life's savings on an adventure to the west, accumulating dings and punctures along the way.

"You know, man, I'd kind of prefer our project to be a book. It would make it more legitimate somehow. At least that's how I see it." Gordy had opened up a fresh notebook to jot down some thoughts.

Cole returned "Hey, it will become what Hollywood decides to make of it. It is pretty much as simple as that. Okay? Man, I'm still digesting my pizza, and you have to bring up a potentially sore point. Why? Remember that your 'brothers,' as you like to call them, already gave us our marching orders. So we can't get off course too much, or it could be a mistake, and a very dangerous one at that." He had been about to say 'fatal mistake' but was able to retract it at the last moment.

"Okay Cole, I agree with you. It's just that being a writer it is hard to conceive of anything better than seeing the story in print, a hefty paperback. Real weight to it. Movies pare down-"

"For a reason," Cole shot back. "When verbiage gets in the way of a natural flow, movies can distill the essence through images and sounds. Anyway, if it comes, the book will have to be produced later. I'm not saying to give up. Just make notes for future use, that sort of thing. But we've already discussed that. I know you hate to hear it, but I'm going to mention it one last time. I'm painting houses, inhaling fumes, and you're living behind your granny. Neither of us is going anywhere fast, right? We've caught a break. That's the way I see it. Really. So let's not screw it up."

Gordy replied "You're a real s.o.b. when you lecture. But that's another topic, right? Look here. We're arguing over-"

"Peanuts?" Cole could not help but interrupt.

Gordy maintained "Let me finish. We might have an opportunity to hit both bases, if you know what I mean. There are all sorts of titles we could use. Some that I have considered? The New Vampire: The LAPD and Law Enforcement in the City of Angels; Panthers Unbound: Chronicles of true black militants-"

It was a loud knock and a deep voice followed in short order: "Police. Detective Mankins. I need to have a quick word with you." Cole was thinking that Gordy occasionally smoked marijuana and hoped he did not have any on the premises while Gordy briefly considered calling Dr. Winfield. The next knock was a more violent banging and a repeater voice: "Police. I hear your television and see a light so I know you are in there. You can open up or I'll have backup in no time. Your choice but I suggest you open your door straightaway."

Mankins was crouched over slightly to the left of the doorway, his right hand hovering near his holster. He did not anticipate any gunplay but he was being extra cautious because he was alone. He had nosed his Charger at a slight angle into the driveway with a thin vanilla folder containing the files he had ordered Stevens to procure for him on the dashboard. Stevens, the young cop looking to help wherever and whenever needed, had attempted to join him on the mission, but Mankins had swatted him down: "Not only will it be dangerous, it is also not authorized by the department, so it comes with other risks as well. You haven't been trained for intrusions, for instance. Okay, you know what the word means in general, but you have no idea how it works in a real life police action."

Stevens drove home to Burbank with a feeling of rejection and resentment toward Mankins for not rewarding him for his unofficial, unpaid assignment without a chance to participate in the interrogation of a prime suspect.

"Okay. Listen. I'm a cop" Mankins yelled through the door. I will slide my badge under the door. It has-"

"You don't have a warrant" Gordy boldly returned. "You don't have the right and-"

"You and your pal are in some sort of trouble. I'm sure of that," Mankins answered while sliding his badge along the floor. "And I'm not trying to force my way."

Cole spoke up. "You don't have probable cause for anything. There haven't been any gunshots, no screams, or anything else, and there are no warrants out on us. But leave us your card and we'll call you if something comes up."

Mankins had his fist raised but relented before it could strike the door. "You sure? You won't be afforded any protection in that case. I can't promise you anything."

Gordy said "Yeah. We're sure, and we're not in any trouble. So we'd like to have our own counsel on the matter."

"Okay. But after this I won't be able to offer you two any sort of deals. That's now off the table, because I feel you are withholding information. And I won't disclose what I already know about you two." Mankins waited and had already pulled his hand away from his holster. "Okay. I'm leaving. But don't be surprised if I pull you over in the next day or two with probable cause."

Gordy and Cole remained standing near the door, listening for the clear signal of the cop departing. Gordy spoke first: "Damn. The badge looked legit. So does the card. We'll still check it out, but it looks like he's the real deal." Gordy plopped down on the couch while Cole studied the card of Detective Logan Mankins. They heard the fading roar of Mankins' car engine and the sharp, isolated cry of "Honky!" Cole went to the fridge and pulled out two cans of Pepsi, and threw one to Gordy. "Pop that open. I just hope the next pop we hear isn't from a gun."

"Right, Mr. Sharp Wit," Gordy deadpanned. "Don't you have anything more smartass to sum up our situation? Or any slick ideas to get us back in control of the situation?" He tapped the sides of the Pepsi can with a thick forefinger.

Cole said "We could sign, make copies of the contract, fulfill that part, then skip town. I realize our 'friends' of the militant persuasion would not be thrilled."

Gordy snickered. "You're actually talking of running away? I'm a bit surprised by you. It would make it hard for us to survive, you know? All the logistics involved and such, how would we ever get paid for the script and all? No. We can't do that. But we could at least get our story straight between the two of us."

Cole replied "You're talking about complete denial when we don't know what the cop knows. It won't hold up, but I guess we have no other alternative at this point."

Gordy finished his Pepsi and crushed it with his strong grip. "All we can do is try to convince the brothers that we've done enough for them already, but we also don't want to be involved in any shenanigans. Of course, we've got to find some way to put off the detective, and other fuzz if it comes to that."

"'Fuzz', huh?" Cole chuckled. "Now you're sounding a bit militant. Props to you, brother, we'll just have to hope we don't get more action than we can handle. And if this keeps up your granny will eventually start asking questions, too...or slashing cops tires."

Gordy spluttered laughter. "That would be great, huh? Granny finally getting revenge for being treated badly by a couple of crackers decades ago."

Cole replied "Well, comic relief is always welcome. At least around here. I've already almost filled up one notebook with impressions of our project. Who knows, but maybe one day they will be worth thousands of dollars. Well, at least one can hope."

"Whatever happens from here, I'm going to keep the latch on the door," Gordy said. "More specifically the lock. It will be a long time before I open the door outright. But I'm thinking we should be open and truthful about the cop's visit. They might get cold feet a bit, which will give us more room to maneuver."

"Yeah, you could be right. We've just got to be careful how we break it to them. I don't want to be the token white guy strung up on a light pole." Cole reached into the fridge for another Pepsi.

Gordy chuckled once more. "Yeah, right. That would draw far too much attention. You know that. Haven't we discussed this already? My death would just be chalked up to a gangland hit, or a quarrel over a lady. Yours would be played by the media as the start of a race war. They'd have an attractive blonde with tears in her eyes and a catch in her throat report from your funeral. There would be old girlfriends interviewed, even if you never actually screwed any of them. And your mother...and the tv news crews would be scarfing down hot dogs and fries inside moldy vans..."

"Alright, alright." Cole held up his hands. "Enough. Don't make a complete farce of the situation. Either one of us could be caught in a crossfire of some sort, manmade or otherwise."

The police chopper dipped and dove in sound. Gordy considered opening the door to get a closer look, but was restrained, in part, by Cole's brooding, negative look. He also wondered, even though it seemed fantastic, if the helicopter was essentially the backup that Mankins had threatened to summon. A few pistol shots rang out, as well as shouts of disdain from the street.

Cole thought "We're trapped. We could leave the city but eventually the trouble would catch up to us." He felt again like the mountaineer he once was, visually charting geometric patterns toward some version of ascent. But that occurred mostly over two summers in his early teens, when his idealism had led him to believe that he could carve out a career as an alpinist, and remove his mother from a virtual life sentence in a mental hospital by convincing his bosses to employ her as a housecleaner. She had, in fact, a degree of obsession with cleaning products. "Did she believe she could somehow cleanse herself of demons in such a cosmetic manner?" he thought. He felt a bit nauseous, and stood to go. He said "I'll pick you up tomorrow, pal."

The therapeutic effect of yelling at the top of one's lungs without fear of being reported for disturbing the peace has probably been underreported throughout history, in part because of societal fears that once one exults in terrible fits of anger, these otherwise isolated episodes might lead one to different thresholds of release, including physical violence toward others. In a man of Cole's temperament, often in tight control of his emotions, it can serve as a necessary balm for mentally scarring exposures. Cole's most wrenching screams began on the 405 Freeway off Century Boulevard, and did not wane until he unleashed one final roar while exiting off the 10. His voice would be hoarse the following two days, and he would soothe the scratchiness with throat lozenges, but he would feel less burdened. And he would conduct himself with more composure at the studio meeting.

He made a heaping plate of spaghetti with Italian sausage when he arrived home, timing it so that when his water boiled he had already finished frying the sausage with olive oil and onions. It was his favorite variety of what would later be termed "comfort food." In other words, a recipe so delicious to the palate that one is able to eat far beyond normal bounds, and relish leftovers for at least one day afterward. He made a few notes of the day in his notebook: "Fiasco day. Again, what more can be expected to strike us? No, really, me?" and resolved to make his spaghetti specialty more often. He wondered if the recent events had urged within his subconscious a mood of solemn celebration. "I'm not that worried, am I?" he thought. "Am I going to celebrate like a dumb lummox merely because I continue to breathe on this planet?"

For the first time in months he opened his windows wide. Initially his nose wrinkled from the potent chlorine smell of the complex pool, as if the chemical intensified in flavor as it ascended the sky. His eyes watered, and he felt a minor headache invading his cranium. The immediate thought was "Did I inhale too many paint fumes?" He went into the refrigerator for the perfect antidote-chocolate milk.

He felt alone but too lacking in initiative to pick up his phone. "Self- sufficiency is the only goal worth striving for," he thought. "I'm not sure about Gordy, but I'm convinced I could complete the project on my own. It might require fleeing to Canada or Europe first, but there it is." Images flooded his mind as he laid back in bed with his windows opened and his fan buzzing on high. "But when does focus on self-sufficiency become egocentric and destructive to compassion for others?" The self-reflective mood progressed with the slightly hypnotic effect of the fan blades. He closed his eyes and visualized standing comfortably at the edge of a cliff above an ocean, bare feet in slightly wet grass, and an ideal breeze barely parting his thinning hair. He added an old tall ship sailing vessel, negotiating a small pristine coral reef at the extreme periphery of his vision. His mother dominated the foreground, yelling to him to help her from drowning. Yet he hesitated. Afterall, what if she was lying, and hoping to manipulate him? Would she try to drown him if he swam out to save her? Or, perhaps, bite him in order to produce blood to draw in nearby sharks to the scent? Such thoughts at least partially accounted for his mild, dull headache. He opened his eyes with an almost compulsive wish to rush to the bathroom and stare at his own face. Instead he made his way to the kitchen and poured himself a glass of chilled milk. In his experience the lactose either lulled him to sleep, or roiled inside his stomach an entire night. And, when he could not sleep, his dreams were haunted by snowy black-and-white images of thick, snowy static, and the end result of this was that he would awaken with a live wire throbbing inside his skull.

Twenty

Inside the movie executive's office a fleshy, middle-aged man in a slightly wrinkled suit held forth: "A philosophical thriller perhaps? Pulpy love story with a touch of the Shakesperean? Or a buddy film with a tinge of superpowers? Momentarily I might ask you gentlemen to give me some valuable input, but for now I'd like to propose this framework: Two young guys, one black, one white, from decidedly blue collar backgrounds happen upon a criminal incident that is purposely overlooked by the LAPD. Honestly I have not much sympathy for the Korean owner who had his place torched. What do they think they want here in the US anyway? My father fought in the Korean War, shagged some little demure Korean fox, said the people reminded him of the best Americans. Good sense of humor, unpretentious, tough but loving. They give that up to come to the shit hole of Watts? No offense, Gordy, but you realize what the extremes of capitalism do to people, poverty and all that, what they wreak on people. I mean, how effing naïve can these Koreans be, opening stores in poor black neighborhoods? Resentment festers. This project could be shot as a bare bones documentary, black-and-white, of course. I've got the ear of the owner of the company. It could be shot a la The Battle of Algiers, real trenchant view of a modern inner city conflict. We could even use you guys as guides of a sort. Rod is going to be the intermediary. He will keep the project moving smoothly. Now here it is: ten thousand each for the two of you, but keep in mind you will get a slice of the gross, one percent apiece. Honestly, gents, it's a pretty nice deal for two newcomers like yourselves." He paused and placed his elbows on top of his executive desk, his already thick neck bulging under the collar's fabric. His eyes were a bit rheumy and partially bloodshot from a booze fueled limousine ride along the Sunset strip.

"You men seated before me. You have a knack for finding action. I'm sure of that. Always a good thing in my book. Rod there will tell you I can be a bit hasty in pulling the proverbial trigger on a project. That's when I'm really enthused, okay? Like now, my adrenaline is pumping really good. Under such circumstances I'm known to be a hothead but right now I'm decidedly ape shit over your project's potential. I'm sure of it. And I believe you guys also believe in the power and magic of movies. That is my domain. Never mind my last name-Duckworth-in my early years competitors said all I'd ever be good for was some schmaltz and comic book movies"(here he raised a gold-plated lighter and flicked on a flame quickly with a thumb) "but one day I surpassed all the bastards. Just like that. And I see the same defiant spark in you two. Even how you smile tightly, not some He haw sort of crap either, but with an edge at the corner of smug mouths. I love it. You two are entertaining me. That much I'm sure of. But don't just stare at your 7 Up cans. Go ahead. Pop them open, let them fizz, then pour them down." Charles Duckworth picked up his full glass of whiskey and raised a toast. His lips were purplish and a vein stood out on the right side of his forehead, in a zigzag pattern. "Here's to a business pact, one that should last until at the very least we see our project up on a screen. Bottom's up! Hah. I would offer you some, uh, special Scotch, but I ran out last week. Never mind, it does burn the throat so! It makes me wonder where the soothing ice went! Bear with me, gentlemen, I'll try to slow down a bit. It's hard under this kinetic influence, that's for sure. It's not been ironed out yet but we might have our photographer ride shotgun with you guys.

But that stock footage would be cut into black-and-white film. Get it? It would kind of be the best of both worlds. A documentary inside a more traditional motion picture. What more could be better? Hitting on all strides is what it is about. What the creative instinct is all about. Do you know that I'm going to write a history of American cinema, par excellence? Because we perfected it, the French like all this avant-garde nonsense. Leave it to us to take it to another level. That's for sure. I knew it might feel like I'm telling my life story. But this is abbreviated actually. I'm here because, well, frankly, because I'm rich, numero uno. Most guys won't admit it, but I do. I wouldn't have the opportunity to do what I'm doing without a lot of capital. I'm willing to lose big in order to become big. And I'm political. A lot of people wouldn't want to touch such an incendiary subject. But I'm more than willing. That's it. I don't begrudge taking chances like the French, just in a different way. I'm taking a sharp cut into some new territory. That's where you guys come in. Just your luck. I'm tired of vigilante films and other conventional material. This will bring a whole new twist. I might even check into you guys wearing miniature cameras, will make some of the footage blurry, but there it is. I'm unsure. I'll have to talk to one of my techs about it. Well, I guess I got everything off my chest that I needed to get off. Maybe not. Rod here will attest, because we have had marathon discussions in the past that lasted well into the early morning hours. Free flowing associative kind of thing. We drink steadily but we don't get plastered. You, we, you get it, right? We can all partake of the philosophy and swill to our hearts' content. That's our only modern fountain of youth, fellows. And it's the one that has remained true and constant for centuries, no, even millennia. Talk the shit out, then burn it at the end of a joint if you can. That's where it's at. Not this modern bullshit, where everyone is supposed to get together in a pig fuck capitalist quagmire. Just doesn't work out, folks. Brings too many spices to the table. Speaking of flavor, Rod, how is it you prepare your famous tri tip again? You know, the thinner you cut your tri tip the more you can eat? Yeah, no kidding."

"Uh, yeah. Garlic, vinegar, salt, pepper, worstershire, a touch of ketchup. That's the combination. A really slow cook is another key component." Rod gauged by the furrow between his boss' eyes if he should continue.

The clacking of a postal machine on the other side of the office wall filled the space created by the lapse in conversation. Cole was studying a wall bank of photo portraits on the wall behind Duckworth, featuring men wearing thick fur next to dead beasts and skimpily clad women in action photos accentuating their cleavage. Gordy's eyes were wandering, from a case of cowboy boots near the door, to the polished brass of the small private bar. Rod was tapping his thigh with a ringed finger, relieved that his boss had winded himself through a lengthy monologue. At the same time he thought he would humor Kit later in the day with a spot on imitation of him.

"Tri, tip, tri tip," Duckworth was saying. "I do my best thinking and planning in the bathtub. But that is neither here nor there"(here Rod's finger started tapping again). "As for the setup, Rod and I will discuss more of the photography strategy with cinematography, or, uh, our cinematography strategy with photography. Hey, everyone just keep doing what they've been doing already, and we should be fine."

"So?" Rod rejoined.

"Uh, yeah, meeting adjourned until further notice. It will be set up the same way, and, uh, good luck gentlemen."

Brief handshakes were exchanged and Cole and Gordy were escorted past the secretary clicking away at her typewriter. She stared stolidly forward although she smiled out of the corner of her mouth.

Once they were outside Rod said "He likes you guys. I'm sure of that. So you should feel encouraged. I'm not one for celebration, but this could call for one, mates. I figure no one here has any objections?"

Cole's eyes squinted from the brief, harsh glare coming off a passing car's windshield. "None here. But I think that Gordy and I are both in a bit of shock. I mean, ten thousand?"

Gordy said "Well, we're definitely wanted men now. It's a bit weird that people might actually lean on us. But ten thousand? That's a lot of money for me. Maybe too much too soon?"

Twenty One

Detective Logan Mankins surveilled Cole from a perch in a tree overlooking Cole's apartment complex, and Gordy from a rusty van, staring through gaps in its mustardy yellow shades. And he spied on both from the bus stop across from their preferred Bob's Big Boy location on Century Blvd. Of course, he was hoping they would soon rendezvous with others in order for him to be able to start fitting the pieces of the puzzle together. At present he had their photos mixed in with assorted photo clippings of former and current militant and revolutionary Californians, but especially Los Angeles based criminals. But they had yet to graduate from the maelstrom of clippings on his floor to the more prominent cork board on his garage wall. When he lifted weights on his padded bench near the garage door he glanced almost wistfully at the pins clustered along the left hand side.

Police brass often chided him for his "one track mind," but privately marveled at his ability to quickly marshal information. Rawlings, the communications and electronics specialist, related him to a rapidly developing machine: "Mr. Computer."

He saw Gordy's grandmother outside the main house periodically, when she came to collect mail, briefly sit on her porch, or water her azaleas. As he became more familiar with his subjects, his notes became briefer, in part because he sought to limit the psychological channels where his own perversity could flourish. Because he did not want to view them as pure villains. The jungles of Vietnam had possessed an unlimited font of malicious material for him; and back stateside he was determined to rid the city of as much random entropy as he could. In such a manner he could reconcile some of the misgivings he had about leaving the military. Many people reasoned "Hey man, fine a cushy desk job, get your pension early, you deserve it. You want to quit and go back to the shitty rat race out there? What for?"

Janelle, his longtime on and off girlfriend, wanted him to arrange for some kind of sinecure in Southeast Asia, since she studied Japanese and had an affinity for the Far East. She wanted them to escape the "violence obsessed US imperium." To her mind the only laudable aspect of American culture was its wide array of culinary possibilities. 'But hey,' she put it one time in her blunt manner, 'it does just become stuff we shit out anyway.' She blurted it out while in the warrior yoga position on the balcony of the inland empire Riverside flat they shared at the time, which they both quickly came to loathe, even though it was considerably cheaper than anything in LA proper.

He replied "No, my angel. This is my turf. I've had enough of compromising foreign situations. You should realize that. Hey, in twenty years we can retire with the LAPD loot."

Janelle smiled quizzically. "You don't talk like a cop, L. You should realize that and adjust accordingly. It will get you in trouble down the road. For sure. Why don't you work in a gym or something? That will help rid you of the 'Nam karma,' as you call it. Push it away, you know, with your psyche, instead of embracing it by wearing it every day on your belt."

Mankins retorted "Wear it on my sleaze? Just kidding. But it is what I want to do, not my what my country or government is trying to convince me I need to do in order to remain patriotic. Screw that. I don't need or want anyone telling me the so-called 'score.'"

Janelle was no longer his lover. She wrote him postcards from Athens, Istanbul, and Berlin. He saw her briefly when she had a layover at LAX, and the rushed urgency of the meetings stirred him to the point that it required him a week to regain firm footing in his police work. He called it "reignition" of their connection over plates of lukewarm airport food, soupy nachos and soggy grilled cheese sandwiches atop small circular silver tables. On one occasion he arrived in full official black uniform, and drew some nervous glances. He thought "If they knew how many men I killed in 'nam they would all get up and quickly leave."

He thought about Janelle over the course of a couple of days while he became familiar with the daily movements of Cole and Gordy. But in the middle of the night he found himself in the sticky embrace of the Southeast Asian jungle, not the soft flesh of a woman.

Cole strode across the central courtyard of his complex and, as he neared his truck noticed a short, stocky guy wearing a Hawaiian shirt, who was studying the pool area intently, then looking up and down his street. When his back was turned, in fact, he had a striking physical resemblance to Rod Owens. It looked as if he was a bit hunchbacked, but partly because the muscles between his shoulder blades were thick. He was wearing bright white canvas and rubber deck shoes. Cole refocused on his truck, but was interrupted by Mankins' voice: "Hey buddy, this place looks pretty cool." Mankins walked toward Cole.

"Not bad," replied Cole, opening his truck door but not as yet climbing in.

Mankins approached to within five paces and said "I'm looking for a new place. My old lady is getting too fussy for me. You see a lot of action here?"

Cole was unsure what Mankins was hinting at. He replied "Not too much. Pool privileges recently scaled back due to some nonsense on weekends but other than that it has been pretty good. Most people pretty respectful around here."

"So not a lot of pot and other stuff moving through?" Mankins said and took one more step forward.

Cole said "No. It comes and goes from time to time, but it's never too bad. Manager is pretty good. Office is just behind the pool. I'd chat longer but I've got to get going."

Mankins pointed as he already started backing away. "Those are painter's whites you're wearing, aren't they?"

"Yeah, got a couple of small jobs today. See you around." Cole hesitated, and decided to not give him his name.

Mankins smiled but the tightness of his mouth and face made it come out as more of a grimace. He was thinking "Guy doesn't seem jumpy, so not as if he is hiding something important. Interesting. Could mean, also, that he is more professional than I anticipated or he is just actually pretty square."

Mankins walked around the block a few times, thinking "Guy seems alright, but I've been fooled more than a couple of times in the past, so I've got to be careful." He looked for drug paraphernalia in bushes, small pieces of paper with phone numbers scrawled on them, and even gang graffiti. He had changed his voice register in order to distance himself from the one Cole had heard from behind Gordy's door. And he had cautiously parked his car three blocks away down an alleyway. He made a few notations on his notepad then headed to Ernie's, a greasy spoon diner along Hollywood Blvd. He had been craving their meatloaf and mashed potatoes platter. Along the way he picked up the morning papers, focusing on unsolved robberies in Orange County and abductions in Baldwin Hills. "Connections," he thought with urgency. "I need more connections."

Gordy's phone rang at about nine in the evening, while he was engrossed in thumbing through a history of the Los Angeles Rams, which he had found in a library sale bargain rack. He had also repaired some of the torn pages with Scotch tape, and sealed up a widening crack in the seam of the binding.

"Yes?" he said in a fading whisper, because he had failed to take his usual afternoon nap.

"Hitch the bomber is dead. This is only a statement, not a binding admission of a conspiracy afoot. Good night."

Before he could respond Gordy's line connection was severed. But he was almost certain that the voice belonged to the strange character who simply dubbed himself "The Statement."

He dropped his book on the floor, re-damaging the spine. Some of the brittle clothe peppered the floor like confetti. He absently dispersed the chaff with the toe of his shoe.

The second call came a bit before ten. "You won't believe this, buddy," Cole said. "I saw a guy gunned down today near your place. I was watching the news."

"Yeah, I saw-"

"What?" Cole's voice raised an octave. "How in Hell-"

Gordy said "I was getting ready to leave the donut shop, heard the blast, and saw the guy fall. One of the onlookers mentioned him being called Hitch. Then that tripped out dude named The Statement called. A guy I've never seen and probably never will. He mentioned Hitch dying."

"Crazy," Cole said and paused. "Too coincidental I think. You know, a bit like the movie we are hoping gets made the right way, or at least our book published. It's as if you were meant to witness the killing."

Gordy continued "Yeah, well, I guess it won't change the project much. And since it is common knowledge now, even the papers having covered it, we don't have to hesitate in bringing it to the attention of Rod and Kit and the studio folks."

Cole said "Alright. But this is all getting a bit more serious and twisted. Don't you think? We are going to really have to watch our backs, watch who we talk to. Just this morning a complete stranger asked me about my complex, about moving in. I should've been tight lipped, but I guess I couldn't help myself."

Gordy heard the police chopper, and the rotor noise had seemed to increase in volume. His mind was agitated by the aerial frenzy, and he returned to repairing his book in an attempt to distance himself from his anxiety. "Okay, Cole. Listen. We have to watch our backs. Now I'm getting back to my writing. We'll catch up later tomorrow."

He thought "Hitch the bomber? Damn, maybe we could've warned him, if we'd only known. Someone might be sending us a message, that we are partly responsible for his death."

Twenty Two

It was a predictable development, one which either Gordy or Cole could have easily written in a fact based movie scene: A party at a beachfront Malibu property hosted by the movie producer, attended by sun-browned beauties and fledgling motorcycle racers and set designers and anonymous inheritors of tremendous amassed wealth. The barbecue sizzled for hours, producing hamburgers, grilled shrimp, chicken, sweet onions and thin potato slices coated with garlic and cheese. Vast quantities of alcohol were consumed, although the host was shrewd enough to keep a limit on hard liquor and wine. Guests lolled on the beach, threw the Frisbee, peppered around a volleyball, and went barely knee deep into the already chilly Fall surf. A handful lounged in beach chairs around a portable stereo, blasting the small speakers until they crackled with protest. Cole found himself tending to the barbecue grill, and being provided with choice bottles of beer at his steady command. Gordy found a comfortable seat on a beach towel in the deep, soft sand, a bit hungry and anxious. The slight pangs in his stomach piqued the vision of Hitch's midsection being blown to shreds by the shotgun blast. A splash image of Hitch as a younger man came involuntarily: Goofy, wide-splayed feet around the horse shaped plastic Big Wheel tricycle he was always at pains to keep shiny. He wondered "How many years ago? Was it during the same year my folks took me to the beach and actually took the time to take me into the shallow water?" He knelt down in the soft sand and scooped up some sand crabs nestled near the shore break. He felt his hands tickled by the mix of water rushing and the frenzy of the crabs' miniature limbs digging in without pause or effect. The sea breeze was a level of comfortable chill, buffeting his face with an invigorating palm, and the distant glow of the oil tankers on the brow of horizon between sea and sky revealed and concealed a mystery at the same time. As ephemeral as he knew the moment and place must be, he hugged his shoulders as the sun completely disappeared. At first he did not respond to the loud summons to participate in the feast. A few crushed beer cans were thrown half-heartedly toward his back, and giggles were cushioned by the sound of yelping seagulls. Finally Cole's voice could be heard above the others' crashing against his back: "Get your ass over here! I'm not saving any chow for you."

There was a ribbon of juice around his burger as well as a sliver of cheddar cheese which had slightly hardened into a type of cheese Fondu dip for his silvery onions. He nodded as Cole handed over his plate. "Thanks, Mr. Chef. I guess you're making yourself as useful as possible." Yet he noticed that Cole was a bit too preoccupied with his self-appointed grilling duties, to the point that he was hardly paying attention to the tawny female bodies flashing past. He thought "See? Another one track mind." Gordy moved around the fire in a clockwise direction, because the wind-wafted smoke was irritating his eyes. He almost tripped over a metal trough of cooking implements before knocking over an abandoned beer can, which made an amoeba like paste of the sand.

"Hey, man" he began, tapping Cole on the shoulder. "Have you ever heard of 'Sherm'?" He followed Cole's adept spatula wristing motion, flipping over a couple of burgers. He thought he also had his first glimpse of the party's host, who was holding court in front of the picture window. He was gesturing toward one of his recent art purchases, wearing a white linen suit.

"'Sherm?'" Cole parroted. "Short for General Sherman of Civil War fame? The one who rampaged through Atlanta? Or, perhaps, a goofy new cartoon character?"

"Good try, smartass," Gordy answered. "It's not a shrunken man from outer space either. A 'Sherm' is a joint dipped in embalming fluid. Not sure why it came to me now, but people swear they had a whiff of it immediately after Hitch was gunned down outside the donut shop. Some cats said the shooter 'must have been 'Shermin'. Those are his exact words. Some cats say that drinking a malt forty and smoking Sherm is the ticket to the first gang hit. That it helps get the juices flowing" He moved a bit closer to the fire, because the sun had flamed out over the ocean's crest, only a long purple-and-black streak lingering.

Cole said "I see. So it's a type of inner city high then. This puts yet another twist on our story. Perhaps we should pass it on to our movie connections right away. They might want to have another chat about it."

"Doubt it," Gordy countered. "They just want to run with it at this point, and-"

"Come on, man." Cole spread some condiments on a side table sticking into the sand. "Gangbangers get shot regularly, but the one who might have torched the grocery itself was the victim this time. That's a whole other level of development as far as I'm concerned. Maybe someone was worried he was going to tell someone about his involvement. It puts a whole new level of suspense into the story. That's what I'm trying to say."

Gordy said "It's a good twist to the story, but I'm saying that we might want to expand it into something more typically 'Hollywood,' you know what I mean? Kind of bring in all sorts of people and groups, G men and the like."

Cole returned "Alright. So you're actually suggesting that they would like to enlarge the storyline, but in a slightly different way? Fine. But have a beer with me and mellow out a bit. The way you were sitting near the water, you looked obsessed about something. No, really. Sometimes I can read your body language. It actually can be pretty loud. You were trying to 'fly away' to some other place. You get that way usually only when you are talking about trying to write a good poem."

Gordy grimaced. "Sure, but hey, give me a can near the bottom of the barrel. Yeah, you know I like the ones that have been sunk deep. Anyway, you realize we're still outsiders here, right? Until and unless our story gets make into a film we will remain nobodies. Although we can use the cash to build up our writing resumes, get our feet more firmly inside the door. Still I hear Portugal is a really cheap place to live, so I might work on my next big project there."

Cole popped open his can and sucked down the beer froth exploding off the top. "Portugal? I don't know, man. Next door dictator Franco is still in control. Not saying Portugal has to be necessarily all bad as a result, but it's a definite possibility. Troubles easily spill over boundaries. Stay home, man. You know your boundaries and challenges here."

Gordy was intrigued by the idea of taking a road trip, and frequenting the Bay Area haunts his parents often visited around the time of their demises. But he was virtually certain that Cole would have a less favorable impression of the concept. Of course, he would accuse him of wanting to run away. So he brought up their shared passion-sports-in the guise of critiquing the way a couple of the lissome girls peppered a volleyball back and forth. Then he added "You know Wilt the Stilt plays volleyball? He towers over everyone else, of course. Saw him practice at Pauley Pavilion, he had a wrist guard on, still he spiked the ball straight down, man, like he was making a mockery of the game. He wouldn't have been allowed to play that game when he was younger. Unstoppable isn't the word. This goes far beyond that. He would never be blocked at the net, not after gathering himself and spiking the ball.

Cole said "Perhaps. Him and Kareem could spike shots off each other's heads for public amusement while James Brown music pipes in to the frenzied crowd staging a roller derby on the side." Cole grimaced.

Gordy replied "That's wicked. But you are plainly nuts. No way around it and no way to solve it. Sounds like a game show concept to me. And talk about 'flying off the page' with madness. Yours does, indeed, trump mine. Hey, put some more cheese on top of my burger, why don't you? Yeah, make that shit drip a bit before pulling it nice and juicy off the grill."

Cole patted the top, then added another slab of cheese before mashing it down with the spatula. "You like layered stories and burgers alike, huh? But, hey, it looks like our pals Rod and Kit finally arrived.   Look at that satin dress she's wearing. Wow. She won't make it out here for a while, though. See, even other women are approaching her? Admiring some fancy necklace she has on? We'll have to remind her to wear it to the Academy Awards show next year when our movie is nominated for best picture."

"Sure, when we're still just unknown 'ghost writers.' But that is good enough for me, at least for a start." Gordy took his burger and found a spot a few feet behind the barbecue, on a thick cut off portion of an oak tree. He thought "Still don't see even one other black face. Well, I'll just have to cope as best as I can."

Cole's eyes were fixed momentarily on the prisms of light created by an oil tanker steaming in the deep sea, and he imagined pockets of sea life underneath fleeing to a more serene locale. "Hey, Gordy, I think we should do a boat trip in the next year or two, when we can afford to reward ourselves for our hard work."

Gordy said "What about going to some Rams games? Or at least the Trojans? I've got to get my sports jones on, you know? Don't forget about that. But, hey, you think because the original Trojans were seafarers that the trustees decided the name was a good connection to ancient history, with LA in essence on the coast? Anyway, looks like someone here is pulling out some sparklers. And it always seems like someone in La la land is trying to spark some action."

Cole finally prepped a couple of burger buns, and sat down cross legged in the sand to eat his fill, grease from his paper plate coating his upper thighs. "Whatever. But I like it out here on the beach.

Even though we are not in the middle of the party we can act as if we are part of it. You know, make all kinds of critical comments from the outside. But just wait. Soon we will be on the inside."

Indeed, once inside they were met with mostly polite reserve. Gordy and Cole milled around with relief that they were not treated with false indulgence. Some witty comments flew their way, but personal questions were kept to a minimum.

"Hey, they're still feeling us out," Cole said in a slightly apologetic tone. "But don't worry, we'll soon have our shot at fame. Just a matter of time." He sensed that the beach party in a bungalow was just the first step on a ladder which might reach the Playboy mansion in Bel Air, or a sumptuous mountain lodge in Aspen, Colorado, with men dressed in seersucker suits and deck shoes and the women in sun dresses.

"Yeah, we've made our appearance, alright. So let's scoot out of here soon, after we say a quick "hello" to Kit."

Cole said "Okay. I've only got a small buzz on, but I'd still like to stop at the first coffee shop to sober up." He took the wood planked walkway up the side of the house two at a time.

Detective Mankins noticed the van ease in behind the small pickup driven by Cole, which would interfere with his clear field of vision. He had decided to continue following the truck when it breached its normal boundaries of Santa Monica and Watts. While Cole and Gordy indulged in beach barbecue, he had sampled a couple of teriyaki tacos at a new eatery a couple miles down PCH, which was drawing in casual surfers, debonair millionaires, and actual food aficionados in droves. The tile roof was surmounted by a giant marlin which had a curiously papier-mache look to its blue-silver skin, as if it would disintegrate under the first heavy rain. Mankins ordered ranch sauce to dip his fries in, and devoured the tacos within five minutes, putting him firmly back on the road within twenty.

He was close to dozing off when the elongated shadow of Cole leaving the party crested the hill. And it only required about one mile for him to realize that the van was also following them. The driver expertly accelerated back and forth, from lane to lane, never remaining behind the pickup for long. Once they were off the highway, the stop and go traffic made it more of a challenge to maintain close contact without risking detection. The truck proceeded south on Lincoln toward LAX airport before heading toward the ocean once more, the van at a comfortable following distance behind it. After about a mile, past a group of smoke belching industrial buildings to the left, the van crept up behind the truck, and red taillights blinked. Mankins slowed to a stop, and watched both vehicle's occupants step out into the gathering dark. He thought "It would be nice to have a police radio right now."

This time there were only two men. "Let's take a stroll," said the tall, thin one. He was partially bearded, had on dark sunglasses, and his blue bandanna was pulled down lower over his brow. The combination prevented the periodic bouts of flying sand stirred by a sea breeze. His colleague stayed back about ten yards, and kept an eye on the road and the van. In part because he had been concentrating such energy on not losing Cole's truck, he had not noticed the trailing Dodge Charger, which now had an excellent vantage point from a natural bluff extending from a curve further up the road.

They walked down to the water's edge. Later Gordy opined that this was a precautionary measure, in case they were wearing wires, the crashing surf would overwhelm any possible audio feed. A lone seagull squawked overhead, its white and gray feathers protecting its fuselage shaped body. "Damn birds," the leader remarked. "Anyway guys, I just had to confirm for myself that you guys are making inroads with the Hollywood crew. And to remind you guys that the rules can change as we move along."

Gordy said "Alright, brother. We've got no problem with that."

"Good. Great. Nice day on the beach, right? Spiritually renewing, and with tranquility to boot. Almost like a nap inside the womb's amniotic fluid." He briefly turned his back to them. "Makes it all seem petty, right? Well, I guess it is really the lot of all men. And I'm sounding like a philosophical weakling."

Cole responded "Far from it. We stayed near the water and the barbecue during the party, and-"

Gordy interrupted "He does cook a mean grill, and it was a nice spread, from steaks to seafood."

"Next time invite me" the leader joked, patted Gordy on the shoulder, and started quickly trudging back up the beach. "We'll be in touch again shortly." The van took an immediate U turn, heading north once more, and the driver did not notice Mankins ducking underneath his own dashboard. The leader turned to his driver and said "That was good. Just put a slight scare into them. Nothing too extreme."

"Agreed, boss. Should keep them on their toes. But now what do you want for dinner? Some burgers, perhaps? I know of a new joint on Pico that has a chili burger." He waited for a response, but his boss just pointed in a general, northerly direction, toward a 747 banking in over the Pacific ocean, gliding into LAX international airport.

Cole sat on the soft sand and waited for Gordy to plop down beside him, watching a thick ball of sea kelp roiling in the surf, the glistening bulbs bobbing like buoys through the white churn. He stretched his legs out in front of himself briefly, then pulled them back to sit Indian style and. He took a few deep breaths and thought "How much attention is too much?"

Gordy cursed under his breath as he sat, then spat. "Did you get the sense he might have been playing with us. No, even taunting us?"

"A bit," Cole replied. "It's a bit strange, I agree. As if he wants us confident and nervous at the same time."

Gordy replied "That's the thing, man. We've got to get through to the other side. It's almost like we're in some sort of creative limbo where we can't see the other side."

Cole motioned toward the sea. "Yeah, kind of like we're adrift, just floating around between places. But let's scoot out of here, alright? It is getting chilly with the wind whipping around."

Gordy chuckled. "That's how we do it, right? Philosophize when we should be concentrating on moving forward. Sitting on a beach while others are busy plotting, even some against us."

Cole shook his head, more in consternation than denial. He counted off a handful of waves, then stood. "Okay. I think we should go before my driving foot and leg fall asleep."

Twenty Three

Two weeks later the proposed film-Black Lords of the City of Angels-was in pre-production, and Cole and Gordy had cashed the first of their monthly installment checks. This required fingerprinting at the Bank of America's corporate headquarters in an earth toned downtown glass tower, and various forms confirming their identities. The elevator man was unfailingly polite, the office receptionist genial, and the bank executive, a silver-haired suit with fresh, polished shoes, polite and commanding at the same time. They were questioned quickly and efficiently, and offered unlimited quantities of a choice coffee roast percolating reassuringly in the corner. Afterward they purchased fish tacos off of a catering truck, and ate inside Cole's truck. "What a celebratory meal," Gordy quipped. In the interim they went to their respective bank locations after the money was wired, and withdrew cash to celebrate. Unbeknownst to both, Mankins had been able to put a trace on their respective bank accounts, even though he surmised in the event of large transactions, they might opt to simply cash their checks to avoid such potential trouble. Although normally hewing to the strict police code, he had latched onto the case in a manner that subdued his normal reservations. He thought "After all, this case could be blown open at any moment." On the other hand he knew that delving into bank accounts could potentially be discovered by federal authorities.

While dusk quickly emerged on the horizon, they sat in the car and blithely ate their tacos off the temporary table of the truck's sloping dashboard, which was parked in the shadow of a drugstore off Alameda. Cole reported on the people walking past on the sidewalk, because the car was angled in toward a brick wall, not allowing Gordy a viewing angle. "Hey, man, I should be able to see all the derelicts, strawberries, and sleazy haberdashers, too." He spiked one of his tacos with a dose of Tio's hot sauce. "This is about right. If the movie doesn't do well, we'll be back to our humdrum routines within the year. Maybe two years at the most."

Cole said "Yeah, you can stay where you are for a while, but I don't have any back ups. If it's not house painting, then it's drywall, if it's not drywalling it's painting, or maybe just driving a truck." Cole winced as an old man fell and with brief assistance barely made it back to his feet again, tugging at the thin cord of a disintegrating belt to keep his fading brown corduroy pants from falling.

Gordy said "Let's get out of here. Eating food off a dashboard? What are we, gumshoes or something? Private dicks in training?"

Cole said "It's not such a bad idea. Neither of us has a criminal background, and we have no dependents who count on us to put bread on the table. We could use our experience as a marketing tool to get clients."

Gordy replied "So let me get this straight. If this project does reap great rewards, then we're going to troll for desperate people looking to get even with someone? And that's not even accounting for some licensing, which would, of course, be mandatory."

Cole only shrugged in response, and started crumpling up the trash accumulating on the dashboard. An old dread, one he associated with his mother, surfaced, and he fought back a mild case of panic. "Well,

I hope we are invited to the pre-screening at least." He revved the engine and started maneuvering out of the alley.

"Got me," Gordy said. "Nothing in the contract binding in that regard. We went to the beach party, so I don't know if we're promised anything else."

"You've been reading legal texts or something?" Cole joked, turning into the street past a rusted out, abandoned VW van. It appeared as if someone had half-heartedly tried to widen the narrow windows, so that it looked a bit like a huge, jagged can.

"Zip it," Gordy shot back. "I think we will be invited as a matter of course. Though we might not be feted like you hope."

"'Feted', huh?" Cole accelerated around a city bus belching smoke. "Good word. Celebrated, honored, what have you. As long as we find a way to continue the story."

"Not that it's really ours anyway," Gordy shot back. "It has kind of been co-opted, right? Nothing wrong there, I guess. And they never made us drive around with a cameraman in the back seat like they threatened. That might have been too stressful, in my opinion."

"Right, Mr. Earnest," Cole said, chuckling under his breath. He accelerated onto the freeway onramp, and rolled his window partially down, which kept their conversation to a minimum.

Once Cole approached Lincoln Boulevard, he fought an urge to turn the wheel to the left, and not stop until San Diego. Instead, he found the traffic artery that led all the way to the ocean, one which skirted a burgeoning beach community. In fact one worker was hovering over a sawhorse, and holding a circular saw near the curb of a construction site. He waved toward them uncertainly as they passed, sawdust leaping off his forearms like wheat chaff. a half empty beer can perched atop the sawhorse.

"Hey man," Gordy said. "Let's get out of here. It all looks weird to me. Cottages and such just don't seem right. We aren't looking for Mary Poppins and strudel, you know?"

Cole pressed the accelerator further to the floor. "Okay, okay. Getaway fast enough for you? Huh? And do you want to make this thing a submersible or something? Drive the fucker straight into the saltwater?" Still, when he reached the beach frontage street he slowed into a small slide into two parking spaces. As if on cue a beam of light shot at them from the other end of the lot. Gordy's cloudy vision made it move spectrally while Cole's less impaired lens transformed it into a giant, hovering moon. There was a brief kind of gloaming at the edges before it faded out. A moment later it reappeared, but in a more diffuse manner atop the small breakers along the shore to the south.

Cole finally punctured the silence by saying "See. Just another couple. But I don't know what point I was going to make, 'cause I was kind of spooked." They were back on the frontage road in short order, chasing dogs gamboling down the grassy slope of a park, a terrier leading the pack with a half chewed away tennis ball in its mouth. Cole slowed for a stop sign, and the dogs overtook him. About a quarter mile up the road another headlight appeared a bit higher and brighter than the first. Now the lead dog ran out ahead, running a parallel course to their vehicle.

Gordy said "Hey, man, I think that's a greyhound or a whippet. The type of dog they run at Hollywood Park. Man, I wonder if it can go any faster."

Cole responded "We'll see about that," and pressed the accelerator. The dog kept pace. They were rapidly approaching another pair of bright headlights. They blinked off once, twice, then paused. The greyhound actually surged ahead. Then the headlights blinked again. The dog surged ahead a bit further, then leapt into the windshield. Cole instinctively wrenched his head to the side below the dashboard, but could not keep the wheel from turning to the side. The truck tipped onto its side, spilling partially, and completely empty, paint buckets onto the street. Metal cans clattered, some contacts softened by contact with gelled paint.

The truck slid to a stop.

Cole regained consciousness to the whimper of the dog lying in the road, which had lacerated skin and damaged ribs at the very least. Meanwhile Gordy's hand clapped him on the shoulder. He blinked rapidly, and the first thing he saw was the spider webbed, cracked glass of the windshield. He wiped his forehead, checking for blood.

"Wake up, man. Come on. We've got to drag our asses out of this thing. Damn dog made us crash. Now look at our sorry asses." Gordy already had a slight twinge of pain in his left shoulder, which would worsen over the following days.

"Yeah, yeah," Cole answered, and struggled to free himself from his seat belt. His weight falling to his side was keeping him wedged in. He only briefly registered that the headlights of the opposing car were still on. Naturally he started asking himself about a connection between the flashing lights and the dog. He recalled the distinct series of flashes before the dog collided with the windshield. "Yeah, get out of here...out of here," he mumbled under his breath.

"Now, Cole. Now." Gordy's voice was amplified inside the small truck cab. He unsnapped his belt and lifted himself. "I'm going to get myself through the opening, then I'll help you out." His right hand found purchase of the door frame before his left followed. When they were both safely free of the metal and glass they noticed the headlights of the opposing vehicle come back on. But this time, instead of flashing they remained on. They both leaned over, so that only their heads were above the upended truck cab. Gordy muttered "Motherfucker, come and get it...mf, come and get it."

"Leave it alone," Cole said, also seething. "But just for now." He had his pistol out already, and was making sure it was still loaded.

Gordy deadpanned "Man, you're the one who is really, really anxious and ready. Let's just wait, I guess, and see what the bastard tries to pull next." They heard the vehicle's engine start, rev, then turn off again, then do the same series of motions once more.

Cole said "We can't sit like this forever, that's for sure. As he began to stand, he felt a keen soreness in his right knee which would soon turn into actual swelling. "Unless someone else comes along we could be stuck here all night."

Gordy replied "Yeah, but maybe the bastard will leave soon. I mean, this whole situation seems pretty fucked up and weird. The blinking lights and a dog? Maybe we should discuss the situation before making any rash decisions. I mean, at least right now we have a kind of cover, and neither of us is bleeding, either. So it's not an emergency situation, and-"

Cole blurted "What! Easy for you to say. I don't have insurance on this thing, or AAA, for that matter. So it's going to cost me major. Plus my shoulder already feels tweaked, and I don't have health insurance, either. Someone is definitely after our asses. That's for sure. But is that the deranged guy who claims he's a cop or someone else entirely? That's what we need to know." About once a minute the headlights blinked on and off, then remained dead for about three minutes. Both Gordy and Cole glanced over at the dog whimpering on the ground from time to time, sorry for its plight, because its suicidal leap in front of the truck and the flashing lights could hardly be coincidental. Periodically the dog struggled to stand, howled out in pain, and laid back down.

"Well, another car has got to come around here eventually," Gordy said.

Cole replied "Yeah. But what if our enemy has friends in the area? What if they blocked off the road further up, and are wearing orange vests, acting like city workers? Because this is definitely some 'weird shit,' if you know what I mean?"

"Agreed. Agreed." Gordy turned his back to the headlights, and leaned his head back. "You don't think it's the militant brothers pulling a prank on us, do you? I mean, what would they have to gain by it? If it's not them or the imposter cop who knocked on my door the other night, who could it be?" Both started at the sound of some crackling noise coming from some nearby undergrowth, but nothing followed. Although they both wondered if it was the dog that had veered off after the other's suicidal leap.

Cole winced as he tried to straighten out his arm. "Who knows, maybe they want this scene written into the movie, or else our book when it is eventually published. Anyway, I'm not going to sit here in the dark for more than thirty minutes or so. I'm timing out this whole ugly scene. As it is I'd like to challenge him to a gunfight."

Gordy returned "Hey, don't show our hand yet. Be sure you're going to use it when you show it. But I don't think you've taken enough target practice lately, either. So just trust me, put it away for now." Gordy felt his first chill of the night, and wondered how long he could counsel patience. He thought "I've been waiting years to find out what happened to my parents, so we can wait at least an hour here."

"Hey, if we don't get a license plate number, we won't give the cops a chance of catching him," Cole mused aloud. "I don't like that idea one bit." Again, he stretched out his left arm to try to unloosen his banged up shoulder, but did not find any relief. Instead he tried to blinked away a few tears.

Gordy laughed, but his humor had a nervous edge to it. "We could be dealing with a psychopath and you want to talk macho? The guy could be a true lunatic for all we know, but what does that really matter one way or another? He could have a night scope and a rifle. He might have been planning this for weeks, even months, and we just happened to be who showed up on his stretch of road at this specific time of day. Although he probably does not live in the immediate area." Both looked intently in both directions, but only saw some hazy lights, which could be heralds of either streets or houses. What appeared to be a steeple of a small church was far to the south, upraised like an avenging sword.

Cole said "That sounds too normal for this guy. We could walk back the way we came in, but we'd lose our cover. We could walk off the road and risk getting lost. We could wait for him to leave at his leisure, which could take a while. Or we could advance on him, take his vehicle-"

"You're saying 'we,' because you've got a gun. Remember: I don't." Gordy rubbed his hands together. "I could try to pull the tire iron out, but that's about it for me. I can't swat away bullets with a stick, even a steel one, you know?" He shifted slightly with his back to the upturned truck's back wheel, maneuvering the small of his back past the loosened corner of a hubcap. "I'm feeling thirsty all of a sudden. I wonder if that's a bad sign."

Cole said "You're not dying. Trust me on that score. You're thirsty like me, maybe because you're pre-diabetic, although I doubt it." He held his arms in to retain more of his own bodily warmth. "Okay. It's about time we seriously consider doing something." The headlights shone once again, and flickered in the branches of the nearest tree, a stately oak thick in its maturity. Cole wondered if the green canopy might be his last rich mortal view, and thought "Maybe I should ask Gordy. He's the poet. Not me."

At some point over the following few minutes Cole realized Gordy was not wearing a watch. "Should I call out the thirty minutes being up a few minutes early, and see if he notices?" he thought. To pass the time he removed and reloaded his bullets, over and over.

"You know, you can't convince me or yourself you are good with guns just by doing that over and over," Gordy said disconsolately. "Instead you just look more and more desperate by the moment. You're looking for quick deliverance, but it's not going to happen. Come on, man. The guy has got to leave in a few minutes, at least not many. Okay. What is he going to do?" Gordy felt a slight panic beginning to grow inside his abdomen, threatening to make the words flow even more impulsively from his mouth, and make him appear ever more foolish. And he had to fight the impulse to yell out a challenge in order to at least generate a response. He thought "At least then Cole might get one clear shot off."

The image came suddenly, and with overwhelming force: a thunderclap of a picture, of a burning tire rolling down the road. Cole chuckled to himself and wondered "Would something that crazy actually work?" As upended as the truck was, it would only require him to puncture the fuel line with a tool, leak the gasoline onto the released spare tire, light it, and roll it down the slight hill toward the glimmering headlights. He thought "How would the creep deal with that?" It did not faze him that a failure would likely result in an even more merciless enemy.

So he started cautiously reaching into his upturned tool box for the implements. Gordy had been napping, but finally awoke. "Hey, it's not time yet," he said.

"I'm not waiting anymore," Cole replied, and briefly chuckled. "And I've got an idea." A rifle report burst through the air, and the whimpering dog settled to the ground. "And now you finally see what kind of maniac we're dealing with." A darker shadow pooling out from the fallen dog indicated the thick pool of blood flowing out of the animal's body. Then the opposing headlights blinked once before going off again. "This has got to be some mercenary type or something."

Gordy said "So now we're going to take the battle to him? Alright, so what do you have brewing in that brain of yours, renegade? Looks like you're fishing for the small gas can, matches, and, uh, what's that you're struggling with now, the spare tire? Well, if you're planning on trying to pull something like that, we are on a downslope. Although you might try a quick one behind the protection of the truck as a test."

"Okay," Cole replied tersely. "As long as the burning tire gets somewhat close to him, we will have a much better field of vision to work from. But we'll take it one step at a time. No telling how the bastard will react, but we've got to start taking some initiative. That I'm sure of." He soaked the outside of the tire, then poured most of the remaining gas into the inside. "The rest of the gas can provide us with a back-up plan," he reasoned. "At least take him down with us, if it comes to that."

Gordy responded "As long as my hands are clamped around the bastard's throat." He fished through the tool box at Cole's side and fished out a tire iron. "This is something that might come in handy."

"No practice required," Cole said. "But take the flashlight out to the corner and flash it off and on when I start the tire rolling. Unless he has his eye on the scope of his rifle, I should be okay. I only need a couple of seconds to get its momentum true. I've got these gloves, so my hands shouldn't get burned, at least not badly in the time to get the flames going and the tire rolling." He recalled a story his mother had told him when he was a child, about a trapeze artist who became bored with simple tightrope walking. Eventually he decided to perform stunts with the suspended cord on fire. "Was it really more a product of her deranged imagination?" he thought. "Or was there some truth to her trance-like visions?"

Gordy asked "You really sure of this? Maybe not? Either way, let's go." He crouched against the side of the upended truck bed and hesitantly raised his head to get a better look. The two beams of the opposing truck's headlights were still shining.

Cole breathed in and out deeply a few times, gave Gordy a nod of the head, and flicked on his camping lighter, the kind that was like a long wand. He burst from cover while Gordy aimed the flashlight. At first the flames only licked along the edges of the tire as it rolled toward the opposing vehicle. Then a hissing sound grew, and as the tire increased its speed, the flames erupted from inside. Cole and

Gordy both yelled choice obscenities. A few rifle shots rang out, but were ineffectual. The tire continued on its course, and its light soon revealed the grille of an old Ford pick-up, peeking out of the lowest branches of a wide mesquite tree. Gordy noticed the figure inside the truck was wearing a mask. He cursed under his breath and, tire iron in hand, rushed out.

"No, man!" Cole, too burst out, as the figure jumped out of the cab and aimed his rifle. "Get down!" he shouted to Gordy, and felt a slight impact at the top of his left shoulder. It was a glancing shot, but he lost balance nonetheless. "Go back!" he shouted.

Gordy briefly hesitated, then crouched over slightly and ran the fifty yards back to the safety of the truck. He immediately grabbed the gas can and the lighter that Cole had flipped back after lighting the tire.

Cole stood, but another shot rang out, almost hitting his left leg, and he took protection near the ground again. He watched the arc of the burning can, and was already running back to cover when Gordy yelled "Run!" The can landed near the burning tire, accelerating the already licking flames, which surged toward the truck's bumper. The hooded figure hopped back inside the truck, reversed, and sped off.

"Come back! We aren't finished with you, bastard!" Gordy yelled. He watched Cole strip off his shirt and inspect the damage to his shoulder. The bullet had cut a narrow, neat groove through the flesh, causing only minor damage and a negligible loss of blood. He shrugged, figuring he would take care of it later. "Okay, let's start walking. We'll walk as long and as far as we have to, maybe take a bus back to your place. The truck isn't blocking the road, so we can decide what to do as far as the authorities are concerned later."

Gordy said "Did you notice the mask the guy was wearing? I hope it was not one of the brothers acting on his own, you know? But the alternative, that he's some psycho acting on his own, isn't too appealing either." They walked past the tire, which was still smoldering, while Cole winced with pain from the injury to his shoulder.

They walked quickly, and did not turn their heads toward house lights or faces looking cautiously out of windows. "We've got to keep a low profile," Gordy mused aloud. "Two dudes, one black, one white, can't look good to people around here, walking through their neighborhood at night. Especially one with a bloody shoulder."

Cole answered "Yeah. And I don't think anyone would believe the story of how we got in this bad way. And the police? Well, we'd rather leave them out of it, right?" He estimated that they had three to five miles to walk before they reached the first bus line. They passed isolated sand dunes and bleached beach cottages in minor disrepair and small boats moored inside of carports. Cole no longer felt wetness on his shoulder, and hoped there would not be an infection once it scabbed over.

Gordy said "Strange stuff going down, indeed. Almost hard to believe. Bet we're already getting close to more streetlamps, which is always a good sign." He noticed a steak house with a half full parking lot, and quickly searched for signs of the truck. There was one in the back corner of the lot but it was a late model Chevy.

"He's smart enough to get out of the area," Cole said. "At least for the immediate future. We might come back around later in the week. But my guess is he found this a good out-of- the- way place. Now he'll probably move on to another area. You know, look for more convenient victims."

"But," and here Gordy's words finally spluttered out, "what makes someone use a dog, flashing lights, and a rifle? Could be more to it. I just hope he doesn't go off on a long killing spree, and we have to read about it later in the paper. Since he wasn't successful this time-"

"Damn right he wasn't," Cole answered, "but at the same time remember I'm the one who had his truck virtually destroyed. I will restore it, it's the cost of the towing that has me pissed off, unless I can get a pal to help me out." Up ahead about three blocks a trail of red taillights turned onto the road directly in front of them, and he wondered aloud "Is that our bus line?" The receding red lights appeared like slowly flickering out flames.

They sat near the back of the bus, with Gordy directly ahead of Cole to partially shield him from the possibly prying eyes of the bus driver, who might notice the silver dollar sized blood stain on Cole's shoulder. To distract him, as they boarded Gordy paid for both their fares while Cole slid behind to find safe seating as quickly as possible. A couple of youngsters were entertaining each other with their own sign language, at times breaking off from their game to gaze out their respective windows. Their periodic outbursts were further welcome distraction for Cole and Gordy, who spoke to each other in a kind of strained, harsh whisper:

Gordy: "We don't want to contact the cops. I actually think that's pretty obvious, whether the guy who attacked us is with the militant group or not. They are all deranged expletives nonetheless."

Cole: "We'll get home and make some plans. That's the only sure thing."

Gordy: "I might contact Prof Winfield again. Maybe he's actually someone we can trust."

Cole: "Be careful if you do that. In the meantime I'll be pouring some hydrogen peroxide over this wound in the bathroom sink." He replayed the strange attack, in his mind reconstituting the bony limbs of the greyhound dog leaping to its premature death, and the sickening crunching noise it made upon impact.

Gordy: "We'll have to compare notes on what happened. Maybe the dog is a wild card in the whole scenario, and doesn't belong to the guy."

Cole: "Strange business all around. And who would use a dog to throw people off, then injure and kill it for good measure? Seems like too much energy invested in one incident."

Gordy: "Yeah. But it could be more than one. Right? We kind of agreed on that. Spree killers like this city, that's for sure. Targets of opportunity everywhere."

Cole: "The open, Wild West, right?" Anyway, I've already got an idea, calling an old buddy of mine. He's got large trucks and winches to get my truck upright again. Just hope his old lady doesn't yell at me for calling so late."

Ellis arrived early in the morning as promised, knocking gingerly on Gordy's door while Cole hurriedly dressed, and poured himself a small glass of soda, which he guzzled on the way out. Ellis was driving his 4X4 Ford, with a large winch on the backside. Unbeknownst to both, Detective Mankins was parked directly across the street. He had played back the talk Gordy had made to Professor Winfield the previous night, utilizing his unsanctioned bug on the telephone line. He was as puzzled by the sabotage action of the unknown assailant as the rest. He thought "Who is this lone wolf maniac? Is he a patsy in the employ of someone else, or is he actually part of the militant black crew?" He noticed that Ellis was lighter skinned than Gordy, with a larger afro, as he and Cole climbed into the truck's cab.

Twenty Four

After the bullet- grooved shoulder had healed, Gordy and Cole had numerous talks about small adventures that would deplete some of their recent earnings, and provide them with a rest from their local pressure. One revolved around approaches to the Bay Area, another took the exact, opposite direction, ultimately taking in San Diego and possibly one of the Channel Islands on the way back. But ultimately they nixed the idea, sensing that the militant leader would insist on maintaining contact for the immediate future. The premiere party was rapidly approaching, and neither had purchased clothes for the occasion, although Cole already had a pair of two-tone wing tipped shoes, which he planned to polish, and Gordy had a silk purple necktie he insisted was suitable for a "white tie" dinner.

"Speaking of which," Cole returned. "We still haven't had our dinner. Why don't we head to Venice and pick something up there?"

Gordy replaced his liter of Coke inside his small refrigerator. "Okay. But I'd still prefer Denny's. If you don't know of a place with a better milkshake I suggest we go there."

Cole lingered for a moment just outside the doorway, where he had not long ago been struck unconscious. "We might discuss some money issues. For the time being I'm going to start a savings account, and see some change added to my stack of loot."

Gordy answered "I don't have that much faith in financial institutions, so I might stash some in crevices of granny's place, and leave it at that for the time being." He had to twice pull at the car's door handle to open it.

Cole paused in park after starting the engine. "I might actually sell this GTO, and put that money away also, so I have even more time before I have to go back to another day job grind."

Gordy laughed. "Don't be pessimistic, man. Both of us might be surprised. I guess technically we won't receive an Oscar, but think of this: A tell all non-fiction book about our experience, with the current crew on board. We've brought it up before, but I think we need to get serious about it."

Cole answered "That book is the idea, alright. Let's do it regardless of whether the movie scores big or not. And we'll probably be more in our element, too, that way." He winced as he shifted from first to second gear, because there was a slight catch in the gear box, making a screwdriver wedged inside his dash rattle around a bit.

Gordy watched the after school crowd make faces at the car traffic, do impromptu jigs on the cracked sidewalk, and skitter empty cans toward fire hydrants. One short youngster with an oversized Rams windbreaker leapt atop a fire hydrant and declaimed to the crowd. Gordy commented "Well, there are all sorts of entertainers about. That's for sure. I've kind of always preferred to let my athletic feats do the talking."

Cole said "Yeah, the stoic man. One with few words. I like that. Fits in with the whole hardboiled detective type. It's only a few skips to a career in something like that, you know? But I guess that's part of what we're doing now."

Each block they proceeded west the sea breeze became more fresh and vigorous, producing a spigot of air that burnished their cheeks with a red glow. And each block closer to the ocean revealed more convertibles with sunbathers anticipating a patch of burning sand. One car in particular, with a deeply tanned blonde trailing red ribbon from her hair, sparked cinematic associations. Cole thought "Her silky legs promise pleasure, but her tongue probably cuts deeper than a meat cleaver."

Gordy was thinking about his deceased parents. "If they had a reprieve from early death what would they do? Would they want to see me? Would I care? But I guess a part of me certainly does care if I'm still thinking about them. And what kind of trouble did they get themselves into to cause their murders? Did they talk back to the wrong type of brothers in the Bay Area? Or did they refuse to do business with some other 'bad' types?" He marveled at the natural pastels chalking the sky as sunset slowly transformed the horizon.

Cole asked "What do you think about cruising PCH with some good tunes? See what action is happening. Stop occasionally for a snack and watched the tanned babes?"

"Sounds good to me," Gordy replied. "Fish and chips would be a good start, I think.   Just sit back in a soothing sea breeze and ponder all the quality time we will soon have from our hard earned fame."

Later that afternoon Detective Mankins was driving an unmarked police car south on Vermont. A few hours earlier he had responded to a long running dispute between neighbors in the Pico district. Because there was a report of gunshots, he placed his siren atop his roof, preparing to supervise the scene. He unknowingly passed the safe house where Cole and Gordy had recently been interrogated. Its overseer was an elderly black man who enjoyed sitting on the front porch, and keeping notes on local action. When black-and-whites followed Mankins' unmarked car a few minutes later, and indicated by their still wailing sirens that their destination was nearby, the man put his sandals on, walked back to the largely empty kitchen, and made a phone call.

The disturbance was a classic case of disputed territory. One neighbor claimed that the other purposely told his numerous visitors to park in front of his house, when the more polite course would have been to suggest using his own driveway, or numerous open parking spaces across the street. Mankins and the other officers had calmed everyone down before Mankins decided to conduct some of his own investigations in Watts when he crossed the 10 Freeway, the natural divider between rich and poor LA. He pulled off on a cul-de-sac, pulled a shotgun out of his trunk, loaded a few shells into its chamber, and placed it snugly in a hollow of the deep front seat. Barrel pointed outward, he smiled to himself, thinking "O'Dool would appreciate my moxie on this. He always liked working alone, too. Although many in the department cited it as the reason he tailed someone recklessly to the edge of the desert, and was taken out permanently by a sniper's bullet."

He satisfied his craving for a chocolate malt at the quiet counter of a Denny's, then proceeded down Vermont as day turned to night with subdued flashes of orange and violet and purple, and the drooped shoulders of sidewalk walkers thickening their own shadows. "I bet I could find a Tarot reading very quickly around here," he thought. The quivering blending of the bright neon store signs briefly reminded him of the red light district of Saigon, where cheap food and sex abounded. But there in Vietnam, as here, he only felt comfortable viewing the tawdriness from the safety of a moving vehicle. "Not just a moving target, but a faster one," he thought. At a stoplight he was looking toward his own blurry reflection in the picture window of a fast food Chinese restaurant when the squealing of tires made him turn to his left. Already ducking, he saw the barrel of a large caliber handgun. Ducking further under the dash, he pulled his revolver from his holster and instinctively held up his left hand to shield the side of his face from the inwardly exploding glass. He rolled onto his back and instinctively fired off two rounds, but the car had already sped away. He heard the screeching of tires again, and a revving engine, surmising that his assailants had turned off Vermont quickly in an evasive maneuver. He accelerated quickly, and turned left after the first block, and began looking for unusual movement. But after about ten minutes he concluded that they were safely out of his reach. A trickle of blood was beginning to run down his left hand and sully the cuff area of his white dress shirt, so he used the first available gas station restroom to clean and dress it. He used toilet paper to stanch the sluggish flow of blood, and a paper towel as a crude outer dressing. Meanwhile he cursed himself for not having seen his assailant sooner, or the car he was driving or riding in. He thought that either it was a professional hitman, or at least a gangbanger with past experience in the ambush of human targets.

Although his right hand was shaking slightly when he bought a tall can of beer at a 7-11, his instinct told him that he was on the right path, that delving into the connection between a certain Professor Winfield and Gordy was compelling a response.

Mankins thought "Someone is feeling the heat," as he poured in a liberal amount of cream and sugar in an after beer coffee an hour later at a Winchell's Donuts. By this time he had re-examined the small wound on his hand, which was beginning to flare a bit. In the Winchell's public restroom he carefully pressed down on a few tender spots, and thought that likely there were a few pieces of small glass shards lodged underneath the bumpy skin. "Bastard" he hissed through his teeth, and rewrapped the hand once more, this time without spongy pieces of toilet paper. He reflected that as adept as he was at impressing soldiers with life saving strategies on patrols, he found it difficult to actually administer first aid in a confident manner. It took him time to realize that the failure had already occurred when one of his men was injured, even if it was the result of an exceedingly crafty booby trap. He called it "the commander's burden."

He smiled to himself thinking about the irony of coming the closest to mortality on the streets of a major city in America, not in the forbidding humidity of a dense jungle in Southeast Asia. In a certain manner he thought that random death was actually less relevant in war than in the conflict and confusion of civilian life.

He skimmed over the LA Times sports section, which he had neglected in his morning paper reading routine, and had a coconut sprinkled donut, which he dipped into his cup of coffee. The waitress looked amused, giving him a wink as small pieces of coconut floated to the top of his cup. "You must be coming off some sort of high, mister," she said, short and chunky in her blue smock.

"Yeah, an adrenaline rush alright, but not from an upper. I could have been hurt much worse than I was," Mankins continued.

"Yeah, you're a cop or a narc," she replied. "It's written all over you. You had a close shave is what you're trying to say."

"Yeah." Mankins fought a surge of sociability within himself, and returned to his donut and coffee. The shock to his system had almost worn off, and he was considering driving home.

"You might be a cop but you're still in a bunch of trouble," she said. "And you look like you're ready to fall asleep where you're sitting." She wiped the countertop with a damp cloth. "Trust me. I might not be much to look at, but I have my own bag of tricks." She gave him a mock salute and smile, and returned to the kitchen.

His right hand clamped around the steering wheel and became numb after a couple of stoplights had passed. Once he realized the extent of the numbness he still did not pull it off and replace it with the left, which had been partially clawed in his lap. He wound his way back to Hollywood, trying to slow his speed in a gradual manner. But his temper was instructing him to turn around and discover, despite all of the evidence to the contrary, that on pure instinct he could find the lair of his assailant. But his more relevant consciousness informed him that an environment of steel, brick, concrete and asphalt dulled his natural senses, not allowing him to sense more subtle, yet more primal wavelengths, like the web of intertwined wires that had connected his main military base abutting the China Sea. He thought "Have my wires been crossed?"

"Okay, get a grip," he said aloud.

He was entranced by the white flurries of old floodlights along Beverly Boulevard. He thought "If only I was Sam Spade responding to a blonde dame in distress. Instead of a harassed cop." When he reached home he washed his small wound with soap and watched the peroxide bubble up until he covered it with gauze and white adhesive tape. He cracked open a can of beer, watched the late nightly news, then went to bed. He awoke briefly during the early morning to a slight pattering of rain, but was asleep once more within fifteen minutes. Around four in the morning he awoke to his hand throbbing, took an aspirin, and quickly fell asleep.

Twenty Five

Three shootings, and one fatality, and not one was reported by the main organs of local and national press. But this was before murder became a polished media sell, before the city's spiraling homicide numbers became a kind of narcotic for the masses. Detective Mankins, however, tutored himself through the limited circulation of inner city papers, temporarily shunting aside the traditional Times and Herald. He found a short article on the shooting death of a young hustler nicknamed Hitch at a local South Central library. He simply approached the personable female librarian that Gordy was familiar with. She was alarmed and afterward made a call to Professor Winfield from her guest house in Baldwin Hills:

Mona said "A cop stopped by. Friendly but tense. Young but a bit rough around the edges. Looked like he hadn't shaved for almost a week." She poured a portion of vodka into a glass.

"You don't say?" Winfield adjusted himself inside his favored leather chair. "He didn't ask about you or Gordy, did he? Because Gordy called me just the other night, and it would be too much of a coincidence."

"No. But he had a 'knowing look,' I know that sounds a bit farfetched, even a bit paranoid, but there it is. Like he had figured out, finally, the secret all of us have been hiding. Wanted info on all the local papers. Strange, though, he did not strike me at all like the typical racist cop. He almost apologized when he flashed his badge at me; it was like he was still a bit unsure of himself."

Winfield placed a half read academic text aside and sat forward on his haunches. "Intriguing. A pensive white cop? Well, I guess we should stay away from stereotypes. Like Gordy, who straddles two worlds, the harsh and stark ghetto on one side, and the rarefied world of the artist/critic. But he told me a strange story over the phone, about him and Cole being sabotaged on the road. Some deranged psycho of some sort using a dog to make them crash."

"What?" she blurted.

He replied "Yeah, weird on an almost epic scale. A dog jumped into their windshield, the dog survived initially, but then someone in a truck further down the road shot it. So Cole decides to confront the guy, ends up shot, while Gordy pulls out a tire, lights it, then rolls it toward their attacker, finally scaring the twisted individual off."

She said "You trust his word? Sounds like something out of a Hollywood action film. Gordy always tells me *The Count of Monte Christo* is his favorite book of all time. Sounds a bit like a modern iteration of the famous prison escape scene where the chief white character seals himself in a bag, steals the key of the jailer at the edge of the cliff, and after the long fall into the water extricates himself from the bag like the original Houdini, and drowns the jailer. Yet he has never struck me as being the dishonest type." She pulled the telephone cord to its limit and turned the television sound down on the nightly news.

Winfield said "Okay. That does provide more insight. He does strike me as the idealist type, and not just because he is young. On the phone he hinted at being in some sort of trouble, him and Cole, but refused to go beyond a general hint. He did mention the gangland murder that occurred in broad daylight. So he's run afoul of an individual and/or group." Winfield stood up briefly to close the shades to his small living room window, and flinched from a lone motorcycle headlight spearing through the dark.

Mona commented "Well, I've always given him fuel to add to his ideas. He's changed a lot from the high school kid who first made inroads into political literature. Even though it's necessary to move beyond idealism, seeing him develop a cynical sense of humor has been a bit depressing. But I'm digressing. I feel like people of our generation had it easy, in a way. Less confusion back then..."

Winfield grimaced behind the phone. "I agree, but sometimes it's necessary for people to be confused before they come out the other side. I was the last person people thought would emerge from the ghetto to become a professor. And you've told me about how people thought you were 'too nice' to be more than a dutiful housewife, cooking wholesome meals and all that-"

"You saying I can't?"

"No, no, sister. Far from it. Although I propose we have a dinner one of these nights on my dime."

Mona conceded "I guess, I mean yeah. Next week's free for me."

"Monday?" Winfield pressed.

"Fine. Unless that cop stops by again and disrupts my whole train of thought, and I forget to call you back to confirm. By the way, I'm pretty sure I knew the guy everyone called Hitch. And gunned down for what?" She realized she had partially lapsed into street language patois. "It seems even having curiosity has become a crime."

Winfield said "Curiosity is both sublime and dangerous, right? But I'm getting too pedantic. The kid Hitch's curiosity got him into some sort of trouble, and he couldn't be rescued. I just hope our pal Gordy isn't headed down the same path." He repositioned his feet inside his black felt slippers. "This real life adventure business does trump my new so-called 'revolutionary' thesis in radical power relations. Hard for me to admit, but there it is. Lately adventure outside academia has meant a drive to Oxnard and lunch at the Wagon Wheel."

Mona said "So you're not a romantic afterall? Oh, well. We're kind of back to where we started. So I guess till next week then, comrade?"

"Good enough. And good night to you. Now don't get yourself kidnapped, okay?" After hanging up, Winfield wondered "Was I too short with her?"

As he strode over the washed up sea kelp he paused to remember his mother's words: "Smell the needling of the wind, its challenge to race alongside it. So run, Cole. Because we are made to run, not walk. Notice your body's balance is best when you move more swiftly." As he scooped up a palm's worth of freckled sand he wondered "How much do I recall purely, and how much have I fabricated with my roving mind?" He plucked a shimmering brown bulb off the leaf of a spongy sea growth and knelt in the sand as one thumb punctured its shell of skin. He obtained a kind of resinous, slimy pulp in this manner. Cole's short sleeve shirt was flowing out of the back pocket of his surf shorts, and the sun was sinking into the ocean on the burning horizon, only the insignificant steel hulk of a cargo ship marring a perfect, unimpeded view. Cole sat on his haunches and reveled in his solitary time, finally separated from Gordy and his persistent references to the inner city. He thought "Am I really suited for the project anymore?" Such was his concentration level that he did not notice the stocky man approaching stealthily from behind, who stood just out of sight over his shoulder.

Mankins shrugged his large shoulders inside his baggy windbreaker and wiped some sweat from the corners of his eyes. "Hello, Cole," he said. "It's Detective Mankins, in case you're wondering. But you can turn around."

"I know that," Cole shot back over his shoulder. "And I understand that I'm in some trouble. But what are you supposed to be able to do for me?" He turned around slowly, and glowered. "Don't tell me you perform miracles, either."

Mankins smiled. "You're angry. That's good. So am I. Both of us here had potshots taken at us recently. The group you and your pal have connected yourselves to talks a good game, but they either can't keep you safe, or they are actively seeking to confuse, even hurt you."

Cole took a few steps forward. "Perhaps that's true," he responded. "I was trying my best to get my mind off it momentarily by contemplating the waves, then you bring it all back to me." He watched a seagull hover, gather itself, then dive bomb the water, bringing up a fish with its beak, some of the ocean escaping and drifting down in an ethereal mist.

"It's what I do," Mankins said, taking a step forward. "Since 'Nam I've realized that trouble finds me, so it's no use trying to avoid it. It is decidedly better to confront troubles head on rather than biding your time, waiting them out."

Cole said "You might have that luxury 'cause you're a cop. People like myself don't. We don't boast a steady paycheck of warrants and arrests, we're out on the margins really." Cole advanced to within a couple steps, watching out of the corners of his eyes for onlookers. But all he saw was sand and surf.

"I guess so." Mankins took a step to the side, and waited for Cole to pivot, so that they both faced the ocean. "I do my homework. You definitely have a knack for drama. But I won't say more on that subject. Suffice it to say you're an adventurist. But 'Nam is essentially over, so going to war isn't an option for you."

Cole said "Sounds like you're making some sort of recruiting pitch to me. Save yourself. I'm not going to work for you-"

"If you get yourself in more trouble you might not have a choice. You know?" Mankins' voice raised its timbre a notch. "It can be voluntarily now, involuntary later. Your choice."

"No choice really," Cole shot back. "I'll take my chances. And you seem to be working alone anyway. You don't ever mention a partner."

"Okay, I'm gone for now," Mankins said, and started trudging back through the thick, deep sand. "But I guarantee you you'll be seeing me sooner than you'd like."

Cole muttered an obscenity under his breath and thought "Has the cop talked to Gordy, too?" He shifted mental gears, preparing himself for an early dinner with Rod and Kit later that day. He had to maintain composure, because they would be discussing movie premiere preparations, and possibly even more controversial obligations. Gordy would be at home recuperating from a series of headaches he had been suffering from since the night of their crash/attack. Cole stolidly returned to watching series of waves crash into the sand, periodically having to back up a few steps to keep his feet dry. Although he had an inner compulsion to look back over his shoulder to make sure Mankins had, indeed, driven off, he did not. He pulled out his small writing pad and started a free verse poem, allowing the words to lean in and fall out both horizontally and vertically. When sand spit onto the lined pages he tried to find a shape on the page, and follow it with words as faithful to the original design as he could. Mustering such concentration only freed him from his contemporary dilemma in a temporary fashion but it allowed him to access dormant recesses of his mind. "Seek the quickest path, as blurry and as messy as it might be" he thought. "Use the mental paint brush freely." Only the first hint of sunburn compelled him to rise and head to his vehicle. He fired up his GTO and headed to a nearby café.

He had already ordered a plate of fried calamari when Rod and Kit arrived. They had to weave through the tight spaces between the small circular tables. Kit was wearing a white jumpsuit and had her hair fastened into a bun while Rod wore a natty seersucker suit, with thin blue pinstripes, which complemented her perfectly. Cole watched the nonverbal reactions of other patrons to a decidedly handsome and stylish young pair. Kit pranced over and gave Cole a hug.

"Glad to see ya'," she said, lingering briefly over the plate of calamari. "And good to see you started before us."

"Yeah, cause we are a bit late," Rod added, taking a seat. "Kit's shift ended a bit later than usual, some bloke decided he had to follow an ocean swell to the south."

"I was just there," Cole said. "At the beach, I mean. Didn't look like there had been, or would be much of a swell to ride. Otherwise I might have had to bodysurf and be late myself." He pushed the rest of the calamari into the center of the table.

Kit said "I've been working less shifts, though, because Rod has found some projects for me to work on at the studio. I kind of thank you and Gordy for that. Your input lit a fuse under the people who Rod works for. So I've found myself coordinating costumes, and even doing some set designs. Never thought I'd want to work in Hollywood, but suddenly there I am. I've actually found it pretty invigorating."

Rod added, "Yeah, she's been a real spitfire, I believe the English would call her. But frankly, mate, we're not working on your project. Rumor has it that in case yours collapses at the gate, our comedic adventure will pick up the slack at the box office. We can't be specific about the cast, but it is pretty impressive, not established stars but up-and-comers."

"So our project is kind of top secret?" Cole said, and ate the last plate of calamari.

"Not really, mate," Rod answered. "I think part of why I'm not involved with it is that the studio figures I'm too close to you and Gordy, that details would leak out. Hey, we're still invited to the private screening, all of us, that is, in case either of you is worried."

Cole replied "No. Not really. It's just that the story is still escalating for Gordy and myself. I don't want to get into the details, but I'm hoping that as soon as the movie is officially out they'll back off on the pressure."

"You do seem a bit more stressed than usual," Kit commented. "One thing Rod and I might be able to do is make sure someone from the press makes it to the preview. A favorable review could get these people off your back."

The waiter arrived, and Cole tried to relax, but he kept thinking that Gordy would excuse himself from the upcoming preview party, putting all the pressure on him alone to represent a new, renegade spirit to the movie industry. Rod and Kit were exchanging jokes about the chaotic side of movie making, but Cole found himself distracted, unable to respond quickly and naturally. He found himself nodding his head at inopportune moments, and putting on a mask of negative chagrin when Rod and Kit took turns drinking from a glass of whiskey sour. Kit puckered up her lips in a comedic "come hither" motion.

She said "Listen, Cole. We are all 'on a roll,' I think you Yanks like to call it. So try to ride the wave, mate. Don't be a crank, okay? The party is coming soon."

Rod flexed a bicep and said "An Aussie Steve McQueen? I'm talking about myself, of course. I can play a man's man pretty well, indeed. By the way, Cole, do you surf?"

Cole saw himself leaning in to reply, but shapes, faces, and glasses and wine bottles were becoming more blurry by the minute. He wondered the last time he had enjoyed a full night's rest.

Twenty Six

A few mornings before the tentatively scheduled movie party Mankins was poring over old police files of local black militants. As usual he spread them out on the floor of his living room. Over the course of the morning hours he arranged them into two small, separate piles: 1. Suspects deemed tenuous 2. Suspects solidly suspect. He had a large cup of black coffee resting in front of his husky form sitting cross legged in Indian fashion. A small storm lashed rain across his living room windows. It struck him how a large percentage of militants had either moved on from the Black Power ferment, or had opted to operate underground instead. Looking at the case and himself objectively, he wondered why he was involving himself in a perhaps convoluted plot. "It's as if I'm organizing another jungle rescue of a lost platoon member. Someone who refused to listen to my counsel." He made small notations on the photocopies with a stubby pencil, and looked for some connective tissue to a certain black academic-Winfield- or men who on the surface had straightened out over time, and joined law enforcement, or become urban mercenaries. So he also delved into unsolved bank heists and grand larceny cases, reminding himself not to oversimplify the crime calculus. Afterall, he reminded himself, an expert getaway driver could be found inside any racial group. His experience in Vietnam had taught him that, placed in comparable environments, blacks and whites were hardly different. In the jungle both were possessed of an affinity for courage alongside sometimes exceeding cruelty. Both could reminisce, but rarely did, about the thrilling times they experienced in the transition to manhood. At times Mankins found himself appreciating in a queer manner the bizarre quality of the war at the same time that he loathed it. One time during a long patrol he announced that whoever pulled the longest leech from his skin would receive an extra six pack during the next beer rationing. He had a permanent visual imprint in his mind of his men under the thickest canopy of trees available, yet still being drenched by a storm, which made their leech impressed wounds into spots of blurry pink slithering down their bare forearms.

Eventually he had so much material spread over his floor that he had to shove his plaid couch to the far wall to allow for more space. He worked under a kind of self-imposed deadline, since he was not at work, per se, and his so-called "case" was of his own devising, without official departmental support. He ate bologna and cheese sandwiches, and took various naps throughout the day, because he hardly slept at night. Moving the pieces on his living room floor, he attempted to sift out those suspects most likely to be involved in the current caper. Eventually he found three very encouraging individuals, men who lived near the Korean grocery bomb site, had definite, past links with black militants, and were definitely not currently incarcerated. He was simply following classic procedure, to never assume that what is closest to the obvious is not to be trusted when conducting an investigation. Eliminate the most obvious clues first, then work outward. At the same time, knowing the target, and being able to keep tabs on the same individual, might bring one into direct, physical contact with the suspect as well. And here Mankins sensed that something was coming. So he stocked a cooler full of sandwiches and sodas alongside a coffee thermos, and prepared himself mentally and physically for a probable long stakeout.

On the south side of town Gordy chatted with his grandmother while waiting for Cole to arrive. They had a tenuous plan to have dinner at a new café recently opened up near the LA Coliseum. Over the phone they had joked about starting to budget their financial windfall, but toward the end of the talk they broached the idea of buying Rams football tickets while in the area after dinner. His talk with granny had predictably ended with her raising a finger and saying "Just don't bring any trouble around here, you hear?" He briefly wondered "If she knew the trouble Cole and I were in, would she blame me more than him, and even threaten to kick me out of this place?"

Mankins was driving a different unmarked police car, and parked halfway down the block. He was still arranging his food items inside a large duffle bag on the passenger side of his seat when Cole's GTO shot past, then quickly slowed to make the turn into Gordy's driveway. He waited for the omnipresent Chevy van to appear, but it did not. A half hour elapsed before the GTO reappeared, backing out of the driveway in the twilight, its red taillights a smooth red smear in the chalky darkness. Heading north in pursuit he watched his mirrors closely for a sign of the van, as he passed throngs of people on the sidewalks of Vermont Ave. The activity reminded him of his one visit to Saigon, although there he was pulled around by a rickety cart while a prostitute virtually poured beer down his throat. Here there was an almost comparable sense of desperation in the wandering throngs, a thirst for sexual danger and money making scores. Mankins saw how relaxed and insouciant the two sexes tried to adapt into a movement of style, and the sly smiles exchanged between street intersections.

With the before dinner traffic Mankins remained only two cars behind the Pontiac GTO, because he worried about being separated by a traffic light. A few blocks north of the USC campus he followed them into the parking lot of Pat's Steaks, and pondered his next move while he waited. Around the time he figured them busy on their main courses, he reloaded two pistols, and resolved to start making his way across the parking lot. He thought "Maybe I'll have dessert myself."

Mankins was about thirty feet away, sitting on a bench, when Cole and Gordy walked out of the restaurant into the shopping promenade area. He had expected to retreat to his car and continue to tail them on the road, but was surprised to find himself walking behind them in a southward direction toward the Coliseum. One thought advised him to continue, another warned him that he might have a long night ahead trying to rest on campus lawns or steps while they visited a militant professor or a radical student committee or set up some kind of drug exchange in a niche of the campus. Yet they passed brick dormitories and what appeared to be university office complexes without pause, and only made tentative gestures toward female coeds wearing their short skirts and burgundy-and-gold USC sweaters. Mankins felt vaguely tentative, like the first time he led the interrogation of a robbery suspect, a feeling that he was slightly out of his element.

Surrounding the football stadium was a chain link fence that appeared to be temporary, before a more permanent obstacle was created, and as Cole and Gordy walked through an opening in it created by a swinging gate he quickly decided to shadow them from outside, since in the event of an emergency he could easily vault over it.

He watched them take a turn at the Rams/Trojans ticket sign, and walked blind for the equivalent of one block, shaded by tall palm trees, until he was afforded another long view. He sped up to be ahead of them, but they never appeared, so he decided to wait at that spot; because if they exited back in the direction they had come in from he would still have enough time to run back and catch up with them before they reached the parking lot.

Muffled shouts issued from the interior, and he quickly vaulted the fence and ran toward the uproar. He pulled out one of his pistols when he was safely out of view from the lawn area, and he heard shouts and curses subside as he approached the noise of a giant scuffle underway. As he neared the corner of the ticket office building he slowed. He heard a final scuffling of shoes, then the slamming of a door.

Twenty Seven

Catching his breath after helping his men subdue and drag Cole and Gordy into the small office area, with its squat safes holding football tickets in the corner alongside still sealed boxes of Trojans and Rams programs, the tall leader leaned back against a wall. "Sorry for the rude action but I've got to be sure you guys are still going to work with us. In fact, I'd like to be introduced at some point to your colleagues, but in a way that doesn't implicate me, either. A way to give some credit for the inspiration we provided for you." His men nodded their heads and squeezed their black leather gloves and smiled and grimaced in agreement.

Gordy was inclined to curse. While fighting his two eventual subduers he had wrenched his left elbow. He measured his words carefully. "Brother, we have done all you've requested of us, and now you surprise us like this? Cole here has a bit of a scrape on his face. How is he supposed to act casual at the upcoming party and not have people ask about the mark?"

"Have someone apply some makeup, that's all. Maybe that tight little chick you've been seeing can do it." He motioned for his men to not stray too far from the door.

"You want money, right?" Cole said. "That can be arranged." He caught himself before he could blurt, "Maybe not quite the amount you're looking for, but still…."

"Now that you mention it, yeah. We probably could use some of that, too. We're not really football fans anyway." The leader smiled impishly and tapped a poster of Jack Youngblood on the wall. "But the Rams have to finally win it all one of these years. Right?"

The knock was subdued, even hollow. Guns were pulled out, and a louder, more insistent knock did not follow. Mankins had briefly considered trying to draw them out, but considered it too risky. Because he could only guess how many men were inside with Cole and Gordy. He had not heard any shouts or screams or gunfire from within, so he considered it an unpredictable hostage situation, one very volatile and difficult to deal with. Therefore he retreated beyond the fence for the time being.

Inside the leader resumed "Don't worry, we don't want or need any close contact with any of your Hollywood types. And we don't want anything to do with Blaxploitation films either. You dig?"

"Yes we do," Cole stated flatly.

The leader resumed. "There is something going on, all right. But we don't want any of your money. We do want, uh, some immortality, is the best way I can put it. We want you guys to write a book about it-"

Gordy blurted out "You read our minds." He gingerly rubbed a knuckle across his slightly puffed out lower lip. "An expose of the seamy underside of LA politics, and how the inner city is often purposely neglected." There was another small thud, this time on the roof.

One of the militants shrugged and said "Nothing but a small branch, brothers."

"Good. Good. The trick is to write it so none of us are implicated." The leader raised himself onto a counter. "But we'll spare you the trouble and conflict by keeping these black ski masks on. It's all, uh, academic, I guess you could say." He paused and made a nervous gesture with his hands. "Hispanics and Asians are ascendant in this huge town, blacks increasingly getting the short end of the stick. Everyone realizes it at some level yet no one will actually come out and document it."

Cole responded "Gordy and I have kept voluminous notes on it, so we will be able to reconstruct the events without much sweat."

"Sounds like a pact to me" one of the militants said.

"Trust is earned, right?" the leader resumed. "And in our case I believe we have done something comparable. Across racial lines, too. This could lead to a kind of long term alliance, you know? Anyway we are going to lay off you guys for a while. We'll be in touch in a month or so. Just keep truckin.'"

The five militants left first and it was quickly evident that Gordy and Cole would not be following in quick succession. Mankins did a quick calculation and followed them to their vehicle and beyond. After the van was deposited at the Pico District safe house he tailed the presumptive leader, whose face, now uncovered, he studied from a distance through his cloudy windshield glass. But twilight quickly turned to complete dark. He followed them onto the 10 freeway then exited south on Centinela, trailing him south to Baldwin Hills.

The dark Ford Fairlane entered a nondescript parking garage.

Mankins sat pondering his next move, and quickly pulled a couple of sandwiches from his cooler. Technically he did not have the law on his side if he planned to arrest the leader. Secondly he did not know his identity. So he sat wondering what kind of pretext he could use to question him. He wondered "Should I go back and speak to Gordy one more time? Maybe he and Cole are finally fed up with the obvious harassment." At 10:15 he watched the tall figure emerge from the house and climb into the car for what Mankins thought was almost surely a liquor run, because his experience was that aggressors in criminal drama both warmed themselves up and cooled themselves off with alcohol. Of course during the cooling off period was when he often laid in wait. As he often paraphrased "Sometimes it is better to be the fox than the tiger." For his part, Mankins bolted upright out of a partial sleep and spilled some of his soda on his floorboard for his abrupt efforts. He cursed under his breath, because if he decided to follow he would almost certainly be spotted by the driver, since the late night streets would not be crowded, and it would be visually easy to latch onto his following car. Ultimately, though, adrenaline overcame his inner doubt.

Cole splashed the kitchen sink water across his left elbow, which was still partially crusted with blood from being thrown to the ground outside the Coliseum. Gordy was brewing some tea and beginning to document the day's events in his notebook. On the drive back they had discussed the probable timeline for creating the book, gauging how much time they had before their money from the screenplay contract ran out. They posited Kit as a potential literary agent, and Rod as their presiding manager, with Ellis as their first chauffeur. Cole walked out drying his arm with a towel. "I think you should write most of the narrative," he said, smiling. "I'll do the speaking parts, because I have a better ear for dialogue."

Gordy tapped his pen on a half-filled sheet of Mead composition paper. "Well, maybe it will be our final payment to our de facto masters, if you know what I mean?"

Cole did not answer verbally. He simply nodded his head and reached for a Band Aid box inside a narrow kitchen drawer. Then he briefly poked his head outside the front door, half-expecting to duck another sudden blow. Gordy's grandmother had begun to water plants in the corner of the yard and he had a brief moment of standing rest, watching the shape of the water spray gently swayed by a breeze, and the sun refracting the yellowing of the flowers.

He placed the Band Aid in his pocket.

Gordy was writing "Two of the militants look the same, same height and build. Comportment is the same, too, mannerisms and the like. But they're still pretty stubborn about keeping their masks on, so we'll have to struggle to figure that out. Rod and Kit snuck a copy of the film home, say it's kind of a Sergio Leone spaghetti western transferred to the city on amphetamines, all kinds of outrageous chase scenes, a la Bullitt with Steve McQueen. Also there is some kind of extraterrestrial robot that goes around killing cops. Sounds a bit too sci fi for me. But what will the threads be between the movie and the upcoming book? And how much more controversy will we create in the meantime?"

He thought wryly "If it gets too hairy, I'll have to write up my first Will and Testament."

Mankins followed his quarry from the 405 Freeway to the Marina Del Rey highway. At the last instant the Ford sedan shot to the right and Mankins had to quickly apply the brakes and wrench the wheel to the right. By this time the Ford was well on its way to the curving-to-the-left overpass. Mankins floored the accelerator, and was surprised that he could barely make up any ground. He thought "Guy must have a police Interceptor engine under the hood." He passed a woody station wagon with a load of unruly kids, a few sprouted middle fingers at him and laughed as he passed. He calculated the distance closing between their two vehicles, watched his speedometer approach one hundred, and for the first time felt uncomfortable about not wearing his seat belt. He squinted in the glare of an oncoming truck with high beams as the lanes merged down to only two. When the gap had closed to about two car lengths he noticed the light ahead turn to yellow. At first he thought that both of their vehicles would easily make it through in time. But he miscalculated, and he estimated they were seven car lengths apart when the light turned red. The Ford swerved around a small truck crossing its path, veered left, right, then right again, skidding, then recovered as it almost hit the right curb.

Mankins pumped his brakes, and executed a long right curve around another vehicle inside the intersection. He was surprised that he had actually lost some ground in the transition. They proceeded onto Lincoln Boulevard, where the Ford alternated between speeding up and slowing down, as if unsure how to proceed. Mankins kept the distance to about five car lengths.

Thoughts raced through his head: "Does he really want to lose me? Am I actually being drawn in for an attack? Does he think he can lull me into a false sense of security? Is he a getaway driver for the militants or something more?" Strangely, they traveled for miles without one red light intervening. But at the left turn onto Century Blvd. he could have sworn that the driver tilted his head to the side and stared at him in the rearview mirror as if to say "You are familiar with this route, are you not?" As the Ford turned it accelerated one last time, then settled into another cruising pace. Cole began to wonder about the message: "Come on, go right ahead. I would prefer you to not follow but I'm not too concerned either way."

The Ford then took a meandering route at a slow pace through the outskirts of Watts then turned right once more and headed back to Baldwin Hills. Its taillights briefly went red beside a liquor store, the man hopped in and out quickly, then the pursuit continued. "You think you have some kind of upper hand, don't you?" he thought. "You trying to convince me that you're safe?"

Eventually the Ford returned to the confines of its garage, and Cole was left with a decision: "Call it a day? Accept the taunts of a civilian? Have his quarry thumb his nose at him and respond by falling back? Wait another day or two? Inform the department about his extracurricular activities and face the threat of a serious write up? Or worse?"

The fact was that he had been working outside the lines of his official standard policing book all along. He found it difficult to avoid true action when he was summoned on a deeply psychological level. As he acknowledged the volume being turned up on soul music inside the house he reviewed the steps that had led him to this point. He felt the distant opprobrium of his soul mate Janelle: "Pull yourself together, little tiger. You're messing with a dangerous mystery, love." He pictured her on a beach in Thailand alongside some lusty Brit or Aussie, executing yet another of her "spiritual float escapes." And he wondered for perhaps the hundredth time if his experience in 'nam had damaged him beyond repair and further if he should have joined her permanently with the support of his paltry military pensions on her travels abroad.

He found himself opening a small notebook and doing something he rarely did, write out some inner torment: "Sitting here faced with a decision, Janelle. Should I stay? Should I go? Or should I go permanently flee to another place, one more suited to me?   But then do I really know myself well enough? Do I have any more of a sense of my prey since 'nam? And if you read my palm, Janelle, would you tell me that regardless of the current decision I am predestined, and therefore there is nothing to prevent me from doing what must be done, for better or worse? But is that really a load of Zen crap? Is accepting reality just another way of ignoring self-reliance? Tell me if you can, we used to have a really potent connection, as you called it.

A way of reading each other's thoughts. But even though we still talk and see each other once in a while, have we been losing the thread?"

He threw the pad on the floor and guzzled some of his still cold soda. Wiping the dribble off his chin he made a few last calculations.

Then he went in.

He crept along the outer edge of the property quickly because to his thinking he figured anyone inside the house would not expect him to make a hasty intrusion. After all, he could have exerted more pressure as a pursuer out on the road, but he had not. He took some comfort in the deep pocket of oleanders along the left hand side of the structure. He had one lone grenade inside the left pocket of his jacket, just in case. He was also wearing a Kevlar vest, military (not police) issue, which he had ensured was strapped to its extreme level of tightness by the Velcro straps.

He found a slight gap in the oleander which he could utilize as a viewing prism. His head shunted aside a few docile bees nestled in the buds of flowers and he saw the distinguished looking older black man with a goatee engrossed in a paperback book. Periodically he let loose a short, dry cough and reached for a piece of tissue paper from a side table, upon which rested a meaty hardback book and a glass of what at first appeared to be iced tea, but which Mankins came to believe was actually watered down rum or whiskey. As he watched his ears were pricked for audible clues of activity from next door, a possible hazard he could not neglect to monitor. He noticed a light flooding in toward the back of the reading chair and figured it was coming from a dining room/kitchen area at the back. He crept around, leery of small animals, noticing a tree swing at the back, an old, neglected shack with peeling gray paint and a dusty milk crate full of old beer bottles.

He sauntered onto the planks of the back porch, treading carefully, and looked into a kitchen area. There was a red coffee mug on the center of a table, some steam rising from it, and a .38 pistol. He quickly confirmed a squat shadow in the corner as a beefy man. Gauging the likelihood of there being yet another man in the area, and a potential firefight, he stood on his heels. Then someone inside shouted "Reynolds!" and the beefy man started to come into view as another, tall and lanky in a suit, make the corner of the kitchen doorway holding a sawed off shotgun. Mankins fired, already running, and did not notice the two bullets hit the wall outside the kitchen door frame. He ran around the corner of the property back to the front, and held the grenade in his hand, his fingers poised to pull the pin at the top. When he reached his car he opened his door and pulled the pin in one motion, as the goateed man and his two guards were framed in the front doorway. He threw the grenade, and two leapt into the bushes as he fired up his engine. The wispy smoke from the blast disappeared slowly in his rearview mirror as he sped away.

Later he thought "Those two looked professional, organized crime, or maybe even the FBI? If law enforcement, exactly how did they become involved?"

Professor Winfield led the men back into his house. "That's probably a rogue cop," he said. "Sticking his nose in. I might be a Judas to the brothers for working with you Feds, to help clean up this city, but that cop must have a crazy hair up his backside, if you know what I mean. But I think we'll be left alone for a while, and by that time things will be wrapped up, and you guys can return to your points of origin."

The burly one snapped his suspenders and paused to admire his reflection in a window pane. "Harris and I will hang around for the time being, make sure the renegade cop doesn't return again. As for the two young upstarts, they are still small fry to us. We'll leave them alone."

Winfield said "It's too bad we didn't get to the bomber before the militants took him out. He would have been a very valuable piece, indeed. Hitch. That was his moniker. And as for Cole and Gordy, the book they are threatening to write will only help our cause."

The lanky one snapped his fingers. "Well, you did a pretty spot on impression of the militant leader, along with that group of SC students acting out the part of followers. Luckily we were quickly able to find a van that we could make look like the original. As far as we know the LAPD is still not onto us. Our boss in DC disdains everything about the leadership here. Reckless and self-serving to the extreme. Old, sordid Hollywood connections, even mob ties. Yet it's hard to break those connections. Maybe in the future the timing will work out for all of us, and we'll make a huge collar."

The false dawn was provoking strips of purple light, streaking across their faces like dark centipedes. A few miles away Mankins sat in his car, temporarily parked in a cul-de-sac of wealthy suburbia. He was thinking "This mission is getting heavy. And who were these guys? Hired muscle? Undercover cops themselves?" He replayed the scene and thought it probable that he could have prevailed in a firefight. But it would have been reckless to the extreme, legally and otherwise. In a dark recess of his mind was an unsettling thought: With worse timing he could have found himself cornered inside the house, with only one choice: fight to the death.

Twenty Eight

Cole arrived a bit past nine in the morning, anxious to show Gordy his work package. Over the previous two weeks, during which Detective Mankins starting doing surveillance on the Los Angeles FBI field office, Cole had typed up his and Gordy's collected notes on an IBM Selectric Gordy had been able to wrangle out of his friendly local librarian Mavis (it was simply a back-up until the rest of the library office's machines were upgraded). Unbeknownst to Gordy and Cole, she had been in the back room of the house with Professor Warfield when Mankins had snooped around, then been forced to retreat when agents appeared And, after only a few days of typing, Mankins told them about Winfield's involvement in the conspiracy. Gordy thought "Crazy. He impersonated the other guy and had us roughed up at the Coliseum. Somehow he met the militant and with or without the Feds pressure got a handle on his speaking voice. But, damn. Strange coincidence that they are the same height and body build."

"This is it?" Gordy said, flipping through the pages.

"What's the matter with you?" Cole shot back. "They are all single spaced, so it is far from brief, if you catch my drift? I haven't typed in years, since junior high actually, and to make matters worse sometimes the space bar is sticky, forcing me into mistakes, so I've been trying not to run through the correction tape too quickly. So give me some credit here, where it is due."

Gordy shrugged, flipped though one more time, then leaned back. "Okay. I've got to admit I'm pissed at Mavis and Winfield. I mean, working with the Feds, and playing both sides? It gets to me, feeling manipulated. And you know, the movie might not be successful like we all anticipate. Okay, it all makes for one wild story, but we might have to consider that people are getting tired of the whole conspiracy business, Watergate, Patty Hearst, and all that sort of stuff."

Cole replied "Nonsense. They never will be. It is how the material is presented, okay? Not how it might jibe with a story that has already been released. And our story has a little bit of everything. It touches on all kinds of corruption, not just in one or two areas, okay? We will just have to make sure that people can follow it."

Gordy leaned back into his couch. "Okay. But we have to be careful about what we might be responsible for, okay? Mr. Kim was lucky to not die in the bomb blast, we were fortunate that lunatic did not shoot one of us to death on that dark stretch of road, and we have not been officially interrogated by the LAPD yet. Don't look at me like that. There could be other cops like Mankins in the shadows. He wants us to think that he would know if he is being followed, but who is perfect? We both have a nice load of cash, and yet we're supposed to turn around immediately and dig for more dirt that might get us into even more serious trouble?"

Cole said "Look. I understand, but I also don't want to go backwards. Again, I can't live rent free like you. So my current money will soon run out. Simple as that. I don't think it will do us any good, simple as that. And remember, Kit and Rod still want to help us out on marketing the book project, even after we decided to skip the latest Hollywood shindig."

Gordy stood, walked around to the kitchen counter, and poured off more soda into his ice chilled glass. "We've done it, though. We are finally on the map, as they say. Now it will be hard for anyone to kick us off. But let's take at least a week off before we start in seriously on the book project. With all the recent action I need to get my head around where we're at."

Cole answered "Well, I'm done typing for the time being. That's for sure. Who knows, but maybe I'll start taking my gun to a firing range. Not that I anticipate an immediate need for a weapon."

When the stocky young man strode into his office without warning, Professor Winfield started to reach for his phone to alert security. In his haste his left hand swept aside a student's essay, the majority of its pages falling conveniently enough into a wastepaper wire basket. The intruder pointedly watched the remaining few pages flutter to the polished floor, and stooped to pick them up as Winfield paused holding the receiver. He said "The other night was almost a tragedy for both of us, Mr. Winfield. Myself or one of your bodyguards could've been killed. How would you have explained that to your librarian girlfriend? I can't arrest you, but I could in the near future. But that's beside the point. You see, I want in." Mankins finally took the wood chair directly opposite Winfield, who was slowly returning the phone receiver to its cradle. Then he stood and closed his office door and sat down heavily in his office chair.

Mankins continued "My bosses always say I have a knack for getting involved in major action. I guess that's true. I learned from an older cop named O'Dool. But that's another story entirely. Back to the present. You can't really refuse my help now, can you? At the very least you will use your job if I disclose what I know to various authorities. No, you don't have to say anything. In fact I prefer you don't. But here is my card. Call me before midnight tonight, but only if you agree to let me work with you and your government ties. Okay? In the meantime I'm going down to the beach and dive in the ocean for a while and clear my head. Admire the tanned chicks and such. Think it out. You don't have much of a reason to refuse me. It is just not logical. You will have more opportunities to get out from behind your desk. Your only hope is that between now and later on I drown while swimming, get in a fluke fatal auto accident, or one of your Feds decides to go in full psychotic mode and hunt me down and kill me. Highly unlikely on all counts, don't you agree? I'll get out of your hair then..."

Winfield began to speak, Mankins briefly stood in the doorway once more, and Winfield kept his silence and sat back down. He wondered "Is my career actually in jeopardy now because I let myself be drawn into this mess? I could get blacklisted in academia and lose everything over this. The business card looks legit and he fits the description I got from the Feds. And now unless I get some late breaking news I'll have to respond to this Detective Mankins." Slowly, laboriously, he pulled the essay out of his trash can and reordered the pages on his desk. "This has gone beyond serious, almost beyond describing," he thought. "And now I might be forced into decisions I don't want to make. But how could I go up against the FBI anyway?"

It was ten minutes before midnight when Winfield set aside his chilled ice glass and tumbler of whiskey. He had already contacted the Feds, who had deemed clearing Mankins from the picture too risky, whether permanently or temporarily. At such a time, Winfield reflected that a constant female companion might alleviate his strain. He shrugged, took a few breaths, and picked up the receiver. "Where is my sexy librarian when I need her?" he thought.

"Just in time, professor," Mankins said. "I gather you have consulted your people and they have given you the green light. Good. By the way, that was quite a show you put on, acting the part of a militant. Do you, too, have a future in Hollywood?"

Winfield stood more erect in his chair. "Don't gloat now, young detective. You don't hold all the cards, you know? Fact is part of my discussion with the agents was how you might still be suffering from shell shock, or you sustained some damage which renders you incapable of making the most logical, clear-headed choices. For instance, could you be trusted to make clear testimony in a court of law?"

Mankins paused momentarily. "So your people might have looked into my file. I doubt it. But either way you and your Feds have more to lose than me. Don't forget that. Sure, you could guess that I fought in 'nam and such. That's not too difficult to gather I suppose. Anyway, I think we'll get along in the long run."

Winfield grimaced. "Maybe," he responded. He felt overwhelmed by emotional indecision. "We are both well versed, I gather, in the corruption of our systems-"

Mankins espied a tanned, nude bather sashaying pool side in the center of his condominium complex, slightly bathed by deck lights. "Sure. My police mentor was killed due to police corruption. But I've got a new target, Professor. Sorry to cut this short but I might have to go outdoors for a while."

"Uh, wait, detective. I've got to warn you in advance that the Feds work both sides, if you know what I mean. It can be an awkward place to be in, that's for sure."

Mankins sat back down. He said "Double speak? Misleading intel? I know all about that, believe me. My military experience was really no different. And don't think for a second that I'm obsessed with only one angle. For instance I would like to know who tried to take out the two young writers recently on a lonely stretch of coastline road. Okay? Well, either way, whether you understand me or not, good night, professor."

Mankins thought that Warfield might have some type of personality disorder, which enabled him to adopt different masks for various situations: Researcher; teacher; writer; demagogue; criminal. He wondered if his own almost fatal encounter with a drive by shooter in south central was connected. But, like certain searches he had conducted in Vietnam, he figured there was much he would never uncover.

Twenty Nine

Three months later, Cole returned to his fifteenth floor balcony overlooking the Pacific Ocean, carrying a tray of takeout pesto ravioli. Crossing his small living room, he only had to negotiate past a couple of suede couches and a teak side table.   He had inhabited the apartment for only two weeks, and had immersed himself in the Venice Beach vibe to the extent that he had largely neglected the development of his bachelor pad. Recently he had lunched with Rod and Kit, who were eager to see his and Gordy's book released within the year. Presently, as he found a comfortable sitting position, throwing his feet up onto the metal railing overlooking the beach, he thought "If it doesn't take off pretty quickly, I won't be here for more than a year." He wondered if all the psychological confidence builders he had been graced with had overemphasized his likely future fortune based on a still unpublished book. Even Detective Mankins and his fetching on-and-off girlfriend Janelle were ecstatic over his almost assured future windfall, and often invited him to places serving oysters on the half shell and sashimi (Mankins had finally convinced him that he was more of a potential ally than a threat).

For his part, Gordy was in his proverbial "laying low" phase as he called it.

"Look, man, I don't have a regular job to fall back into like you," he told Cole over a burger lunch at Badgro's. "Yeah, I could work, but I've been out of the work force so long that it would be very difficult, you know?" He speared a fry on his fork and dipped it into the mound of ketchup. "But I salute you for getting a better place, at least for the time being."

For lack of something else to say, Cole commented "What's wrong with you? No one eats French fries like that. Do I have to remind you it is not cheese fondu?

Cole spent most of his time, in fact, sitting on the balcony, since spending too much time in his virtually empty one room studio apartment caused him mental distress verging on depression. His first week there, in fact, he had purchased a case of beer, and found himself drinking virtually all day, only venturing out at times to make a pass at women on the boardwalk. None violently reproached him, but he had to admit to himself that it was partly his inebriated state that repulsed them. He returned afterward to his flat and wrote about rejection in forced rushes of largely tepid verse, then scarfed down a leftover slice or two of cold pizza before slipping into unconsciousness. At such times only a loud knock could rouse him from his stupor. Then he would almost frantically calculate that his manuscript was, indeed, still secure inside a special compartment under his mattress, a detail that only Gordy knew about. One morning he awoke panicked, burst out of bed, and, unwilling to wait for the dilatory elevator after he pressed the button, sped down the stairs to the underground parking lot and retrieved his pistol. At the same time he heard Mankins' voice upbraiding him: "At least come to the firing range with that. Otherwise it will scare you more than it helps you."

He did not see or speak to Gordy for over a week. When he felt that Gordy himself would tire of the lack of communication and call him, his phone did not ring. Then he realized he had turned off the ringer at the close of a drinking binge, and immediately considered cutting his intake down to two beers per day. Still, in this gradual drying out period he saw shadows emerge out of the lengthening days, and malicious intent in the twisted smiles of those who noticed him looking at them through his binoculars from his high rise apartment perch. For, although he was experiencing a new level of freedom, he was also anxious about the changes that his writing and natural curiosity and ambition had wrought. And he realized the certain drawbacks that emerging from his anonymity could produce. "I feel somehow that I am being watched all the time," he mused aloud, before opening his second and last beer of the day.

His space was small, but the view it afforded made it seem spacious. "Why don't more people understand this vital fact?" he thought, as he repositioned himself in his chair on the balcony in the gathering twilight. "Are they concerned that being too close to natural beauty will make them unable on far too many days to gather themselves from bed, and face the indifferent world?" His muse was punctuated by a small colony of seagulls emerging off of the boardwalk railing far below, calling out obstreperously before heading toward the foaming shore breakers. One moment he was intoxicated by the feeling of uncertainty surrounding his life, the next he had a deep and galling dread of the controversies that he and Gordy had already, and still might, stir. At the same time he discovered his writing output growing stagnant, which he had long associated with inebriation. So he counseled hard patience with himself, and finished off his remaining two beers over two nights. He ate chips and salsa alongside them, prolonging the alcoholic sensation as much as he could. On the second, final night, though, Rod and Kit dined with him on the boardwalk, which merited a couple more beers alongside a largely mediocre meal of oily ravioli and stiff garlic bread. Cole sensed that Rod and Kit's relationship had developed into something solidly romantic.

They questioned him about the progress of the book, and he commented gently about still being in the research and exploratory stages, which drew a knowing chuckle from Kit, and a shrug from Rod, who exclaimed "I think we need to bring along Gordy next time."

Kit smiled and said "What's that expression?-'Hit it while it is hot?' I think we need to light a fire under you two. You should have heard all of the talk about you two at the movie premiere."

"Yeah," Rod chimed in, "There is definite momentum for that book, indeed. And the fact that you two have hardly been seen I think adds a layer of mystery to the whole project. We will be your cheerleaders."

Cole mused, "Yeah, but with all the strange plot twists they put into the movie, it makes sense it was not successful. The movie executive spouting off like a Hearst should have alerted us the project was spinning off into weird territory."

Cole walked home vaguely uneasy about the future. "Is it fear that the book will fail?" he thought. "Or is it that I will continue to lose women like Kit to men more adept at wooing them?" As he neared the corner of an alley he almost tripped over the foot of a bum nestling inside some bushes, an empty bottle of vodka near his left hip. The leg performed a kick of shock, then was still. He was approaching his building from the backside, skirting a paved lot and a low brick wall, the sound of waves breaking becoming louder as he neared the end of a kind of natural noise funnel. The beginning of a headache pressured the inside of his left eye.

His phone rang just as he was settling in for the night. For two hours he had written, mostly in journal form but also in verse, about his recent meetings, until his stock of soda would require replenishing in the morning.

"Hello Cole. It's Mankins. I want us to meet tomorrow at some point. Bring Gordy along, too, if he is available."

Cole scratched at a small scab on his elbow. "Okay," he said. "I have nothing on my plate at this time."

"I understand you guys like Bob's Big Boy. How about we meet at the one on Century you guys go to at about seven at night? That way I can do some more investigations of, well, I'll tell you tomorrow..."

Cole gazed out the window. "Okay, I'm not sure about Gordy, though."

He debated with himself whether or not to call Gordy right away, and fell asleep still undecided.

Thirty

Cole and Gordy sat in the Bob's Big Boy red booth, playing what Gordy called the "quiz game," because he felt that it was key for them to do a checklist of potential dangers before Detective Mankins arrived.

Gordy: "We only began to trust this cop recently, and now we are considering being wingmen to his cop exploits."

Cole: "Check."

Gordy: "There is no pressure for us to take on new material. We already have enough for a book that will take care of needed future income."

Cole: "Uh, yeah. Check." He reached for his icy soda glass and admired the backside of a waitress he did not recognize. Meanwhile he noticed that Gordy was wearing a chain around his thick neck, and wondered if it was made from sterling silver.

Gordy: "For a cop this guy seems a bit of a loose cannon. I mean, uh, how many times has he risked losing his badge lately? I've done my own research on the guy in question. Sharp as hell, but also kind of a renegade. Takes on all sorts of risks."

Cole: "Uh, check most of that. He took out some robbers one time, but another cop was held culpable for the excessive force charges."

Gordy: "Check me. So you've been doing your homework, too, not just admiring palm trees and bikinis. Good on that, brother. Have a good time, but don't burn your money too fast. As for myself, I bumped some funds into granny's account. I should be safe from her raspy tongue for a while because of that."

Cole: "Check. But I think we're getting off subject. And, look, there's a cop car coming into the lot. We'd better keep a low profile up to and through Mankins being here." He noticed their presumptive waitress looking their way, so he held up his hand to indicate the need for five more minutes. Where he was expecting a black uniformed police officer Mankins pushed through the entry doors instead, sporting a blue Hawaiian shirt and white Adidas Stan Smith tennis shoes. Cole wondered anew if he was related to Rod, such was the resemblance, even the rushed manner of speaking.

"Sorry for the shock, guys. Sometimes I'd rather change out of uniform down at the beach behind a beach towel, that sort of thing, the old curtain effect." He dislodged a vanilla folder from the crook of an elbow and sat down in one motion, almost nudging Gordy aside with his compact form. "I typed this up at night and made copies. It is basically a document of all the intel I've collected over the past month. I've got a few solid leads one people who might have tried to take you two out that night. It also included doing a necropsy on the dead dog."

"What?" Gordy said. "I mean, didn't the guy dispose of it afterwards? Seems a bit weird to me, to say the least."

"Right," Cole added. "Who would leave behind evidence like that? Well, we did repel him pretty well, but still..."

Mankins chuckled. "You'd be surprised how poorly some people plan out their crimes. But it is usually the aftermath where they slip.

He had no experience of defeat the way it was dealt out by you two. I could tell you more, but it's all there on those pages. A kind of road map to get you two up to speed." He picked up a menu, scanned quickly, and said "Double burger and vanilla shake and fries, whenever you guys are ready."

Mankins set the folder in the middle of the table and the way it rested revealed the general thickness of the two copies. Cole thought the expectation was that they would each guess how many pages the document contained. "This case should open up your careers, gentlemen."

Gordy thought the statement sounded rehearsed, as Cole ticked off their orders to a tan blonde with the name badge reading "Cynthia." "Yeah, or put us all six feet under," he could not help commenting. Cynthia was briefly distracted, and had to confirm the flavors of their three milkshakes.

Cole asked "You realize that, as writers, we're still unknown? The film has gotten us some publicity, but we can't guarantee you anything. We're past the point of being intimidated, too. Gordy has been brushing up on his martial arts, by the way."

Mankins shrugged. "You've made your point. But if I doubted your resolve I never would have considered having you on board with me. No one likes surprises, but you guys have an ability to blend in. Good skill not only for battles, but also civilian life." He rubbed a rugged path of fresh sunburn between his eyebrows.

Gordy stated "We've all been close to death lately. But nothing new in the 'hood, you know."

Mankins said "Read through these notes thoroughly. Then decide if you want to get a closer look, and be true witnesses after the fact."

Gordy said "Reminds me of the song 'Can I Get a Witness?'"

Cole said "Go on. We're all ears."

He pulled the folder open, fiddled with the top, stapled edges momentarily, then pushed them across the table. "Strike it while it's hot, guys." He smiled and leered at the ass of the waitress momentarily.

Gordy began "This is, uh-"

"'Extensive' is the word I believe you're looking for." Mankins leaned back and spread his arms across the curved booth. "I was always called a pretty good intelligence collector by my CO. Anyway, let all that info digest at home, all right?"

Cole said "Okay. But don't let us feel rushed now. Kit and Rod want us to start considering a natural cutoff point for our book, meanwhile we can't be sure the Feds or other authorities won't make an appearance, you know, uh-"

Mankins said "I've passed around the message you aren't to be bothered. Understood? You need not fear the Feds. I've been to see your slick professor Winfield, and let him know he needs to back off for the time being."

Gordy gestured toward their waitress for still a few more minutes. "It's kind of like we all have side business. Right? Wearing 'different hats' and all that stuff. Well, I'm in and I'm pretty sure Cole here is, too."

Mankins continued "Remember this, perpetrators never understand that the opposition can be just as persistent in discovering their methods. I've been pursuing this from many angles, okay? But don't take my word for it. Just read."

But Cole had waved the waitress back. He had tired of the cop's grandstanding and had taken the self serve order form and filled it in with pencil. He continued writing "blowhard?" as a message to the slightly amused waitress, but simply passed it on to her as Mankins continued "There it is. I mean, uh, a condensed version of what I've been doing with my free time. I've never enjoyed intimidating with my official power but I've got to tell you it's amazing what a badge can compel people to divulge. But I'm starting to go on too much." He rubbed the patch of sunburn between his eyes once again and glanced over his left shoulder briefly toward the parking lot. The wailing of a few emergency vehicles blared as their plates were brought out.

Gordy commented "Keep the noise down now, guys. It upsets my digestion."

Cole returned "Well, I can't figure out whether to reach for the pepper shaker or my file first."

"In all truth I didn't type all of it out. Janelle insisted on helping out even though she still hadn't gotten herself all prepared for her transcontinental flight." Mankins realized he had likely disclosed more information than they could digest. "Anyway I'll give you guys a couple of days to decide what to do with what I've given you. When all is said and done you might even witness me collar your assailant."

Janelle perked up onto her elbows when Mankins returned to the police cruiser. "You really trust those guys? They're just civilians, as you like to call the non-military."

Mankins nodded his head. "Yeah. They are like me. Renegades. They hate going through a bunch of red tape before taking action."

Janelle laughed. "Well, I hope they have good souls because I won't be able to watch over you from the east coast. And my stewardess wages won't be able to get you out of jail if it comes to that."

Mankins turned on the police cruiser flashers. "Hope we've got enough gas to get you off the airport runway, Janelle."

"Well, just stay under control. Okay? You've got that look in your eye again. I like it, but it scares me, too." Janelle finally sat up completely in the back seat, and began opening her makeup kit. "This is the point I hate, Logan. All the smeared on cosmetics the airlines make us wear. But I can't stand the idea of secretarial school, either." She leaned back fully, muttering "Logan, Logan, what have you started now?" to the clicking noise of her makeup compacts opening and closing.

Separately, and by midnight, Gordy and Cole had read the document in its entirety. Gordy took shorter breaks between reading sessions to watch the evening news while Cole read larger chunks between maps out on his balcony. Perhaps the periodic sounds of sirens and helicopters both distracted and concentrated Gordy's mental energies and the cawing of seagulls and the shouts of randy teenagers became a peculiar form of psychological balance for Cole well into the night. Both considered calling each other, and each committed himself to reading it a second time in the morning. And, finally, at about eight am one was reaching for the phone while the other had barely finished dialing.

"Gordy?" Cole yawned into the mouthpiece because he had hardly slept throughout the night. The meaty piece of reading material had fired his mind with images both vivid and bizarre. In the half-light upon awaking he envisioned a brown couch pillow as a recumbent dog corpse, with the red fringes becoming the extruding entrails of its intestines. And the shadow of a palm tree across his window like a ghoulish character attempting to pick his lock.

"You finished, too, I assume. What a read that was, right?" Gordy clicked his tea cup down on his kitchen counter, noting that in his excitement and haste he had not gotten his Rams windbreaker properly situated over his broad shoulders. Meanwhile he heard his grandmother's shrieking voice scaring off the neighborhood's feral cats. "It kind of even trumps our story, as hard as it is to believe."

Cole pulled the cord out to its extreme length and briefly bit the inside of his left cheek. He was reminded of a pithy comment his mother made to him years ago about a classic of world literature.

"Dostoyevsky invented the deep psychological underpinnings of a crime." He wondered "Was that before or after she was admitted to the mental hospital?" He said "It is quite riveting reading. Not sure I've ever read something so hard to comprehend, yet so convincing nonetheless."

Gordy thought there was an element almost romantic in the document, reminding him of his first joyous reading experience involving the dashing characters of Dumas. "It's that idealized experience of the novitiate, the beginner," he thought. "Well, he has the knack, luck, intensity, whatever," he said. "Also able to operate on the outer limits of what is legal, don't you think?"

Cole had a sensation of being in a kind of subconscious state, one where reality was subsumed by an alternative one. He thought he would not have another drink for at least one more week. "Uh, yeah," he finally responded. "So we have this written record now. The question presently is how and if we get involved on the ground level."

Gordy paused, in part because he could hear his grandmother in the driveway. "So we get pulled in deeper?" he mused aloud. "Agreed. But this is all a bit freaky, don't you think? Working with a cop? Especially a white one? For me it's different. I couldn't walk through my 'hood ever again if word got around that I had associated with the fuzz."

Cole coughed to cover up some humor percolating in his gut. "But this is what we've been looking for, right? Kind of the gift of a perfect ending to our book. Right?"

Gordy said "Maybe." He kneaded a knuckle in the sinus space between the bottom of his left brow and eye, and pulled his single brown window shade completely down. "But, man, a former air traffic controller? I mean, the guy who tried to take us out used to safely direct planes full of passengers?"

"Yeah," Cole chimed in, "pretty strange. Then he invests money in a breeding business for dog racing? I guess he always had a need for a rush of some sort."

Gordy said "Yeah. But then he became addicted to gambling, lost his mansion is Bel Air and yacht, then started that business taking in stray dogs and helped restore them before being donated to kids fighting cancer. It's like he has to eventually destroy whatever he creates. A shrink's dream subject."

"Well, that's where he can be seen as human, right?" Cole's eyes followed a biker weaving through some pedestrian traffic along the twisting bike path. Some of his most twisting journeys were punctuated by shouts of surprise and outrage, and shocked flops of long hair. "Like either from a quest to more fully connect as a human to others, or as a bit of an ego boost proving he is not just supremely self-centered. Reminds me a bit of my mother, at times her better spirit interrupted her crazy mumblings at the hospital."

"What do you mean?"

"She had a deep, unconscious compulsion to reconnect with people on a normal level without the dulling effect of the drugs that helped her cope. Anyway this guy has struggled to keep on an even keel but kept being pulled back to the brink."

Gordy said "An inner compulsion, right? A drive to somehow always prove he belonged. But on the other side it seems events pointed to him not being able to keep on an even keel. Like when he sued the Airlines Authority to get his job back when by all accounts he was sabotaging others within his department. But then there seems to still be a piece that is missing."

Cole replied "Yeah, well Mankins had to really dig for all the intel. Don't you think? The guy can get pretty intense. No doubt about that. Yet the first time he approached me outside my place he was casual, and convincing at the same time."

Gordy chuckled. "Well, he is making a believer out of me, too. But raiding city and police files while looking for evidence? That could have gotten him fired, or still might if someone is ever determined enough to track down and put the pieces together."

Cole said "Well, I'm going to sit down today and read it one more time. I have a feeling he'll be calling us tonight or the next day, and I want to make sure I'm prepared." He watched a tan colored mutt loafing half-intent toward a pelican peeking its head out of a trashcan next to the boardwalk. During his late afternoon nap Cole imagined an arm extending from the can and lifting the dog by its neck.

Thirty One

Gordy realized that every book had an artificial ending; unless, perhaps, all of its main characters died. So Mankins' offer to have them join the stakeout, and whatever else it might entail, was just another chapter, an artificial way to extend the narrative. He thought "I was duped by Dr. Warfield impersonating someone else, and then both Cole and I were almost victims of a psychopath who happens to be a college graduate and a former successful professional."

Phone receiver in hand, Cole hesitated and poured off more soda into his tall, chilled glass. He said "Professional and psychopath together. It is a strange combination, and fit more for a movie. Isn't it is strange how someone seemingly with it all 'figured out' could make such unwise choices."

Gordy kept glancing in the direction of his book shelf as if a volume or two could rein in his disturbed thoughts: "Everything is speeding up and there is seemingly nothing to unwind it; I doubt either anyone in my 'hood or some Westwood intellectual could explain it."

Cole thought along these lines: "In the middle of a plot in which I play a starring role how could I almost get clipped by a man possessed of a spirit witch?" He verbally acknowledged Gordy's parting words over the wire, and was delivered to a corner of his mother's frantic mind, where even the tracery of her favored felt pens over paper once filled him with dread. Because the power of her prose overwhelmed reason and also, ultimately, her tenuous grasp on reality. He thought "Are we just becoming plot points miniaturized for a future book or movie?" He was exhausted but unable to sleep. At one point in the middle of the night he considered putting a sleeping bag out on his balcony.

He returned to reading the document, thinking "What kind of perverse mercenary has been released into society?"

Three am finally found him slumbering in bed.

Perhaps it sounded like a mortar round to Mankins. So thought Gordy. Piercing through metal, even two layers of it, and exiting through a gaping hole on the other side. And jungle cats screeched to the echoing thud of the aftershock, jolting Gordy out of his sleep sack, banging his head on the headboard in the process. Within a couple of minutes the obligatory helicopter arrived and nested in the enshrouding trees holding the pulverized metal can. And a mangy mutt with matted hair came to lick the flames around the jagged edges of damage. When Gordy clipped his right kneecap on the way to the bathroom a lone wolf police patrol car entered the fray. The two cops approached the trash can slowly, even hesitantly, and beamed flashlights into the hole like miners looking for fault lines in the rich vein of a subterranean wall. Gordy was quickly outside his door peering down the alleyway, hoping his presence would not be noted by the cops. "They'd immediately question and accuse me," he thought. The cops knocked on the door closest to the imploded can but no one answered. A series of commentaries followed: "Damn. They know we're out here; Yeah, but they clearly aimed directly at the trash can, not the house, so it was probably just a nasty prank."

Gordy heard the last of the final comments while already ducking back inside, where Detective Mankins' document rested on his dusty coffee table next to the *Times Herald* sports section. Split between the urge to brew tea and shower off a slumber of indecision he settled for a cup of instant cocoa instead, wondering when Mankins would call.

Because it was a near certainty. Gordy was virtually sure that the young detective had suffered during the waiting period. So he figured he would remain indoors and wait for the call. He thought "Even if the cop doesn't dial me, Cole is bound to." His clipped knee throbbed, but only dully.

Now the barking of dogs succeeded the howling of cats. He heard some loud curses emanating from the house across the way, and figured neighbors had finally tired of the cops' grandstanding, and were angling to eject them from their block as soon as possible.

The phone rang at half past nine in the morning, a half hour after Gordy had returned to a deep sleep. A pattering of rain on his thin roof made him especially loath to emerge from bed and make his way to the phone, but he did.

"It's Mankins."

"Good. I was waiting for your call. Yeah." Gordy sat up and put the receiver piece into a better position. "You must be calling this early because of a good reason, though."

Mankins chuckled. "Blunt enough," he said. "And I like that style, by the way. I want you two to meet me later today. At a place not too far from where you guys were attacked. Can't say much more over the line right now. But let's make it five. Here's the address."

Gordy lay back down for a few minutes, almost allowed his eyes to close, sat back up, and called Cole, who had been transferring certain material from Mankins' documents to his own bulging spiral notebook. He thought "I've got to make this a good story."

Cole said "Okay, Gordy. I'll be at your pad by four so we can go through some last minute strategy."

Gordy cracked open his door, as it was still quite humid after the rain. He said "Okay. I'm going to have to hose off the driveway, do some other chores in the meantime. Granny hates stepping through wet leaves, you know."

"Turn here." Mankins laid his hand across Cole's shoulder inside the GTO. "I want the long way in." The road was hardly visible and at first Gordy thought a machete would be required to clear a path through the splaying of ice plants and sunflowers spreading their chaff onto the windshield. Cole flipped the wipers a few times, his ears attuned for any scratches to the flanks of the vehicle. At the same time he gave Mankins a warning look in the rearview mirror. Because Mankins had promised him the way would not be rough. And, indeed, at the very least the road was paved, if in a slightly bumpy asphalt. There were some derelict homes along the way, one practically engulfed by the long branches of sycamore trees. Gordy noted the back end of a boat trailer peeking out from the corner. The road skirted two hills in the topography of two separated camel humps, including the dark sand color circling the cones. Mankins said "Remember, you guys will hang back while I approach the house. There's some weed scrub on that side that should shield me."

The house appeared to have virtually been built into the side of a hill. It was of stone construction with an aboveground basement entrance on the left side near a substantial mulch pile covered by a haze of gnats and flies. Cole had braked the GTO to a stop between, conveniently enough, two large elm trees, their trunks and thick foliage putting the vehicle in a perfectly cloaked position.

"Okay," Mankins said. "This guy is into archery. And for all we know he could be somewhere outside stalking some imported prey. Let's not be the ones in his sights, okay?"

Gordy grimaced. "And what, exactly, is the plan again? You've already pointed out this can't be official police business."

Cole said "Listen, he's on an evidence collecting mission. Okay? It can't be admissible in court but it will support the theory he's our guy."

"Right." Mankins was already half out of the vehicle. "I need you guys to note the exact time anything happens, first time when and if you see him, exactly when I enter the place, any noises whatsoever. When in doubt retreat. As long as you have wheels, that is. Pull out the guns only if you're trapped. This guy is tricky, don't forget that." Mankins quickly checked his gear. "He parks his car in his garage, keeps his blinds down at all times, so I won't know he's here until the last moment." Mankins loped toward the structure, and quickly arrived the exterior wall, where he was shielded by some undergrowth.

Cole deadpanned, "We should have brought a movie camera and used Rod as the cinematographer."

Gordy said "Did you hear that? A small crunching and cracking noise? I think he broke a window because he couldn't get into the basement from outside."

Cole answered "I guess. I hope it is not booby-trapped. Remember the guy has a couple of chemistry degrees and could probably make a small bomb."

Gordy replied "You just keep an eye on the front side, I'll keep an eye on the back. Look out for decoys, you know he has used dogs but there could be other animals to deal with."

Cole said "I know, man. There's no consistency in what he does, either. It's like he's still searching for the perfect way to entrap people. Maybe he's read just one too many books about psychopaths like himself. I just wonder like Mankins if he has a keeper."

The sound at first was a scratching kind of droning, and they wondered if it was the loud exclamation of approaching airplane propellers. Without speaking they exited the car. Within a minute they realized it was approaching from the north/back side of the small abode. Gordy thought in all probability that it was a dirt bike while Cole considered it being a small military jeep. Meanwhile both glanced toward the house, expecting Mankins to appear at any moment. Cole began "We should" and Gordy nodded his head and climbed back into the car. Cole fumbled for his revolver while Gordy nervously pawed at a .9 millimeter automatic he had purchased a week before at a gun show inside the Inglewood Forum. He quickly checked to make sure the safety was still on, because, as nervous as he was he feared an accidental discharge.

Initially, because of the thick clumps of weeds surrounding the abode, it was impossible to determine what type of machine was making the noise. One moment it looked like a large Harley motorcycle, the next like a squat dune buggy. Mankins appeared at the front door and walked around to the back. The raised dust of the machine for a time still prevented Cole and Gordy from being sure. Mankins was creeping along the exterior wall. Cole's hand briefly reached for the car's ignition, then fell back to his lap, near his gun.

Gordy adjusted in his seat. "Man, this is looking sketchy to me. I know Mankins can handle himself, but what if this quickly turns messy?"

Cole did not respond immediately. Instead he gazed at the landscape and slowed his breathing. Finally, he said "We'll manage. I know it sounds simplistic but it is about all I have to say."

Gordy said "Look. See Mankins creeping around? Like a sniper or something. I hope he doesn't lose control of himself and just go off and shoot the guy."

Cole mused aloud "Yeah. I guess we could be considered accessories after the fact. Not a place either of us wants to be in." He wondered "Should I get us out of here now? Hey, there was no talk of actually confronting the guy yet."

Gordy said "Hey, wait. Looks like he's got a larger dog in the passenger seat and, uh, it's some kind of old-fashioned motorcycle with an extension on the side. At any rate he is coming quickly. Okay, now he's slowing. And I think Mankins is not quite sure what to do." At the last moment the cycle went into a gentle slide, raising some dust. After a moment a Great Dane burst toward the corner of the house, barking. But Mankins had somehow scrambled up the outside wall to the roof. There he crouched, patient, until man and dog were safely inside the structure. Mankins only remained briefly. Then he ran back to the car.

Mankins said "You see how casually he walked inside? But don't let it fool you. Trust me, he knows someone is around. Let's wait a few before we take off, though."

Cole replied "This sure has me on edge, man. The guy is like some panther creeping around his property. And now you can't snoop around anymore."

Gordy added "In other words let's get out of here. The guy is clearly insane, okay? And you still don't know when he was born, but he likes to attack people in weird ways. He uses a dog one day, and who knows what the next?"

Mankins shrugged and draped his arms over the front seat headrest between their shoulders. "This is kind of a test run, guys. To see how the three of us, uh, 'can get along' I think is how Janelle put it."

Without asking Cole put the car into idle, and did a slow three point turn from under the tree canopy. He almost cursed, because a small branch had fallen onto his hood, although there did not appear to be any obvious damage. Mankins arched his eyebrows but refrained from speaking, because Cole did not continue forward from that point. He merely smiled back in acknowledgement of his cautious approach. Meanwhile Gordy took some hurried notes on his writing pad.

Cole put pressure on the gas pedal slowly while Mankins looked out the back window, and briefly inspected a shotgun lying at his feet. "Sector looks stable," he said under his breath. "Once you get around the next bend, speed up a bit."

The truck appeared as a mere speck in his rearview mirror by the time he realized it could not be mistaken for something else. Mankins became aware and his fingers drummed atop the driver's seat.

Gordy said "I believe that is him coming again" and held his pistol between his knees. The rural road was ending, and Cole prepared to put more separation between the two vehicles.

Mankins said "Slow down."

"What?" Gordy blurted. "You actually want to 'engage' this lunatic? What are you on, man?" In his mind he reflected that they could not be sure that there was not an accomplice that had been helping out their antagonist all along. "It is beyond risky."

Cole temporized in a calm voice "We could let him catch up a little and see if he's carrying someone along."

Mankins clapped him on the shoulder and said "Spoken like a future Fed."

"Yeah, but then you're risking ruining your fancy ride." Gordy's voice was loud inside the compartment. "And this isn't some kid

Vietcong you're trying to smoke in the jungle," he added, turning briefly toward Mankins. Cole could tell that the primed over truck pursuing them was at least ten years old based on its hunched over and almost globular look, which was enhanced by the midday sun rays. And the driver's head, only the outline clear, was scraping the roof of the inner cab. "I thought he was short?"

"He is" Mankins asserted. "He's just got extremely short legs plus he's probably propped up on pillows. Yeah, he's a vain little bastard. Also wears a different toupee each day of the week because he's prematurely bald."

The stretch of road lacked lights. They passed a decrepit dog racing park on the left and a sleepy farmer's market on the right while the truck gained on them, and a shopping area festooned with traffic signals rapidly approached.

"Yeah, let him catch up," Mankins said, cocking the shotgun in the back seat. "If it takes him more time, you might pull a U turn."

Cole said "Forget it," figuring they were only about a half mile from the first light. "This is his only chance."

Gordy said "Shit. Three against one and we're trapped in a car. This wasn't in the plan, right?" He noted a fire station, wondering if its assistance would be needed after their fiery crash. "Now what are we supposed to do, Mankins?"

Mankins said "We'll have to see what he does first. That's it, Cole. Reel him in. Yeah, let him come up on your right or left tail..."

The shroud of the truck became close enough for Cole to see scratches on the dull hood and he saw their pursuer's mouth opening and closely widely, as if he was shouting out in pain. He only half-acknowledged Mankins' commands punctuated by his stiff hand gestures. Meanwhile Gordy cursed softly under his breath, gauging how many seconds would elapse before they entered a potential impact zone, with beach bound pedestrians jaywalking with unleashed dogs.

Then the truck veered off into the sand-flecked parking lot, almost clipping the back of a sun blaring silver Winnebago RV. The driver watched the taillights flash on the GTO, then followed it as it it circled back around to get a closer look of him

. The man strode out into the deep sand with a pistol tucked into his belt. Even when he heard Cole's car approaching the lot he continued resolutely walking toward the ocean. When his three pursuers reached the edge of the lot and took their first steps into the sand he pulled out his pistol, stared at it momentarily, and shoved it back into his shorts. Then he stripped off his shirt and shower shoes and walked into the ocean. By the time Cole and Gordy and Mankins reached the shore break, where sand crabs could be obtained by reaching down and scooping up the wet, mud-like sand, their former pursuer was swimming through the small waves. He started in the general direction of a small fishing boat, which was bobbing off the slightly agitated ocean with a solitary man leaning back in the fisherman's revolving white chair, his pink scalp recently scalded by the sun shielded by a red visor. He turned almost casually after a couple of minutes and trained a pair of binoculars on the swimmer, who was laboring a bit. The fisherman turned on the boat's engine and let it idle while Cole and Gordy conferred in agitated tones.

Cole: "Now what is this, Mankins? At first it looked like he might be going for a long swim, but now a boat seems to be coming around."

Gordy: "Yeah. This wasn't in the plan at all. So he might have at least one accomplice now. That's clear."

Mankins: "Take it easy. So he might have some help. We have him on the run. That's the main thing in my view. You can't overestimate that fact. We'll flush him out soon, that's for sure."

Cole: "Well, I think that might be the topic for a new book. Gordy and I already have enough for at least one slim volume. Let's head back. He is clearly being picked up by that boat. And I don't expect to see him bludgeoned with an ax or speared by a pole at the last moment, either."

But they continued to watch as the boat came into position. A circular float was thrown out at the end of a red rope. The swimmer struggled to bridge the final five yards through the rolling water. After he was hoisted up onto the deck, and had gathered a solid breath, he extended his hand. "We fooled them this time, but I don't expect we'll be able to do so again."

The other shrugged and pulled off his visor briefly and wiped the sweat off his forehead with the back of his right hand. "The wind is picking up. You feel it? We might have a small storm within a couple of hours. So we should get back to the harbor." As the boat turned sharply, cutting through the small waves, the sun glinted off the letters stenciled onto the back of the boat driver's yellow windbreaker: FBI. Twenty minutes later, as he maneuvered the boat into its slip at the edge of the Marina Del Rey harbor, he asked, "How again did you manage to have that dog attack their moving vehicle?"

"LSD, my friend," the other replied. "I have spent countless hours in labs over the years working on hallucinogens, and I decided I might test them out on animals over time. A pal of mine who used to work in psych ops for the CIA set me up with a lab and enough dogs. It took a while but I was finally, after much experimentation, able to get the desired result, a rabid dog that is able to attack without the slightest bit of hesitation. I cannot help it. You should know that. I am easily bored so I must cause mayhem. And as long as the highest brass in the company stays in the dark I'll be free to do as I wish."

The other's hands were a bit shaky on the wheel and he almost collided with the stern of a large clipper ship. "I see. I'm just trying to figure out exactly what you-"

"I seek to trouble those who are causing trouble. That is all. I have done my own research on these two wannabe detectives. And the actual attack, by the way, was done by an associate of mine who is highly trained, but still a bit hotheaded. I fear he is also involved in causing all sorts of mayhem on the side, including murder. But that is for the local authorities to deal with. Hey, no one will cause more trouble than us, the Feds. Agreed? And since the two upstarts survived my triggerman's assault I have reconsidered my approach. I'll watch them from a distance for a while, and when the time is right

I'll pull them back into the loop, so I can have my hands on the strings again.   But for now let them write the book they need to produce."

The pilot leapt off the lip of the boat onto the dock and tied off the rope. "So how and when will it all end?" he asked, his voice a bit shaky.

"Ah. That? Never mind that. Let's see how crazy it can get first."

Thirty Two

It was a small theater on Beverly Blvd. that was in the process of being renovated. Cole and Gordy knocked on the front doors, which were a thick brocade of dark wood and glimmering brass. A shadow approached and Cole stooped to be on eye level with the figure. A dead bolt clicked, and before the door was completely open Rod's voice sang "Welcome gents to your private screening of The Dark Lords of Los Angeles. Come on in and Kit and I will get your popcorn and soda pop."

Cole said "Will do," holding the door so Gordy could enter first. Instinctively he looked up and down the street before he closed and secured the door.

"Well, that's a mark of trust," Gordy commented, taking mental notes about the lobby, whose marble floor had been recently polished. But the concession area was still a pile of construction materials. Cole briefly caught himself wondering if painting contractors had already been secured for the remainder of the project. He reminded himself "Hey, you've moved up, pal, in case you hadn't noticed."

The theater itself was finished, with flowing red curtains and thickly cushioned seats. Gordy said "This is something else."

Kit said "Isn't it, though? She skipped down the left hand aisle carrying large tubs of popcorn. "I didn't ask before, but I figured you two would like butter, but it's only lightly salted. I brought a salt shaker in case one of you two likes to load up on sodium."

Rod had a tray of drinks out from a side room. "Hang on a sec', gents, while Kit and I fetch our own snacks. Then we'll get the film rolling." There was no ice machine yet, so Rod had brought in his own cooler.

"Remind me again," said Cole, settling into his third row seat. "Is the film any good?"

Gordy said "That's a bit irrelevant. This is something the two of us have definitely been waiting for. Of course, being a writer I doubt it can hold up to our book. But we'll see."

Rod commented "Don't compare. That's the main thing," and headed upstairs to the projection room. He almost collided with Kit, who was holding yet another large tub of popcorn and two extra large cups of soda. "If the movie had already started I would've shrieked in surprise,' she deadpanned, which drew a couple of chuckles from Cole and Gordy.

Cole asked "Is he coming back?"

Kit sat and said "He is staying up in the projector room in case something acts up."

Cole quipped "Hope he doesn't trip over any cans," and took his first generous helping of popcorn.

Kit replied "You two really haven't seen the picture yet? There is actually talk of doing it over with a larger production team and established actors. And promoting it, of course. Then there are the edits..."

Gordy said "What do you mean by that? Getting rid of some of the more interesting plot twists?"

Cole said "Like the killer robots?"

Kit responded "Oh, the director has taken out that one already. It took some measured reasoning with the studio head, but he finally agreed."

Gordy laughed. "I gather no vampires either? What a shame. So it's being pulled back to reality? That's a bit of a drag."

Kit replied "Well, Rod tells me he did storm around a bit, talking up a storm as he usually does, before he came to his senses. He can afford to have a flop or two but the rest of us in the industry rely on a steady income, you know?"

Cole said "Well, our book is on its way. And Gordy and I have enough funds to fall back on to for the time being."

"Yeah," Gordy said. "But we've got to make allowance for some people wanting some form of payback in the future, too."

"No one's bothered us lately," said Cole. "Let's keep it that way." This statement was a half-truth, because he had slowly taken Detective Mankins into his confidence, to Gordy's slight displeasure. "I can maybe see him assisting us at some point, but does he have to hang around all the time? I mean, with the resemblance to Rod, I sometimes wonder if they're separated at birth twins."

The camera panned onto the back of an Afro inside a car slowly passing a donut shop on an overcast day. The driver nodded his head in acknowledgement of voices behind him.

"He's here. He's got to be."

"Yeah. He wants to be famous. Some sort of star. Selling his services to the highest bidder and all of that stuff. No loyalty there, brother."

"Yeah. Punks like him don't deserve to be called 'Hitch' or any other damn nickname. They can't be trusted if they aren't members of any local crew."

"Especially working with white dudes. That can't be allowed.'

"Yeah. We'll show this clown he has to keep the action between Blood..." A shotgun was cocked as the camera focused in on a stocky figure walking back and forth in front of a bus bench, eating a large cinnamon bun.

"This is what you get for bringing outside trouble to the hood," the shotgun wielding passenger hissed. As the report of the shotgun echoed, a cartoonish dripping of thick blood gelled down the screen:

BLOOD!

As the opening credits rolled down the screen Cole nudged Gordy in the shoulder and said "I thought it was supposed to be called The Black Lords of LA?"

"Shush!" Kit said. "Rod won't rewind it for you guys so watch closely."

To Cole the film still looked raw, too rough for public consumption. For instance, the screen literally went dark between scenes, although Kit noted that at least the snowy fuzz had been wiped clean from the film. Meanwhile she half-expected their private showing to be interrupted by a nosy detective, or the film seizing up after being eaten by the old projector.

The second scene featured a series of conversations, jumping from a seedy south central garage to a generic office space which on closer inspection appeared to be a converted classroom. The first scene focused on the voices of men in hooded sweatshirts, the second collared polyester business shirts. The former passed around a joint while the latter passed around cigarettes. Predictably the first group spoke about "fuzz" and "honkies" while the second focused on "hoods" and "upstart blacks."

Gordy was sneering at the screen one moment, smiling at it in the next, as if leery of acknowledging how certain scenes starkly portrayed the reality of his neighborhood. He also thought that someone might have to remind someone else about the irony of "Blood," because the name "Bloods" was the second iteration of inner city black gangs, after the "Crips." He thought "this is really just the beginning."

Cole had been pondering the same subject, if with a bit more trepidation. "Did Gordy realize that their arrangement was one with the devil? And did he care?"

Kit and Rod were thinking that overall the film was entertaining. Additionally it was shedding light on a new angle of gang and police activity. And as their agent Kit would directly profit from the project's success, while Rod himself might move up in the movie industry.

At the same time Detective Mankins was creating a new scrapbook from cases he thought pointed to FBI involvement. So while the private screening of Blood! ended in a bloodbath he was on his haunches in his living room yet again, cutting and pasting news clippings. His brow was wet, and some of his sweat dripped off his nose onto an already spongy and greasy newspaper page. He thought "this is becoming a real tour de force."

Since the night he failed to eliminate the two young writers, the triggerman had returned to dozing on his employer's basement sofa. In fact, the day his employer had chased the pesky young writers off his property he had been working on setting up a sniper's perch facing the road. It was agreed that he should remain out of sight for the time being, until his employer determined that they were not in any danger of being detected. But he had watched the intruders through a pair of binoculars, hoping that somehow he would be summoned at the last moment.

He was determined to redeem himself in his employer's eyes, because he still held out hope for future assignments. And, according to his employer, Detective Mankins did not realize that were two men, not one, to contend with. So he set up a makeshift target range. He had already been told that under no circumstances would he be involved in a direct manner with Cole and Gordy, although he might be able to do some surveillance work. "At a distance," he thought. "That's it. Distance." It had required patience to coordinate the dog attack. Newfangled mobile phones had to be dialed in so that he could constantly be updated on the target's location. It was a luxury his employer had, that he could test out new procedures and equipment on a mercenary such as himself. And one who fancied himself a prospective field agent.

His employer had accurately deduced that Detective Mankins and others were looking for him elsewhere, outside the boundaries of LA. Therefore he focused mostly on firing handguns, which his employer said he was a bit negligent in the proper use of. Only after he had been "passed" in the arms category could he be taught some martial arts. Until then he would not be allowed to resume any activities involving the two young writers.

"You might become the perfect weapon, afterall" his employer remarked.

"Like an attack dog?" he said, opening the bag of fries and cheeseburgers that his employer had brought him.

"Never mind that. Put some food in your stomach before you get any crazy ideas. And you're sounding a bit ornery. By the way, in a few weeks I will be starting you on a new assignment. You will be on a bus heading east…"

END